ANNULLING OUR PROMISE

BY AUTHOR LIFE LINE

ISBN-13: 978-1-7338641-2-1

This book was printed in the United States of America.

Website email lifelinepresents@gmail.com

DEDICATION

This book is dedicated to my big sister Angela Williams who was called home in December 2019. You lived how you wanted to, always putting your children first. I always admired that quality about you. I'm going to miss your smile and our conversations that was always followed by laughter. We love and miss you.

I can't forget about my older little sitter Lynette Williams who is a breast cancer survivor. I know you still have a lot a head of you on this journey, but you are still here to fight. Enjoy life and take a deep breath until your lungs can't take no more. Then exhale and thank God, I know I do. I thank God I can call you and make you laugh, when I know you don't want to because of the pain you are in. I pray the book take your mind off your situation for a moment. Love you.

AKNOWLEDGEMENTS

Thanks to everyone that purchased my first book Stay On The Line. Friends, family and readers. I will always be grateful for the support and love y'all showed me. Thanks to my team, Lelo, Tab, and Takesha for being my first readers of the novel. I always appreciate the feedback and honesty. And last but never least Salsa, my homie and ears I used in the beginning process of making this book. I love you guys.

I want to thank my kids for figuring it out last year that allowed me the time to focus on writing. Learning to lean on the teaching we gave you guys is a big deal. I'm proud and love you guys.

ANNULLING OUR PROMISE

CHAPTER 1

"This game has been exhilarating since the opening tip-off. Count IT! E.T. has phoned home once again, and the crowd loves it. Eric Taylor drains another three-pointer; the sophomore has 21 points so far. The crowd screams, 'Phone home, phone home!' as he trots down the court with his finger pointing in the air. Taylor is four for six from behind the arc, and more than half his points are from three-pointers. If Georgia Tech keeps this up, I can see a tournament berth. Nebraska Coach calls a timeout," the commentator said.

Eric ran to the bench, giving his teammates high fives as he took a seat. The water boy handed him a cup of Gatorade. He downed it and tossed the crushed cup over his shoulder. Georgia Tech was ahead by 10 points, with 7:40 left in the game. The crowd was screaming at the top of their lungs. The coach was talking in the huddle, but Eric couldn't stop looking into the stands at the fans clapping. He always got going off their energy. The Coach tapped his head with the clipboard to get his attention.

"Keep up the defensive intensity and no easy buckets. Bring it in, guys!" Coach C. yelled as he stood up. The team placed their hands onto his. "Defense on three. One, two, three!" Coach C. sounded off.

"Defense!" the team yelled as they ran back on the court.

Eric tripped over the sneaker mat at the scorer's table. Eric felt his knee twist, and he went down, falling backward in what felt like slow motion. Blood started shooting out from his knee all over the gym as he fell, coating the fans in blood--

Eric woke up from his nightmare rubbing the scar on his knee. He pressed his cell phone to see the time. 2:15 A.M., August 19, 2017. He rose out of bed and went downstairs to the kitchen to get something to drink. He flipped the switch to turn the lights on, only to see his son, Danny, sitting in the dark with his head down on the table. It reminded him of when Danny would fall asleep at the table when he was a child.

"Son. Son," Eric tapped the table. Danny raised his head, then put it back on the table. Eric smirked as he walked to the refrigerator. He opened it and stood there, trying to see what he had a taste for. He pulled out a container of almond milk and sweet potato pie before shutting the refrigerator with his elbow. "Son, you better not be drooling on my table," he said, trying to be funny. He placed the milk and pie on the table. When Eric took a seat, he noticed Danny hadn't yet raised his head or made a sound.

"Danny? Are you okay, son?"

"Yes, I'm okay, Dad. I have something I have to do, and it's not that easy for me," Danny said without lifting his head.

"First of all, sit up while you're talking to me, son." Danny did so, sitting up and facing his dad. "Next, figure the best way to be successful with what you must do. Then, take the shot."

"You right, Dad. Take the shot." Danny had a thoughtful look on his face.

"You damn right I'm right. Now get me a knife and a glass out the cabinet. This Patti LaBelle is calling me." He stuck his finger in the pie, then licked it off.

Danny placed the knife and glass next to Eric, then sat at the other side of the table.

"Dad, you do know that the wedding is in three months? Or,

should I say, 98 days?"

"Yes. How could I forget, the Saturday after Thanksgiving? My favorite holiday, *and* my only child is tying the knot. I'm so proud of you son."

"Thanks, Dad. That truly means a lot coming from you. I just... I wish that you would attend the wedding. I know you don't do weddings but this one of the most special days of my life. I'm trying to respect what you believe in but--"

"'But!' Some people don't do funerals, and I don't do weddings. I have never been to a wedding my whole life, and you know this. Why? Why, son? Would you ask me to do this?"

"To be honest with you, I had to, Dad. Yolanda and I were going over the wedding party and guests. Her parents are playing major parts of our wedding. Her father is giving her away, and her mother will be escorted in. It dawned on me that I won't have any of my parents at my wedding. Can you imagine how that makes me feel?" Danny's voice grew louder. "I've been trying to fill this hole in my heart that Moms left my whole life. Until I realize a hole of a parent can only be filled by another parent. Sometimes I need your love and support more than your guidance," Danny took a deep breath with a long pause.

"What you trying to say, son? So, I guess I haven't been there for you, huh?"

"That's not what I'm saying, please let me finish, Dad." Danny pulled out a letter from his back pocket. "I wrote this letter today at work. I was going to slide this under your bedroom door to avoid having this conversation. But we're here now, Dad, and this is me taking the shot. Do not interrupt me, Dad. DO NOT!"

Eric watched as Danny unfolded the letter and read aloud.

Dear Dad,

You have been my rock, friend, mentor, and even my mother at times. I could spend the rest of my life trying to pay you back for all the sacrifices you made for me. Never putting anything or anyone before me. I am very grateful for you helping me become the man that I am today. All the lessons and family values that you instilled in me are priceless.

In a couple of months, Yolanda and me are starting our own family. We will always be Team Taylor, and you know this. I've held back taking this step for a long time because of our bond. I never wanted to break up what we have. I know if Moms were still here I would have made this decision sooner. With that being said, we must be better, not bitter, better, not bitter. I heard those words come out your mouth numerous times trying to encourage me. Now, it's my time for me to encourage you. It's time to move on. It's been almost 27 years since Moms passed, you must move on. I know you've dated lots of women, and some of them I probably loved more than you did. This is not healthy, Dad. I pray that you move on. I want you to be my best man. You have been my best man all my life, it's only right that you be next to me. Not to put any pressure on you, but if you don't hand me the rings, I won't be getting married.

Love you, Dad, and please help me to be better.

Danny.

After Danny read the letter, he tossed it on the table without another word and went upstairs. Eric watched him walk away a man. That was the first time he'd ever stood up to his father. He picked up the letter and balled it up in his fist. Hearing Danny pour out his heart to him had taken away his appetite. He got up from the table and followed his son upstairs.

Knock, knock. Eric waited outside Danny's door.

"Yes, Dad?"

"Before you go to bed, you need to clean that mess you left on the table."

"Really, Dad? I left a mess on the table?"

"Good night. Love you, son."

"Love you too, Dad."

Eric grinned to himself as he walked to the bedroom. *Danny might have manned up to me reading that letter, but I'm still the Big Daddy around here,* Eric thought to myself. He sat on the bed and placed the balled-up letter on his nightstand. He opened the drawer and pulled out a picture of Danielle. Danielle is Danny deceased mother. Eric kissed the picture and looked up to heaven. He knew he had to be there for Danny, but his heart still mourned over Danielle's death. He kicked off his house shoes and got under the covers. Looking upward at the ceiling again, he started thinking about when they first met.

CHAPTER 2

Eric's freshman year at Georgia Tech was a hard transition academically. This was new to him, being a star high school athlete in NYC had had its perks. Georgia Tech also helped their athletes, but they focused on the hopeless ones. The coaches didn't cut the players any slack, especially not for Eric. After a few of his professors told them how bright he was, they also added how uninterested he was on getting his degree. Eric honestly didn't think he needed a degree to play professional basketball for a living. If he didn't make it to the NBA, he could always make decent money overseas.

As Eric walked from the locker room showers with a towel wrapped around his waist, he noticed a note taped to his locker.

Come to my office.

--Coach C.

"Damn!" he grumbled to himself. Eric didn't know if he'd done something wrong in practice or what. He dried off and got dressed. He grabbed his gym bag and started walking to his office. Eric knocked on his door even though it was open. He walked in to see a beautiful young lady sitting in a chair in front of Coach's desk.

"Taylor, I want you to meet Danielle Danson, your tutor," Coach C. said. Danielle stood up, and Eric shook her hand.

"For what class, Coach?" Eric asked, looking baffled.

"Any class that you don't have a B or higher in. We will start with your weaker classes until your GPA is 3.0 or better," Danielle said, showing him a print out with his classes and current grades.

Eric ignored her as if she hadn't even said anything. "Coach! My grades are already over a C-average. Which is good enough to play, so tell me… What is this about?"

"The same way we push you on the court, we push our student-athletes in the classroom. It's one thing not to have the ability to excel; but you, on the other hand--you have the ability and refuse to use it. I won't stand here and allow that. I have a faculty meeting in five minutes, so you'll have to excuse me. Close the door behind y'all." The coach walked out of the office and left them standing there.

"When do you want to start?" Danielle asked him.

He looked at her for only a second before walking out of the office and closing her up inside. That didn't go over too well once the coach caught wind of that. He had him run so many laps. Eric stayed in the gym three hours after Coach drilled him. He wanted to leave, but his legs were like noodles. Coach had left him the schedule that Danielle made, and he finally accepted he couldn't miss a study session.

Their first session, Eric showed up 20 minutes late. He tossed his book bag on the table and took a seat across from Danielle.

"I know you can read. You're twenty minutes late," Danielle said with an attitude.

"My bad. I got tied up, you know how that be."

"It's ok. We will stay 20 minutes later than scheduled. Pull out your English textbook."

"You think I'm staying 20 minutes over? You lost your mind."

"Either that or you can leave now, and I'll tell your coach that you never showed up. And he might… bench you or have you run 1000 laps. You decide what it's going to be."

"You serious, ain't you? Damn snitch. I don't know if you're possessed by the devil or if you *are* the devil."

"What's it's going to be?" She waited for his response with her arms crossed.

He didn't say a word, just sat up in his seat and pulled out his English textbook.

Their first session was alright after she punked him. The more she spoke, the more he realized how beautiful she was. She articulated things so precise that, despite Eric trying to be difficult, he learned. She had an old soul; she reminded him of his mother. As they wrapped up the session, she gave him a couple of worksheets to work on.

"Make sure you get them done. If not, I will add 30 minutes on our next session for you to finish the worksheets. And be on time, Mr. Taylor."

Eric didn't say anything, he just looked at her as he placed his books in his book bag. He knew that got up under her skin by the way she walked off. He put his book bag on his back, then headed to the dorms. When Eric got to his room, Donald, his roommate, was sitting on the floor Indian-style, playing Atari. He'd known Donald ever since they were 13, both being from Jamaica, Queens. They met at I.S. 8 Park one summer playing basketball. Donald was an 'American Jamaican;' in other words, his accent would come and go. They called him Dee (or Dirty, depending on what he was doing).

"What up Dee?" Eric said when he walked into their room.

"Nothing. I have been stuck here for the last 2 hours playing this game trying to beat my high score. But forget all of that. How was your tutoring session?" Dee asked as he paused the game.

"The worst. Coach C. got the tutor from Hell helping me. I hope this doesn't last too long."

"You sure you're not hiding anything juicy? I saw your study partner; Coach McMillian pointed her out in the cafeteria. She's fly. I know if she was helping me, she'll be the one learning something. Word up."

"I didn't even get a chance to see what you saw. She drilled me so much I thought I was in military school. I'm going to see if they can switch her out for another tutor." He dropped his book bag and jumped into his bed with a huff. He never took his sneakers off.

"You crazy, she's all that and a bag of chips. Just your luck, your tutor will go from Pam Grier to Neil Carter. Then you are going to want a break, a hefty break."

They both laughed as Dee started back playing his game. Eric put on his headphones and played a mixtape he'd gotten from back home. He closed his eyes and zoned out to the music, but he couldn't get her out of his head. If he was an artist, he could've drawn the perfect picture of her face to the smallest detail. Dee was right, she was gorgeous, and smart on top of that. Beauty and brains. He couldn't wait for their next session.

The rest of Eric's freshman year tutoring sessions went the same —him giving her a hard time, and her treating him like a dumb, spoiled jock. Everyone on campus thought they'd known each other for years, the way they teased each other. Eric called Danielle a bookworm, and she called him a muscle brain. Secretly, after every session, he liked or loved something new about her. Eric never tried to talk to Danielle outside of tutoring because he had enough groupies hanging around. High school had nothing on these college girls. Every time she would see him with another woman, she would roll her eyes.

The last week of school, the campus had wall-to-wall parties. All the finals were over, and no one had classes. Most of the students were living out of boxes because they had their rooms packed up to sign out and turn their keys in. As Eric walked back from the cafeteria to his dorm, Larry, the equipment manager, stopped him.

"Eric, Eric!" Larry yelled as he ran towards him. Eric looked back and saw it was Larry. Larry always took his job to the highest level.

"What's up, Larry?" Eric asked as Larry hunched over with his hands on his knees, trying to catch his breath.

"Coach wants to see you in--in his office, immediately," Larry said with a slight stutter, breathing hard.

Eric looked at Larry for a second, and then he started walking to the coach's office. *Every time the coach send for me, I get nervous,* Eric thought to himself. He walked up on Coach C. in the hallway, taking down papers from the team's bulletin board.

"Hey, Coach. You wanted to see me?"

"Yes. On my desk, there's an envelope with your name on it. Your guidance counselor brought your grades over here personally. I didn't open it, but your grades will determine your status on this team next year."

The coach said all of that without looking at Eric. He just kept taking down the papers off the bulletin board. Eric walked into his office slowly. He had never been in a rush to get his grade. Eric picked up the envelope and opened it. Scanning his grades, he started smiling from ear to ear. This was the best report card he ever had. Eric had a 3.50 GPA. Coach walked into his office and caught him smiling.

"Congratulations on your 3.5. I knew you had it in you," Coach sat at his desk. Then, he started looking through his desk drawers.

"How did you... don't worry about it. Thanks, Coach."

The coach pulled out an academic patch from his drawer. "Take this and put this on your team jacket." Coach C. passed Eric the patch. "Work hard on your game this summer--don't wait until training camp. You're moving from our 6th man to the start shooting guard position. Can you handle that starting job?"

"Yes. I can handle that, Coach." Eric said it so fast, almost before Coach finished speaking.

"Great. Stay out of trouble and enjoy your summer."

"Same to you, I mean. Have a good summer, Coach."

Eric walked out of Coach's office and ran down the hall. He ran all the way to Danielle's dorm, even hurdling a couple laying on a blanket on the grass. He had never been to her dorm before, but he knew where it was.

"Excuse me. Do any of y'all know what's Danielle Danson's room number?" He asked some females that were in the day room.

"She's in room 26 on the left," one of them said as she pointed down the hall.

"Thanks." He walked to her room. It was closed, but there was music playing through the door. He knocked on the door, then fixed his clothes. He noticed he had grass on his sneaker. He bent down on one knee to wipe it off. The door opened, and Eric looked up.

"Are you Eric?" The female who opened the door asked. He heard Danielle tell one of her friends that she was going to miss her roommate, but he would have never guessed that her roommate was goth. She was dressed in all black and had on black lipstick.

"Yes, I'm Eric," he said, looking confused.

"Hey, I'm Daphne. Danielle's parents came a few hours ago and took her home. She left an envelope for you." Daphne said as she went to get the envelope. "She didn't know if you were going to come looking for her, but she said if you did to give this to you." Daphne passed him the envelope.

"Thanks." Eric took the envelope before starting his walk down the hall, a little disappointed. He wanted to tell her about his grades, just to see her face. He headed to his dorm, slapping the envelope in his hand as he walked. When Eric made it to his dorm room, Dee had a sock tied around the knob. The sock signaled that Dee had someone in there. Eric walked back outside and sat on a bench in front of the dorm instead. He opened the letter and read it.

Dear Mr. Taylor,

If you're reading this, that means you stopped by my room. I wanted to give my home number just in case you needed some tutoring over the summer. My number is 718-555-5555. Please be on your best behavior calling my house; my father is very strict. I truly enjoyed helping--or, should I say motivating--you this school year. Enjoy your summer, and remember: the sky's the limit.

Danielle

P.S. Use that number, muscle brain.

Eric must have read that letter fifty times or so while he sat there on that bench, smiling.

CHAPTER 3

"What's the score?" Eric asked Bruce as he held the basketball at the top of the arc above the free throw line.

"50 to 45, my way," Bruce answered.

Every Saturday, Eric and the fellas play five-two at 8 Park. They no longer run the full court (or even half court, for that matter). They're all over fifty years old—Donald, Bruce, Maleek and Eric. They have over forty years of friendship. Maleek is the youngest and shortest out the crew. He works for a major record label in the city, with no kids or wife. Bruce and Donald are both married with children. They know each other better than anyone.

Eric took a few dribbles, as if he was getting ready to make a free throw. He took the shot and made it, standing there a second with his follow through still in the air. The ball went through the net and rolled to the left of the rim. He tried to get it before it rolled too far. When Eric finally stopped it, he was past the baseline three-point line. He squared his shoulder, preparing to take the shot.

"Add an extra ten to this shot, boy. You out your range, E--or should I say, Ellis...That's a bet?" Bruce said, clapping hard trying to distract Eric.

"That's a bet," Eric confirmed.

Usually, he doesn't let Bruce talk him into adding to the bet they already have going. But Bruce knew calling him Ellis, referring to Dale Ellis, the former NBA player, would get up under his skin. They're playing twenty dollars a game, and if he misses this shot, Bruce most likely will win on his next turn. If Bruce wins, Eric will owe him $30. He took three dribbles, never taking his eye off the rim. Then, he took the shot. Bruce smiled as he followed the shot; it looked long and high. It banked high off the glass, *swish*.

"Buckets!" Eric said, staring at Bruce while holding his hand up.

"Whatever. That was luck," Bruce said as they walked to the fence in the shade.

Donald and Maleek were watching them play, sitting near the fence in the shade. They'd started drinking, so Eric knew they were done playing. Eric got a beer out the cooler and sat on the ground with his back against the fence. Besides spending time with his son, there's nothing he enjoys more than this. Chopping it up in the park after they play is priceless. A few beers and a lot of laughs, that's what Eric lived for.

"I got a dilemma," Eric said, taking a sip of his beer.

"Oh, God. Who's getting the ax now?" Bruce asked.

Bruce is always throwing shots about Eric and his women. That's Bruce--AKA Batter-up--he's married and still tries to hit everything thrown at him. He'll find the smallest thing to compliment the ugliest girl you ever saw. To say he doesn't have any standards is an understatement.

"There you go. This ain't about no female, I'm talking about Danny. He asked me to be his best man at his wedding. He made it hard for me to say no, but y'all already know how I feel about weddings," Eric said.

"I hear you, but that's your son. Your *only* son," Maleek said.

"Word!" Bruce said, co-signing Maleek.

"Yo! The greatest sign of love is sacrifice. Sometimes it's not about doing the things that come easy. It's doing the things that are difficult and rewarding for someone else, not you." Dee said before he turned his beer up.

"That's your last beer," Maleek said.

They all laughed at Dee. Eric zoned out of the conversation, processing what Dee said. Dee has changed over the years. They called him Dirty when he was younger, because of how he played the ladies. He and Bruce competed to see who could hit the most girls around the way. They went in until it backfired--now Dee has three baby mamas and five children in the same zip code. Now, he's a born-again Christian and happily married. The Crew was so proud of him, but at times he forgets why they called him dirty.

"E! Loverboy, E!" Bruce yelled, trying to get Eric's attention.

"What? I hear you," Eric said to Bruce.

"What I said? Since you heard me."

"Okay. I didn't hear you. What's good?"

"As I was saying. Do y'all remember Catisha from Jersey?" Bruce asked.

"Yeah," they all replied.

"Check this out. I went to her house on my motorcycle about two weeks ago. I got to the house--she asked me to go to her aunt house to pick up this sewing machine. I got in the car with her, I put my helmet in her back seat. We talked all the on the way there; her aunt didn't live too far from her. She asked me to come in, which I did, but I wasn't feeling up to meeting her family. I got out of the car, took my riding gloves off and threw them in my seat. I closed the car door and went into the house behind Catisha. We stayed there for an hour, she introduced me as her guy to her aunt. Her aunt was cool, I pointed at my watch to show her I had to run. Her aunt was cutting into our sex time.

"'Auntie, we about to go. I will call you later.' Catisha said to her aunt. 'Let me talk to you baby, before you leave,' Her aunt said. They walked in the kitchen and talked briefly. I grabbed the sewing machine and we bounced. On the ride back to her crib, she didn't say a word. I didn't think anything about it. Then when we got to her crib, I stood behind her as she unlocked her door. She turned around and took the sewing machine from me as she walked into the door. I tried to follow her, but she put her hand in my chest stopping me. 'Stop playing, baby, and let me in,' I said. 'No! You got me confused. You need to go home to your damn wife,' Catisha said, as she pointed at her ring finger. I looked at her like she was crazy, I didn't know where this is coming from. I know I never talked about my wife, that's the number one rule. Then she pointed at my left hand. I looked at my hand... and I forgot to take off my wedding band.

"'Are you going to at least let me explain?' I asked, trying to stall so I could think of a good lie. 'No need. It would be different if I noticed it. But my favorite aunt saw it first. Do you know the type of talks me and her are going to have over you? You played my face to my family, and I can't forgive that. Lose my damn number!' Catisha said, harsh, then she slammed the door in my face! I stood there for a second trying to rationalize what happened. I walked down the steps to my bike and realized my helmet and gloves were still in her car. I looked in the car through the glass, she had the car locked. I text her asking her to unlock her car door. She texted back, *I wish I would for your sorry ass.* That's crazy! We have been dating for over a year and she did me like that. I went to Walmart and got a cheap helmet until I got home. I thought she was better than. Word." Bruce said and looked at them for a response.

They looked at each other. *That's Bruce for you,* the look said. *He never see his wrongs.*

"And he serious," Maleek said.

They all laughed, except for Bruce.

"What?" Bruce asked, not knowing why everyone was laughing.

You gotta love it; these are my guys, *The Crew*, Eric thought to himself, taking another sip of his beer.

CHAPTER 4

Later that night, Danny and Yolanda were driving home from the movie theater. "Did you enjoy the movie?" Danny asked Yolanda as they stopped at a red light.

"It was better than I thought. I didn't expect it to be that funny with the cast that they had, but Tiffany Haddish is crazy," Yolanda said.

"Yeah, *Girls Trip* was something else. Now I'm feeling some way about your bachelorette cruise coming up. I'm not worried about you, but a couple of your friends are suspect. I hope they don't get you into anything."

"Well, I have heard that whatever happens at sea sinks to the bottom ofthe ocean." Yolanda smiled as she looked out the window.

"What?" Danny looked over at her.

"Just joking, love. You don't have to worry about my friends or me. You are marrying a woman, not a girl still finding her way. Marrying, Lord. Every time I think about the wedding or me marrying you, my heart smiles. I can't ever remember feeling like this in my life."

They both smiled, and then she put her hand on his knee and started rubbing it. He looked at her with his eyebrow raised as he made a right turn on her block. Danny parked in front of her building next to a fire hydrant.

"Are you coming up?" Yolanda asked.

"No. My nana wants me to stop by her place. I haven't been over there in a minute. I'm sure she made an apple pie with my name on it. Give me a rain check tonight, baby."

"No problem. We will have all the quality time allowed once we tie the knot. Tell her I said hi." Yolanda leaned over and kissed him.

She got out of the car and walked into her building. Danny watched her walk away so many times after a date. That view never gets old, but tonight was a little different. Love is in the air. He smiled as he pulled off.

A couple of miles up the road, he realized that he didn't tell her about his conversation with his Dad. "Siri, call Wifey."

"*Dialing Wifey,*" Siri said, and the phone started ringing.

"Hello. I changed your mind about coming up?" Yolanda said.

"No. I remembered what I wanted to tell you earlier about my dad. We had a good conversation last night about him being in our wedding. I asked him to be my best man."

"Why your best man? And what did he say?"

"He still hasn't given me an answer, but knowing him, he's closer to yes than no. As far as the best man, I've been contemplating over that. Plus, I figured if he had a major role in the wedding, he might be forced to say yes. Just trying anything to get him to show up."

"I hear that. Do you think he suspects what you're trying to do? Your father is pretty sharp."

"Not at all. He knows how much this day means to me and how much I want him there. If he ever got wind that I'm trying to get him bit by the wedding bug, he would kill me. I hope that it works, because when I move, it's going to be rough for him."

"You right, Y'all have a certain type of bond that's hard to describe. At first, I was a little jealous. Then we created our bond and it wasn't even close to any other bonds I've had in prior relationships—that's one of the reasons I love you so much. You're very loving. I remember when you told me that you love hard. I didn't know what to think about that, especially after I've had a few stalkers in my life. You were correct. You love hard and precise. Your father, Nana, and I all receive different love from you, but the same. It's genuine and personal."

Danny exhaled, deep. "That's enough, you about to make me tear up. If you think my love is special now, wait until you become Mrs. Taylor. I love you more than anything. I wish I could fast forward to our wedding. I'm ready for us to move to our house."

"That's funny that you said that, the house part. When I told my girlfriends that you already closed on the house two months ago, but refused to stay overnight, they thought you were crazy. I told them that you said you want us to experience the house as a married couple. Their hearts melted, but they said you still crazy," she said with a light laugh.

"Tell them I got good sense. I'm just crazy over you, baby." *Beep, beep.* "Hold on, baby, my dad calling on the other line." Danny clicked over.

"Hello."

"Hey, Son, don't say nothing. Listen, I'm honored to be your best man at your wedding and wouldn't miss it for the world. I 'm not bringing any date and don't try to hook me up with one. Let me know all the duties you want me to handle as your best man. I'm here for you, son," Eric said.

"Thanks, Dad, you do know how you just made me feel. I'm on the phone with Yolanda, so I will see you when I come home."

"When you come home, don't get all mushy. We're going to handle this like men. Also, I'm entertaining Ashley tonight in the basement. We'll talk in the morning. Be safe, son."

"Always, Dad. You do the same, I'm too old to have a brother or sister." Danny said with a smile on his face.

"Whatever." Eric ended the call.

Danny clicked back over to Yolanda.

"Hello."

"Yes, I'm still here. You lucky this ring is beautiful, that the only reason I held on," Yolanda said.

"The only reason. You must have short term memory, or was that someone else on the phone confessing our looooooove?" He drug the word love while teasing her.

"I ain't telling you nothing else."

"I hear you. Oh yeah, before I forget. My dad said, he's honored to be in the wedding. I don't know what made him get a change of heart, but that news made my day."

"I know it did. I'm thrilled that he's going to be there. Now I must see who I can hook him up with. Someone that I feel is marrying material, maybe..."

"I know when we planned all of this, you were supposed to be the matchmaker. He made it his business to tell me not to try to hook him up with anyone. So, let me think about this a little more. If I need you, I will let you know. I pulled up to my nana house. When I leave here, I will call you. Love you."

"Love you, too." Yolanda hung up.

Danny parked the car and sat there for a while. He couldn't stop smiling from his dad's decision to be in the wedding. *I can't wait to joke him about Ashley,* he thought to himself. Ashley's not too much older than Danny. They haven't been dealing with each other in a while because she started catching feelings.

Eric is stubborn and very disciplined. He's honest with The females he dates, but they think if their relationship grows he will change his mind. He has a lot of things with him, but his two biggest haven't changed. Eric doesn't want any more kids, and he's never getting married. Those two are carved in stone--the eleventh and twelfth commandments. Danny's seen so many women over the years cut his dad off, then months, or even years, later resurface. Knowing him, he's all wine and romance right now. His basement has a pool table, bar and stools, TV projection, and a wall bed. He knows how to treat a lady. Danny took the key out of the ignition and got out of the car. He locked the car with the keypad and headed in Nana's building.

CHAPTER 5

Knock, knock! After Danny knocked on his nana's door, he looked down the hallway. One of her neighbors rolled out of her apartment in a wheelchair.

"Who is it?" Nana said through the door.

"It's Danny."

"One second, sugar."

Danny stood there, waiting. It took every bit of three minutes before Nana opened the door. He walked in, hugged her and kissed her on the cheek. She closed the door, and they both sat down. He sat on the couch, and she sat in her recliner rocking chair facing the tv.

"I thought you forgot that I was in the hall waiting."

"Stop being silly, baby. Nana old, but not senile. I had to find my good wig and Sunday teeth. Are you hungry, sugar?"

"What you got, Nana?"

"Don't worry about that, let me get my favorite grandson a plate." She got up and went into the kitchen.

He looked at her wig and thought to himself, *I'd hate to see your bad wig*. He got up, looking at all the old pictures that she had everywhere. Everyone had their section: Danny, Eric, and Nana. She even had pictures of his granddad, from when they were together. He never heard her speak on him ever. Eric told Danny that his dad left his mother for another woman. He had another family, married and everything. Danny had an aunt and uncle on his granddad's side he'd never seen.

"Every time I look at these pictures, it takes me back in the days. Especially the ones I'm in," he said, loud enough for Nana to hear him in the kitchen.

"That's why I keep up certain pictures. When I'm having a bad day, these pictures remind me of some great times. Pictures is what people had before clock lines on Facebook." She walked into the living room and put Danny plate on the coffee table.

He knew she meant timeline, but he didn't correct her as he walked to his plate. She went to her closet to get his tray. Yes, his Spiderman tray. Smothered cube steak, greens, yams, and mac and cheese. Danny stuck his fingers in the yams as he stood over his plate.

"I didn't see you go wash your hands. Now, did I?"

"No, ma'am," he said in a child's voice as he took his finger out of his mouth. Danny walked to the bathroom to wash his hands. When he got back to the living room, Nana was gone. He sat down and started going in--her food was always amazing. Danny was blessed to have two living grandmothers, the total opposite of each other. Nana spoiled him with food and love. Momma May spoiled him with gifts and guidance. Nana walked out the bedroom, rolling a suitcase.

"When you finish eating we can go through some pictures you haven't seen yet. Oh, where's my head? I didn't even get you nothing to drink." She walked back into the kitchen.

"Okay. Just water--nothing with sugar, I'm trying to look my best for the wedding."

That suitcase looked like a treasure chest to him. Danny ate so fast trying to get to the pictures, he didn't even remember swallowing. She placed a tall glass of sweet tea with lemon on his tray. He didn't even say anything to her about it. She heard him, but she also knew he loves her tea. Nana sat down and flipped through the channels. Her TV had been on the whole time with the volume down. He finished his food, placed the plate and glass in the sink, and grabbed a chair from the dining room under the table, placing the chair next to Nana's.

"I can't wait to see these pictures." His face was full of excitement.

"Remember, the only pictures that leave my place is the ones you brought in here. Do you understand, while you're smiling like a Cheshire Cat?"

"Yes, ma'am."

When she opened the suitcase, Danny couldn't believe all the pictures and stories he didn't know. She picked up the pictures, then she passed each to him with a story. There so many pictures of Nana's parents and only sister, Ellen. Ellen moved to Stamford in upstate New York when she retired from Airborne Express. Nana told Danny so many stories about her and Ellen sneaking out to go to the city, always to go to a party. He would have never thought Nana could do anything wrong. As she was talking, he saw a picture of his father and his prom date. He picked up the picture out of the pile.

"Who's this, Nana?" He handed her the picture and Nana fell quiet.

"I'm sorry, baby. You weren't supposed to see that. I try to keep these pictures separated from family pictures." Nana sat that picture on the floor next to her.

Danny picked the picture back up off the floor. Eric was sharp in this picture, and the girl was beautiful. They both were matching with the baby blue. Eric wore a tux and she wore a gown.

"Nana. Who is this, and what grade is this?"

She snatched the picture out his hand, then stared at him with an evil eye. Danny gave her the sad puppy-dog face. He'd mastered this face as a kid, and he knew she couldn't resist. Her evil stare soon went away. She closed her eyes, trying not to look at him. But when she opened them, he looked even more pitiful.

"Okay, boy, you win... You gotta make sure you don't tell your dad I showed you this picture. He made sure I kept it from you. Your dad didn't want you to see him with any other woman when you were younger. If it wasn't your mother, he made me put them away. This picture is from your father's junior prom, and that young lady is Kenya. Kenya Crawford. She was your father's first love--or, first real girlfriend."

"Kenya. I never heard dad speak of her. She's gorgeous, her and mom favor each other."

"Yeah. He does have a type, even though he dated so many types of women. Any chance I got to meet any of his ladies, I always knew the ones that would be around for a while. If she's pecan tan, she got a chance. The apple doesn't fall too far from the tree, he got that honest." She got up and went to the kitchen.

While she was in the kitchen, he took out his cell phone from his pocket. He took a picture of the picture, front and back. On the back was written:

This was the best day of my life.

I love you and wish to have many

more with you.

Love always,

Kenya

"Do you want everything on your plate to take home?"

"Yes, ma'am." Danny put the picture on her seat, wanting her to see that he didn't take it. He stared at the copy on his phone, wondering if she was still around.

CHAPTER 6

It was just over seventy days to the wedding. Eric was sitting at his desk in his office, going over Steve's numbers before giving it back to one of their biggest corporate accounts. Steve was one of the rising accountants at Eric's firm; he was very enthused.

The fellas still joke Eric to this day of becoming an accountant. The last thing they ever wanted to do growing up was to fix someone else's problem. Eric, however, learned to love it. At first, it was hard for him to earn peoples' trust, but a happy client brings many more. *These figures look great. Steve did a wonderful job*, he thought to himself. He placed the paperwork back into the folder, then pressed his secretary button on his desk intercom.

"Yes, Mr. Taylor?" Tina answered.

"Call Steve and tell him that he can submit the numbers to Telodyne International. Thank you."

"Will do," Tina replied.

Eric opened the bottom drawer on the right side on his desk, then placed the folder there. While his hand was still in the drawer, he reached up and grabbed a pouch that was velcroed under the top drawer. Eric placed the pouch on the desk and opened it, going through the pictures of Danielle and himself inside. He smiled looking at pictures. "I miss you so much, " he said to the picture of Danielle. Once he got to their first booth picture of many, Eric smiled so hard with infatuation that he started reminiscing.

◆ ◆ ◆

July 4, 1984

Eric had been talking to Danielle for a couple of months over the phone, but they hadn't had a chance to see each other. They made arrangements to meet at the movie theater. She lived in Nassau County, where the movie theater was. He convinced her to bring three friends along, because he was going to be bringing The Crew. It was Maleek's birthday, and Eric thought it would be cool for Maleek to hang out with some college girls. The Crew met at Bruce's crib.

"What up, birthday boy!" Eric yelled with his hands around his mouth as he walked through Bruce's yard. He opened the gate and gave Maleek dap.

"Yo, I hope my chick is cute. I'm not being stuck with the fat one, not on my birthday," Maleek said.

"Where's Bruce and Dee? They need to hurry up before we miss the bus."

"You know Bruce got his license last week?"

Eric looked at Maleek like he was crazy for saying that. "And what that means? I know a lot of dudes that have their license and be right next to me on the bus."

Bruce opened the front door then, shaking a set of keys with a bottle opener on the key chain. Maleek looked at Eric as if to say, *I told you*. Eric would have bet his left arm that Bruce's pops wouldn't trust him with his '78 Delta 88, with those white walls shining. It was burnt orange brown and a two-door.

"You're playing, right?" Eric asked Bruce.

"Not at all. Call Dee before he changes his mind," Bruce said as he walked down the steps.

"Pa-oh, Pa-oh!" Maleek yelled up to Dee's window.

Dee came out from the side door of his house, next door to Bruce, and they loaded up in the car. As Eric got in the front seat, he still couldn't believe this. Maleek and Dee were mad Eric was in the front with Bruce, but they knew they couldn't argue since he was the one who set this all up. Usually, on the Fourth of July, The Crew stayed around the way lighting fireworks. Last year, they were shooting roman candles at each other until Dee's shirt caught on fire. He still had that mark on his stomach.

Bruce turned left off his block, heading towards 8 Park. He honked the horn to show everybody out there that he was driving. Eric leaned forward, so they could see him bopping to the music. The Crew was rolling like they always imagined they would, once one of them got a car. Maleek kept getting Eric to turn the station if he didn't like the music, but he didn't mind because they were rolling. The neighborhood never looked the same after The Crew rolled through.

Finally, Bruce pulled into the Sunrise Movie Theater parking lot. They got out of the car and made their way into the theater. Eric looked around to see if he saw Danielle. He didn't see her. He checked his watch, only to realize they were a good thirty minutes early. They got in line to buy tickets for Ghostbusters.

"Make sure you buy two tickets. One for you and one for your date," Eric reminded The Crew.

"I hope my date is worth me buying these tickets," Maleek said as he counted his money.

Eric side-eyed Maleek, but didn't respond to what he said. Maleek was the tightest out The Crew when it came to money. Even on his birthday, with a pocket full of money, he was always complaining. Dee and Bruce didn't say a word, either. Everyone got their tickets and went to the video games. Eric put a quarter in *Spy Hunter* and started playing. He was locked into the game so hard he didn't even see Danielle walk up. She put her finger over her lips, silently tellingThe Crew not to say anything. Then she reached her finger into Eric's right pocket from behind. He jumped and stomped his foot on the leg of the video game.

"Stop playing before y'all make my mess up my sneakers," Eric snapped, looking down quick at his Nike Cortez to see if he'd scuffed them. Then, he looked back up at the game. "I'm 1200 points from getting the high score," he said, biting his tongue and concentrating. Danielle did it again, but this time he grabbed her hand and squeezed it. She screamed, and he turned around to see her face.

"I'm sorry, I didn't know that was you. I'm sorry," Eric said, surprised and feeling stupid.

Everybody laughed, even Danielle. Eric was the only one that didn't.

"Give me a hug, silly," Danielle said as she held her arms out.

Eric was so nervous when he moved in to hug her. He could feel his heart beating in his throat. He had fantasized so many times of their first hug, kiss, and everything. Eric stood 6'4", and she was every bit of 5'9". The way they embraced was electric and very intimate. Her arm went under his, reaching up with her hands going towards his shoulders. It seemed like his chest was made for her head to lay in. Then she looked up at him. The moment when their eyes locked was magical, and the entire theater disappeared except for them.

"Okay. Now can we see the movie." One of Danielle's friends said.

"Definitely," Danielle said as they let each other go slowly.

"Fellas, this is Danielle. Danielle, this is Maleek and Bruce. You already know Donald from school."

"Nice to meet y'all. This is Kesha, Tonya, and Jasmine," Danielle said as she pointed to each of them.

The Crew took no time finding their match. It worked out perfect; Maleek and Jasmine were the shortest, so it was only right that they clicked. Kesha and Bruce hit it off, and so did Tonya and Dee. They got in the concession line, trying to get some popcorn and drinks.

"How's your summer been so far?" Eric asked Danielle.

"It's been great. I'm enjoying my internship with Dr. Brown. She's taken me up under her wing. Some of the other interns thought that she was related to me. I could see me with my practice once I get my degree. What about you, how's your summer going?"

"Busy. The coach had me scheduled for so many camps, I feel like a lab rat. Besides that, I'm glad to be home. I love Georgia Tech, but New York City is the place to be. I didn't realize how much I missed it."

"I know what you mean."

They got their snacks and found a row in the theater that they all could sit in. After a few previews, the movie came on. As they watched the movie, all Eric could think about was how he was going to kiss her before she left. Every so often he would look at her, and she would catch him. Danielle would smile and look back at the movie. He finally put his arm around her to pull her close to him. She scooted over so fast, as if she were waiting for him to do that. Danielle smelled so good Eric's mind started racing with his thoughts. *I wish we were alone instead of in a packed theater.*

When the movie was over, they walked back out to the video games. The nerves started rumbling again in Eric's stomach. He looked at The Crew, and they were all holding their dates hand. Usually, he was the one moving fast when they hook up with females. He didn't know what it was about Danielle that was making him feel nervous, but he found he liked it.

"Do you want to play *Pac Man*?" Eric asked Danielle.

“Not right now. I want to take a picture in the photo booth.”

They started walking to the photo booth, just Danielle and Eric. It was the longest walk. His heart started beating in his throat again. He wondered if Danielle was just as nervous; if so, she played it off better than him. Eric put the money in the slot, and they got inside the booth. It was tight trying to sit in there, side by side. They took two serious poses and two silly poses. They got out of the booth and waited on the pictures. Dee and Kesha walked up next to them, and everyone laughed at the pictures once they fell in the picture slot.

Eric put more money in the slot to take some more. He got in first and tried to make some room so that she could sit next to him. Danielle opened his legs, and then she sat on his lap with her legs between his. She leaned in and put her cheek on his cheek.That was the first picture. They turned and faced each other for the second picture. As their eyes locked, it was as if someone turned the volume down in the theater. They moved in for a kiss for the third picture. As their lips met, Eric's heart skipped a beat. Then, his heart started over, synced with her heart. It got heated in the booth; their lips were locked together even after the fourth and final picture was done. Danielle had the softest lips he'd ever kissed. Eric didn't want to stop kissing her.

“Hello? Did y'all die in there?” Kesha asked, trying to funny.

Danielle and Eric wiped their mouths off, fixed their clothes, and got out of the booth. The Crew and their dates were waiting on them. The guys were smiling, and the girls looked upset and confused at Danielle.

“We need to go to the bathroom, ladies,” Kesha said with a little attitude.

“What about our pictures?” Bruce asked.

“We going to take pictures as soon as we get back.” Kesha and the ladies walked off.

"Cool," Bruce said as he gave Dee a high five.

Eric watched the girls walk to the bathroom, still floating from the kiss. He never thought this day would come, after they'd given each other a hard time during the school year. Maleek grabbed Eric's pictures from the machine and showed Dee. Then Dee handed them to Bruce.

"I thought you said y'all never did anything while you all were in school? I can't tell, look at these pictures. I see love in both of y'all eyes," Bruce said, still looking at the pictures.

"Whatever." Eric snatched the pictures from him. He stared down at the pictures to see what they were seeing.

"He right. If a girl looks at me like that, I'm getting some," Dee said.

...

As the girls entered the bathroom, Kesha turned and said, "I thought you said Eric was just a friend from school that you thought was cool. What's going on?"

"He was--or, should I say, is--I don't know," Danielle answered.

"You better get him, girl, he's fine *and* he's feeling you," Tonya said rolling her neck.

"I'm not trying to stop you, but you told me he was messing with a lot of different girls on campus. Just... be careful and make sure he wants what you want. Whatever that is," Kesha said.

"It sounds like you trying to stop her. Do what you feel because we're young and beautiful. Okay! Now let's get back to our dates. I want to go into the kissing booth--I mean photo booth," Tonya said with a little smirk.

"Speaking of kissing. Can Eric kiss?" Jasmine asked Danielle.

"*Yes.* It was like our tongues were dancing and he knew my whole routine. Move for move, hmmm." Danielle said, so softly and passionately with her eyes closed.

"You do know you in here with us and not him, right?" Kesha said.

Danielle opened her eyes, and they all laughed. They left the bathroom and met back up with the guys. Kesha and Bruce went into the booth.

"Can we talk?" Danielle asked Eric.

"Sure." They walked away from the rest of their group.

"Did that just happen in the booth? And what are we doing?"

"Yes, it happened, and... I don't know."

"Well, I don't go around kissing everybody, and I know you have a lot of options at school. You probably have a girl at home, too. Do you have a girl out here? And don't lie, tell me the truth."

"Not really..."

"What does that mean? Either you do, or you don't."

"It's not that simple. See, my girlfriend graduated from high school a year before me and went into the Air Force. The first year we kept in touch with letters and late-night calls. This last year the calls and letters slowed up to almost none. We haven't said that it's over, but you can tell by our actions. That's the only reason I said, 'Not really.' Because our relationship hasn't had any closure."

"I hear you, but until that chapter is closed, we can't start anything. I'm nobody's side chick. I'm the prize, not the parting gift. So, when you're ready, let me know," she said, looking directly in his eyes.

"What's up? You act like you're ready."

"As I said, I don't go around kissing *everybody*. Hopefully, if and when you get ready, I'll still be ready and available," Danielle said, jazzy and confident before she walked away.

Eric stood there, watching her walk to the photo booth with everyone. He knew that a long distance call had to be made tonight. *She's ready, she's ready,* Eric kept repeating over and over in his head.

"You ready, Mr. Taylor? Mr. Taylor!" Tina yelled over through the intercom, snapping him out of reminiscing.

"You say something, Tina?" He asked while putting the pictures back in the pouch.

"Yes. Are you ready for the partners' meeting in 15 minutes?" Tina asked.

"Yes. Thanks for the reminder."

Eric put the pictures back in the drawer and closed it. He grabbed his cell phone off his desk and noticed a group text from Dee. He read it and texted him back.

Dee: *Drinks on me tonight I got a promotion I put in for. Meet me at Fat Buddha after work, I got a space reserved.*

Eric: *Congrats!!! See you there...*

Eric grabbed his suit jacket off the back off his chair and headed into the meeting.

CHAPTER 7

Eric entered the bar, looking at the scenery as he made his way over to the reserved tables. The bar was jumping, full of women getting their drink on. Eric left his suit jacket and tie in the car which didn't help; he still felt very corporate in comparison. He made it to Dee sitting at the table. A red leather U-shaped booth with two tables in the middle. He had four buckets with bottles of Rosé Moet on the tables.

"What up, baller? I see you put the 'happy' in 'happy hour' with these bottles. Congrats!" Eric said, giving Dee dap and sitting down.

"You already know. Drinks on me, and the food on y'all. Pass me that menu, I'm starving."

"I feel you." Eric handed him the menu.

They read the menus over and over, trying to be patient because the waitress hadn't yet made it to their table. Eric looked up over the menu, and saw Bruce was standing over him with a girl on his arm.

"Slide over," Bruce said, without even giving anyone dap.

Bruce sat down, and the girl sat beside him. That was Bruce--he'd kill two birds with one stone. He's always bringing a date to The Crew outings, and never the same chick. She's possibly the finest girl he's ever been with--besides his wife. She soon got up and went to the bathroom.

“You could have told us you were bringing a date,” Eric said to Bruce, trying to get him started.

“This wasn’t my plan, it just happened. That’s my co-worker, Taletha. She’s one of my shortys on the job,” Bruce said.

“One of your shortys. You’re out of control. I don’t even know *why* you got married. For what?” Dee said with disgust. He got up and walked over to a waitress getting drinks from the bar.

“Get your boy before I check him. Dirty forgot all the females he slayed before he got saved. I’m cool with him being saved, but all that judging stops tonight. For real.” Bruce had a scowl on his face. Eric could tell Bruce was heated. Eric hates to see tension in The Crew.

“Calm down, brother. We will talk to him about that, but this is not the place.” Eric started opening one of the bottles.

“I’m with you. This is not the night.”

“Stop! Don’t even open one of those bottles. I paid for bottle service, she on her way.” Dee said to Eric, who stopped.

“Have anybody heard from Maleek?” Bruce asked.

“No,” they both responded.

The waitress came over to the table and started pouring up champagne. After she poured up four glasses, she tried to ease off. “I’ll be back to take your food orders.”

“Nah. We ready now. Let us get three 16-piece fat wings. Two of them spicy dragon, and the other honey ginger. Three dragon fries with dragon sauce and a slammin’ salmon salad. That’s it for me and the table. Place y'all orders in now, too,” Eric said.

“Let me get the Mongolian beef with dragon sauce on the side,” Dee said, handing the waitress his menu.

“That’s all,” Bruce told the waitress. She took the menus and walked away. “Me and Taletha good with the wings. She must have got lost or something,” Bruce said looking around, trying to see if he could spot her.

"If she's dating you, she probably used the bathroom and forgot how she got here. She's in a cab on her way home," Dee said with a smirk.

"Ha, ha," Bruce laughed dryly.

"She probably in the bathroom cleaning up, not realizing that she's off work," Eric said, then he took a sip of his drink. Dee and Eric laughed. Bruce was a manager at MTA sanitation.

"Ha, ha. I see y'all got jokes tonight. Ya, something like comedians, but ya ain't damn funny." Bruce said.

"Whatever," Dee said.

Taletha walked up and sat next to Bruce. They made a few toasts to Dee for his promotion. They went through the bottles and smashed the food. Almost two hours of being there, Maleek walked in.

"Sorry it took me so long, but I had to entertain a new artist. The CEO asked me to do it since the artist heard how many careers I helped go platinum." Dee said while taking his man bag off his neck and set it in the booth. Then he gave everyone dap and hugged Bruce's date. He poured the last bit of champagne in a glass off the table.

"Hold up! I know I ain't the only one that saw him put his purse in the seat. You and this forever young stuff is going too far. That's my word you're losing your hood pass, I'm going to give you a village pass. A Village People pass." Bruce said, then he gave Eric dap.

"Really. First, that's a man bag, not a purse. But coming from your ignorant ass, what can I expect? Sometimes I have to dress younger-- y'know, 'industry fly'--to appeal to certain audiences. And you know I don't have a funny bone in my body. Not even on my elbow. So, kill that," Maleek said.

"Break it up, fellas. I feel you Maleek, we all have to dress differently on the job. Plus, I can see why you got the man bag on," Eric said with a serious face.

"Thank you. That's why I rock with you," Maleek stared pointedly at Bruce.

"So, you feelin' the man bag?" Bruce asked Eric.

"Not at all. But those pants too tight to put a feather in his pocket, more or less a wallet and cell phone. Looking like Cat Woman." Eric growled and made a scratching motion. Dee spit out his drink onto the table as they laughed, including Taletha. Between Dee and her, they both had had too much to drink.

"Forget y'all," Maleek said, leaving to walk to the bar.

Dee wiped up the mess he made on the tables with some napkins the waitress had left. Taletha's head would slowly sink in her chest, before she would raise it quick. Eric tapped Bruce and pointed at her so that Bruce could see what he saw.

"Baby, you okay?" Bruce asked her.

"Not really. My mouth feels juicy and dry at the same time. I might need to get some water in my system. That usually puts me back in the game," she said with a slur.

"Yo, I'm going to get her some water. I will be right back." Bruce helped Taletha stand up. He held her by her waist and wrist as they walked to the bar. Maleek passed them coming back to their section.

"Where they going?" Maleek asked, holding a bottle of Patron. The waitress followed behind him, carrying a tray with a salt shaker and a bowl of lemon slices. She set the tray on the table.

"He said he's taking her to get some water," Dee said.

"Cool. We need to start these shots. If you scared, get a dog. I don't wanna hear, 'I'm driving' or anything. I got a limo and driver outside. No excuses." Maleek looked at Dee and Eric like *what?*

He cracked the Patron and poured three shots. They took one for Dee's promotion, then another one for good health. Bruce got back just in time as Maleek poured the third round.

"Where's your date?" Maleek asked Bruce, fixing the shots.

"I put her in a cab. She not messing up my night because she can't drink." Bruce picked up a shot glass of Patron. "Let take a shot to my guy Dee's promotion," Bruce cheered as he held his glass up. They all looked at him with his glass raised.

"You late. We took that shot to the head two shots ago. This shot is for The Crew. Forty-plus years and hopefully forty more," Eric said, and they each took the shot and grabbed a lemon.

Later, after they'd killed the bottle, they paid the tab and hopped in the limo. Maleek tossed everyone bottles of water. The Crew was wasted--everybody had their own drunk body language. They laid all over that limo.

"I can't go home like this, my wife's going to kill me. I need some coffee. Hot, cold, wet, or dry. I'll *eat* it right now not to hear her mouth," Dee said with his head leaned back in the seat.

"Take us to the USA Diner," Maleek told the driver through the phone.

Eric smiled when he heard Maleek's instructions. That was The Crew's spot, where they'd ended a lot of epic nights. The Crew, in full effect. Everyone passed out on the way to the diner, except for Maleek. He'd started drinking a couple of hours after them, after all. Maleek took all of them home. They went from The Crew, fly and ready for whatever, to the Geritol Gang, can't hang for anything.

CHAPTER 8

It was sixty days to the wedding.

"Good morning, sleepy head! It's Happy Tuesday," Yolanda said chipperly, holding a bed tray. She placed the tray beside Danny, climbing into the bed. The tray had two cups of coffee, a bagel with cream cheese, and sliced fruit.

"Good morning, love of my life. What time is it, and what makes Tuesday 'happy?'" Danny asked as he sat up in the bed.

"It's 6:00 AM, and after work, we're meeting with the wedding planners to confirm a couple of things. Hopefully, this will be the last time that we sit with them until we are two weeks out. Just knowing that makes me happy."

"That's right, it's *that* Tuesday. Cool, I will meet you there." He picked a few grapes out the bowl.

"I know you forgot, but it's okay baby. It takes teamwork to make the dream work and I got you." Yolanda got back up, walking towards the bathroom. "I'm going to hop in the shower."

Yolanda stood in the doorway and dropped her robe with her back turned to Danny. He almost choked on a grape looking at her peach. She poked it out a little more than normal. Danny didn't need more convincing; he got up and took his briefs and tank top off as he followed her to the bathroom. He pulled the curtain open and stared at her for a second from the far end of the shower. She had her face under the shower head with her head tilted back.

"What took you so long?" She looked over her shoulder at him as she licked her top lip.

Danny stepped into the shower and pressed their bodies together. He kissed her lips as she looked back at him, then he kissed her neck. That neck kiss made the bathroom steamy that morning, not the hot water.

"By Thursday, I need at least a 500 word paper on what a forensic psychologist means to you. Not the Google definition or anything from out of the class text books. I want to know what led you to these studies and how you're going to make your mark in this field. Two simple but terrifying components I need you to express in your own words. Have a good day," Danny said to the class. Paul, one of his students, walked up to him as he packed his briefcase.

"Professor Taylor, what if a student has a problem with speaking in lamest terms? Would that hinder a passing grade?" Paul asked.

"Not at all. I want to highlight that the paper needs to come from themselves, not from the internet. I can't grade a person's truth, only their effort."

"Great. Thanks," Paul said, very relieved, before leaving the classroom..

Every time I give them a paper to do I have one of my favorite students that want the specifics. I see myself in all of them. My dad used to get mad when I would make him repeat how he wants me to do something. Danny thought to himself as he smiled at Paul walking out.

"What are you thinking about that got you smiling?" Jack, Danny's colleague, asked, sitting in the last row of the class.

Danny hadn't seen him sitting there.

"Nothing. You're ready to go?"

"Definitely."

Jack stood up, and they were on their way to B Side Pizza & Wine Bar. They went there every Tuesday to get an Oscar the Grouch pizza. Spinach, black kale, garlic, and mozzarella fonduta. You couldn't get that just anywhere, and it happened to be not far from John Jay College where they worked.

At Yolanda's office, Yolanda was going over some work.

"Who's doing your bachelorette party?" Elaine asked her.

Elaine was Yolanda's assistant, a work alcoholic with no friends. She'd adopted Yolanda as a friend, but hadn't told Yolanda. She was a young Asian New Yorker who watched old reruns of *Sex In the City* every night, despite never having had sex in any city.

"I'm going on a cruise with my girls for seven days," Yolanda said as she flipped through a napkin pattern catalog on her desk.

"That's right, but I have to stay here and run the place, so..."

Yolanda tried not to look at her, keeping her eyes on the catalog.

"So, we should do something before you leave on your cruise. Maybe go to our spot, just the two of us. Thelma and Louise, painting the town orange." Elaine was getting excited.

"That's red."

"What's red?" Elaine asked, confused.

"Never mind. What's our spot so I can make reservations?"

"Stop being silly. Kyoto."

"Okay, I will make a reservation. Do you have the numbers from the Picerake account?"

"I will have them done in an hour," Elaine called as she went to her office.

Yolanda shook her head. If Elaine wasn't a marketing genius, she would have been let her go long ago. She could get a bit obsessive. Elaine had said "our spot," but Kyoto was just the restaurant Yolanda had her order from when they worked late. They'd never been in there together, or even by themselves for that matter. Her parents were Yolanda's former employer. They were the ones who helped her get the business up and running. The catch was, though, that Yolanda had to show their daughter the ropes for three years. She'd been there for six years now, and had been a great asset to the business. She was like a gift and a curse.

An hour later, Elaine sat the folder with the marketing projection numbers on Yolanda's desk. Yolanda picked up the folder, and was impressed as she looked it over. The numbers looked better than she thought they would. Yolanda grabbed a courier service envelope and put the paperwork in it before getting the catalogs together and grabbing her purse. As she walked out of the office, she stopped outside of Elaine's door.

"I'm going to take the numbers to Picerake myself instead of using a courier service. I'm heading out anyway to make this appointment for this wedding. I will see you tomorrow, have a great night," Yolanda said.

"Same to you."

Yolanda ran the figures to Picerake's security desk in the main lobby. Then, she headed out to meet the wedding planner. Dipping through traffic, she tried to avoid being late.

Ring, ring.

"Hello!" Yolanda answered her cell phone through the Bluetooth in the car.

"Baby, where are you?" Danny asked.

"I'm outside trying to get a park. I should have caught a cab or an Uber, because this is ridiculous. I will be right there, don't start without me."

"You don't have to worry about that. See you shortly."

Don't start without me, if that isn't the funniest thing she said in a long time. She knows I'm not the least bit excited to be here. I love her enough to sit through this circus to finally have my bride, Danny thought to himself.

"Hey, honey," Yolanda said, breaking him out of his thoughts and kissing and hugging him in greeting. "Why are you out here in the lobby?"

"I was tired of sitting in there with them. I wanted us to do this together."

"Awww, you're so sweet," she blushed.

They walked into their suite and sat in the lounge. The secretary soon notified them that the planners were waiting inside, and walked them back to the office.

"Come in and have a seat," Mr. Couple said as he pointed to a love seat.

They sat down on the love seat, and the planners sat across from them in their chairs. They both had organizers and pens in their hands. In front on Danny and Yolanda was a coffee table with catalogs, all with tabs covering them. The tabs held the items that they'd picked out online.

"As you can see on the coffee table, we have all your requests. If you flip through the tabs, you can feel the fabric of the clothing. We've clearly tried to make this as painful and nerve-wracking as possible," Mrs. Couple chuckled. "Danny, you can start with the groomsmens' tuxedos, while Yolanda goes through the bridesmaid's dresses."

They picked up the catalogs and went straight to the tabs. Danny handed Mr. Couple his booklet before long and gave him the thumbs up. Mr. Couple took the brochure and started writing in his organizer. Yolanda was asking questions to the planners. Before Danny knew it, he was on an island by himself. He tried his hardest not to pull his cell phone out and play a game to kill time. Every few minutes, one of them would ask him a question.

"Ain't these long-stemmed calla lilies beautiful?" Yolanda asked as she showed him the picture.

"They're stunning," Danny replied.

She pulled the picture back and hit him with the side eye as she turned back to Mrs. Couple. Danny watched her closely as they went over the florist, caterer, invitations and aesthetic vendors. He didn't understand what type of vendors they were, but it made her smile. Truthfully, the only decision he made with these planners were the wedding colors. Yolanda decided white, and he'd added the gold. The funny thing was, he'd decided that five months ago. Danny finally pulled his cell phone out and started researching Kenya Crawford on a people search website.

"Danny. It's time for the men to leave the room, follow me," Mr. Couple said.

Danny followed him, thinking to himself, *I'm the only man leaving this room. Mr. Couple is way too excited about planning our wedding.* Mr. Couple took him to the stairwell, then opened the door leading to the back of the building. Danny followed him out there to witness another world. It was like a smoke utopia. He didn't realize this many people smoked.

"Would you like a cigar?" Mr. Couple asked.

"No, I'm good, but I could use a drink."

Mr. Couple smiled and pulled two shot bottles of Jose Cuervo out his pocket. "That was going to be my second question." He handed Danny a bottle.

Danny opened the bottle and downed it. Mr. Couple held his hand out for the empty bottle.

"Before you start wondering how a married couple named

'Couple' became wedding planners, let me tell you the story. My wife and I have been happily married for over thirty-five years. We had a beautiful wedding with a big turnout. Years later, our family always brought up our wedding and how lovely it was. For our tenth anniversary, we decided to get remarried. The wedding, the wedding party--the whole shebang. This time, we planned it ourselves instead of paying a planner. It was even better than the first wedding.

"We had such a great time organizing our wedding that we researched the salaries of wedding planners. My wife was the face of it at first; then, I started helping her. We changed our last name from Capuzzi to Couple. With the help of my cousin, The Couples' Wedding Planners was launched. Twenty-three years and counting, with no regrets. I've had many jobs and even a career as a tax auditor. Nothing I've ever done comes close to this. Helping people make the ultimate memory of the happiest day of most people's lives? For my wife and me to be a part of that puts sparks back into our relationship, and we love it."

Mr. Couple took a long pull from the cigar. As he did so, his cell phone chimed like a doorbell. He looked at his cell phone and read the text.

"That's my wife. Your fiancé is all done designing her wedding dress. She's looking for you. Tell my wife I will be there shortly."

Danny walked back in the building, still thinking about what Mr. Couple had said.

CHAPTER 9

Later that night, as Danny brushed his teeth in the mirror, he thought about Mr. Couple's story. *I've always been a 'marriage over a wedding' person for a long time. I don't know if my father's way of thinking is rubbing off on me or if I've just been seeing a lot of statistics on big weddings. Not sure how I got there, but Mr. Couple's is one of the good stories,* he thought to himself. He spat out the toothpaste and rinsed his mouth out with water. Danny placed his toothbrush in the holder on the sink, making his way into the bedroom.

"About time. I was about to come in there and see if you fell in the toilet," Yolanda said, sitting on her chaise at the foot of her bed.

"Whatever. I had to get that taste off my tongue. I love Mexican food, but sometimes the spices linger longer than they need to. But when I was brushing my teeth, my mind was going all over the place. Mr. Couple told me the story behind them opening up a wedding planning business together." He stood over her.

"Mrs. Couple told me the same story while I was going through the dress catalog. Do you think that's part of their pitch?"

"I don't know, but their story's stuck in my head. The longevity of their marriage and how they were working together for the last 20 years is remarkable. It really made me cherish the moments leading up to our special day."

"I'm glad to hear you say that. Most men do the whole 'wedding' thing for their wives to be happy, not because they enjoy it. Thank you for acting like you're enjoying the planning, on that note. But don't let me catch you on your phone while we're taking care of business. You know better; you're the one who made that rule. I rolled my eyes when I saw you playing that game today."

"See, it ain't even what you think. I was researching something vital. Trust me, it wasn't no game or social media." He sat next to her.

She turned to face him and said, "What could be more important than what we were doing?"

Danny closed his eyes and tilted his head back as if he was stretching. He could feel the heat on his face from her staring, even with his eyes closed. He took a deep breath and opened his eyes.

"I was trying to get some information on my dad's high school sweetheart. I found a picture over at my nana's, and she told me how my dad was into her. She's beautiful--or, should I say, she was." He showed her the picture on his phone. "This woman is hard to locate, especially since her or my dad don't use social media."

"Yeah, that's a beautiful picture. Why didn't you come to me? I have an uncle that's a private investigator. I'm sure--"

"Baby, I told you I got this. Plus, if this whole thing backfires, I don't want your fingerprints on it. My dad has never said anything bad about you, and I want to keep it like that. Plus, if my two favorite people in the world get into it, you know I got to choose him... hey, no, I'm just playing!"

"I know you are, and not, at the same time. But if you don't want my uncle, get your own detective. Or..."

"Or what?

"You should look for a mutual acquaintance--friend, family

member, or classmate. Or, better yet, one of your father's posse. If she was someone that meant something to him, I'm sure one of them know her. What's her name?"

"I will not tell you her name, but I will use what you said. I think I know the person out of The Crew, not a 'posse,' that I can ask. You kill me how you mix up stuff and you're still young. I could imagine when you get old." Danny smiled at her, seeing his Nana all over her.

"Whatever! You love it!"

"You right, and don't want to lose it." Danny moved in and kissed her on the forehead. He stood up and got the keys out of her dresser. "Let me go before it gets too late and I stay over again."

"You act like that's a bad thing."

"Never that. I have a few things at the house I need to take care of."

"I know, I'm being selfish," she grinned. "Call me when you make it home. Love you."

"Love you more."

Danny hurried up out of her apartment before she started something that would give him no choice but to stay. No sooner then he pressed the elevator he got a text from Yolanda.

Wifey: *WHAT'S HER NAME?*

Me: *???*

He followed up his text with the emoji of a monkey covering his ears. After he typed his response, he sent it. The elevator opened, and he pocketed his phone, getting in with a smirk on his face.

CHAPTER 10

Dee walked into the U.S.A. Café. He looked around until he spotted Danny sitting alone.

"This better be important. You're cutting into me and the miss' quality time," Dee said to Danny as he sat down at the table.

"Sorry I didn't say much in the text, but I needed to see you in person."

"Ok, nephew, spit it out."

"Do you know Kenya Crawford?"

"Are you serious? That's why you didn't use text, you needed to see me. Why didn't you ask your father? Oh, that's right, it's none of your business." Dee eyes looked suspicious as he stared at Danny.

"Hear me out, Uncle Dee."

"Don't' Uncle Dee' me. You know how your father is. He hates to be surprised, probably more than he hates when someone lies to him. Now you're trying to bring me in the middle of this. I can't do it, not at all."

"I'm not trying to put you in the middle of anything. I'm just trying to get someone my dad can settle down with. I came across this picture at my nana's place." Danny showed Dee the picture on his phone. "Nana told me how my dad was head over heels over her. Only thing I need from you is to lead me in the right direction. That's all, I promise."

Dee didn't say a word as he stared at Danny. The waitress placed a cup of coffee in front of Dee, along with a menu. Dee started putting sugar and creamer in his coffee.

"You're not going to say anything?" Danny asked.

Dee put his finger over his lips as if to tell him to be quiet. Danny shut up and watched Dee fix his coffee. Dee took two sips of the coffee, then stood up and pulled out his wallet to pay. When he placed the money on the table, it was on top of a business card. Dee left the diner without saying a word. Danny picked up the business card and read it.

"'*Jackie's Caribbean Delights?*'" Danny read out loud, confused.

On the other side of town Eric was entertaining his guest in the so-called Boom Boom Room. "You know your team is losing tomorrow?" Monica said.

"Whatever. Your Buccaneers are trash. We're going to kill them, mark my words." Eric said as he walked towards her with their drinks.

Eric handed her the drink and sat next to her. They were listening to music while watching the college game on the TV. They always made a little friendly wager when their teams played each other, Eric being a die-hard Giants fan and Monica loving her Bucs. Besides her flexible and chiseled frame, her sports knowledge intrigued him. Also, her living in another state helped them not to burn out on one another. She was one of Eric's friends that probably had more rules than him. Eric put his drink on the end table and laid his head on her lap as he stretched on the couch.

"What time is your flight?"

"In two hours. I have the 11:45 flight to Dallas."

"Cool. What are you betting for this time?"

"I want you to cook for me and feed me on demand." Monica took a sip of her drink.

"Wow. You're getting creative. Let me think about what I want..." Eric closed his eyes as he thought. "I got it. I want you to come over in your flight attendant uniform, minus the hat and panties. And you have to serve me on command. On my command. I love how that sounds."

"That's a bet."

Eric lifted his pinky still with his head laying on her lap. They locked pinkies to make the bet official. He tried to pull his hand down, but she held it tight, placing her drink on the end table and using that hand to tilt his chin back. She pecked his lips two times gently before they started kissing passionately. It was weird and exciting for Eric to be kissing her like that. He turned himself around and caressed her face as they kissed. He guided her legs on the couch and slid her down. He raised onto his knees to undress, taking his shirt and tank top off. He grabbed her shirt from her waist and pulled it over her head. They resumed kissing while his hand worked her bra loose from behind.

"Dad. I need to talk to..." Danny was saying, walking down into the basement until he saw them making out.

Eric jumped up and sat in front of Monica so that Danny couldn't see her.

"My bad, Dad, we can talk later." Danny put his hands up, walking back up the few steps he walked down.

"You okay?" Eric asked Monica.

"Yeah, I'm good. I'm glad that we were just in the beginning, or Danny would have found out that his daddy is a freak." She put her shirt back on.

"Whatever. I can't out-freak the biggest freak in the friendly skies."

They both laughed as they got dressed. Monica ordered an Uber to take her to the airport. They finished their drinks and watched the games as they waited for her ride. Then, Eric walked Monica to the Uber and hugged her goodbye. He watched the car drive off for a second, then started walking back into the house.

"Thanks for the invitation," Bridget yelled through the screen door of her house in her raspy voice.

Bridget was Eric's next-door neighbor. She was only two years older than him, but cigarettes had taken her down. She was already going to chemo for lung cancer, and she still hasn't stopped smoking. Danny and her son Thomas were best friends. Thomas had been the first friend Danny made when their family moved back to New York from Georgia.

"Hey, Bridget, I didn't see you over there with all your lights turned out. You know Danny consider you all as family. Have a good night." He tried to get into the house before she started telling him about her last fling.

"You do the same. I'll talk to you later," Bridget called after him.

"Danny! Come down here, son!" Eric yelled up the steps. He walked into the kitchen and sat at the table.

"My bad, Dad." Danny entered the kitchen. "I followed the company handbook. You had the door to the basement open, plus I didn't see any car in the driveway or in front of the house. My bad."

"You good, son. That was my fault. I thought we were done getting it in. That's why the door was open. The funny thing is, she wasn't embarrassed the least bit. We are too similar," he said with a smile, thinking about Monica. "But forget all that. What's going on?"

"It's nothing important, but..."

"But what, son?"

"I need you to tell me more about Moms. She died when I was five, so I remember her until that point. I want to know how you knew that you wanted her to be your wife. Was she your first love? I want to know if I feel the same way about Yolanda that you did with Moms, if that makes sense?"

"Are you getting cold feet, son?"

"No. It's just that... you never talked about Moms. I know we both blocked a lot of things out dealing with her death in our ways. But I need to know more about her life. Ma May told me about her from a mother's perspective. I need to hear from your perspective."

"I will tell you, but promise me that you won't try to compare your relationship to me and your mother's. That's too much pressure. Plus, every relationship has its own love color. You got me?"

"Yes, Dad, I won't compare ours to yours."

Eric sat back and began to talk. "Your mother, without question, was my soulmate. When I first set eyes on her, I knew she was going to be mine. Our freshman year at college, I never made any advances on her because she was my tutor. But I crushed on her hard, son, more than you could imagine. By me being on the team, I had my share of females on campus. None could compare to how my heart would race every time I was in her presence. I realized it was more than a crush when I got my grades, and I wanted to tell her more than anyone in the world. Not because she was my tutor, but because she believed in me more than anyone ever have. We started dating over the summer of '84. I still have the picture from our first date and kiss.

"Your mother didn't take any junk, keeping me accountable. Accountable! That was her favorite word. Most men wouldn't like that quality in a woman, but I learned to love it more and more every day. When I blew my knee in my sophomore year at

Georgia Tech, your dad hit rock bottom. I was predicted to be an All-Conference player that year before that season started. I don't know if it was the expectation or my pride of not being able to do what I love. Whatever it was, it was hard to get out of that funk. Your mother consoled me and motivated me to use this scholarship to the fullest. She stood by me when everyone turned their back on me: teammates, coaches, and many of the fans. Your mother helped me to realize that most relationships come with conditions. Once a person can't get from you, they find someone else they can get it from. That's why, when I was cleared to play the following year, I wouldn't. I focused on my degree and your mother.

"Our love grew and kept growing. One day, I was in my dorm reading a textbook for one of my classes laying in the bed. Your mother was sleeping next to me on her stomach. I placed the book on my chest and watched her back going up and down. Then I looked at the book going up and down in rhythm with hers. I thought to myself while she laid there, *she's going to be my wife*. I whispered, 'Will you marry me?' She woke up and asked me, 'What did you say?' I stuttered and told her I didn't say anything and for her to go back to sleep. She said, 'Okay. But if you ever asked me, my answer would be yes.' I smiled, picked my book off my chest and started reading again. Our relationship was simple, complicated, easy and very loving. When I say soulmate, I mean that. I still haven't connected with anyone the way your mother and I have. Mentally, spiritually, and physically. Our connection was heaven sent, the essence of truth. It was easy loving her--even easier than loving myself. Our love was a special type of love, son."

Danny was silent for a long moment, processing. "... Wow. I knew it had to be special, but to hear this, I'm in awe. I have so many questions. How did you propose? What did she say? Was she your first love? And what does 'love color' mean?"

"What, am I on trial?"

"No. But I have almost thirty years of questions for you."

"I get that, son, but we're not going to make it all up in one night. I will tell you this: she wasn't my first love, but she was my truest love. I'll give you a rain check on the rest, I promise." Eric walked upstairs smiling. Hearing himself tell the story out loud brought joy to him.

Danny sat there at the table trying to visualize the stories his dad had told him. His cell phone rang and knocked him out of his deep thoughts. It was Yolanda.

"Hello?" Danny answered his phone.

"You texted me and said you were going to call me. Did you forget?"

"No. When I got here, I asked my dad about my mother. He opened up, finally. Hopefully that wasn't our last conversation about her. I need this clarity, closure, or whatever this is."

"I hope it's not the last time, either. I could never act like I understand what you been through, but I'm here for you. Love you. Get some sleep."

"Love you, too. Good night." Danny ended the call.

Upstairs, Eric was sitting at the edge of the bed with his legs next to the nightstand, holding a picture of Danielle and tilting it so that the light from the lamp would shine on it better. He knew this day would come--the day when Danny would ask him about his mother. Eric thought the older Danny got the easier the conversation would be, but he was evidently wrong. Staring at the picture, tears rolled down his cheeks. He kissed the picture and placed it back in the nightstand before cutting the lamp off. Even in the pitch dark, he could still see her face. It remained in his head until he fell asleep.

CHAPTER 11

Danny's alarm clock was going off. The noise kept getting louder and louder until Eric couldn't take it.

"Turn that damn alarm off," Eric yelled through Danny's closed door.

Danny still didn't turn it off. Eric finally opened the door and walked over to the clock on the nightstand. He turned the clock off, then shook Danny to wake him up. "Did you have this alarm set for something? Or did you set it to wake me up?"

Danny opened his eyes slowly and stretched. "My bad, Dad. I'm going to church with Nana this morning. It didn't even feel like I was sleeping that hard. Let me get up before she starts calling me." Danny wiped the drool from around his mouth.

"You better, because you *know* she will call repeatedly."

Eric went back to his room. Danny got out of the bed and hopped through a shower. After he got dressed, he headed to Nana's place. On his way, he dialed 'Wifey' on the car's bluetooth.

Ring, ring.

"Good morning, handsome," Yolanda answered the phone.

"Good morning, baby. Are you getting ready for church?"

"Yes. I'm running a little behind, but what's new?"

"You can say that again."

"Whatever. You called to see if I was going to church?"

"Yes and no. I met with someone out The Crew last night, trying to get some information on the female in the picture. He didn't tell me much, but he left a business card. I don't know what I'm supposed to do with the card because he didn't say anything."

"What type of business is it?"

"It's a Caribbean restaurant."

"That's good."

"Why you say that?" Danny asked, baffled.

"That's an establishment that anyone can go to. Take your Nana there after church. Maybe when you get there, you might realize why your Uncle Donald didn't tell you anything. Be friendly and you might get the information that you're looking for."

"That sounds like a plan. I hope that Nana likes Caribbean food. Thanks. I heard you try to be slick and throw Uncle Dee into the conversation. Pray for me at church. Love you."

"Love you more." Yolanda ended the call.

Danny picked up Nana, and they went to church.

Ding dong!

Eric headed to the door wondering who was ringing his bell. He hoped it wasn't anyone selling something. "Who is it?" He yelled aggressively, but when Eric peeped through the peep-hole, he saw Bruce standing there. He opened the door and Bruce let himself in.

"What you doing out here? Don't tell me. You're meeting some chick out here at a hotel. Am I right?" Eric asked Bruce.

"Nah. I dropped my youngest off at the mall. He met up with his friend, so I decided to shoot over here. I wanted to talk to you about something."

"Hold that thought. I'm putting my dinner together, let us take this conversation in the kitchen."

In the kitchen, Eric started washing the beef ribs in the sink.

"Check this. Before you say I'm 'in my feelings,' hear me out. I didn't like how Dee put me on blast when we went to Fat Buddha to celebrate his promotion. You know I can take a joke with the best of them. Hell, I probably joke the most out of The Crew. But for real. I'm starting to think Dee's taking my situation personal. I get it, I'm married, and I could be doing better than I am, but that's my choice. Everything ain't for everybody, and ain't none of us perfect, not even him. I've tried my hardest to let him slide since he got saved, but it's getting ridiculous. I feel like he's judging me to the point where it's almost violating our friendship. What you think?"

"Hmm. That's a hard one..." Eric hummed. "The sad thing is... you're right. I can't blame you for feeling that way."

"What you mean 'the sad thing?'"

"Usually, we don't see eye to eye, you know that. I feel you on this one. I hope that when you confront him you have an endgame."

"I got an endgame, alright. The games stop here. We don't have to rock with each other if he can't stop getting at me on my business. This *my* business, and he need to mind his," Bruce said, looking at him with a sour on his face.

"You're serious?"

"I'm dead serious."

"Let me call Dee so you'll get past this now." Eric put the ribs in the crockpot, then washed his hands and dialed Dee.

◆ ◆ ◆

Danny left before the Pastor gave the benediction it to get the car, and met Nana in front of the church. Nana talked to a few people in the congregation as she headed outside. Danny was starting to get impatient; almost the whole church came through the doors before Nana. Finally, she said her goodbyes and got in the car.

“The Pastor got it in today. He almost got a few tears to run down my face. Did you enjoy the service?” Danny asked.

“Yes. The Word was awesome, but if she said ‘touch your neighbor’ one more time. Lord knows, I was going to go up there and touch *her,*” Nana said.

“You’re a mess, Nana. I hope you’re hungry, I have a taste for some Caribbean food.”

“I wish you would, and I made all that food last night.”

“Let me do something for you. Plus, I don’t remember the last time I treated you out to eat. I’m still going to get my usual plates when I drop you off. Believe that.”

“Well, if you get your plates, we can go.”

“That’s why I love you Nana,” Danny said, then he blew a kiss at her as he drove to the restaurant. Nana smiled as she looked out the window.

They pulled up, and Nana got out while Danny tried to find a parking spot. Danny came back walking, twirling his keys on his finger.

“Why didn’t you go into the waiting area?” Danny asked.

“I wanted to get a little fresh air before we’re in funky town.”

“Huh? What are you talking about?”

“You *know* they don’t wear deodorant.” Nana turned her lip up.

Danny laughed to himself as he opened the door to the restaurant. They walked in and were very impressed by the atmosphere. Red, black, green, and yellow were everywhere. The tables had candles inside of real coconut shells. Even the music was very soothing. Nana looked at Danny with a shocked expression.

“Just the two of you?” The hostess asked, in a Jamaican accent.

“Yes,” Danny replied.

“Follow me,” the hostess said.

She grabbed two menus and walked them to their table, placing them on the table and lighting the candle. Danny and Nana took their seats.

“Your waitress will be with you shortly,” she said before she walked off.

Nana looked through the menu as Danny looked around the restaurant.

“Is Yolanda meeting us out here?”

“No. Why you say that?”

“You’re looking around like you’re waiting for someone.”

“Nah. Just impressed with how they have this place decorated. It almost looks like this spot Yolanda and I went to in Freeport Bahamas. If the jerk chicken taste close to what I had in Freeport, I found me a new spot.”

“I’m impressed, too, that it doesn’t smell like musky refugees in here,” Nana, said a half-smile on her face.

“Shhh! Don’t say that too loud! I haven’t got my food yet. I don’t need them to put anything extra on my plate.”

“What could be more extra than jerk. I wish I would pay for something with jerk on it. Stand for something or fall for anything.” Nana kept reading the menu.

“I can’t win with you,” Danny shook his head at Nana with a faint smile. Then he picked up the drink menu.

“Are y’all ready to order?” The waitress asked.

"Yes. Let me get the jerk chicken with cabbage and yams."

"What's your drink?"

"A coconut water," Danny said, then he handed her his menu.

"I will have the curry shrimp, mac and cheese, and collard. Give me a glass of red wine."

The waitress took the menus and walked away. Two minutes later, she placed their drinks on the table. Danny took a sip while noticing a couple making selections at the jukebox. When they walked away, he went to the jukebox. He put five dollars in and start flipping through the screen.

"Is that you, Mrs. Pat?" a woman asked as she stared at Nana.

"The one and only," Nana said, very confidently.

"You ain't change a bit. I'm Jackie, Kenya sister." Jackie hugged Nana.

"I know who you are. I can't count how many times I had to put you and your sister out of my house. Y'all was too beautiful to follow behind Donald and my son with their foolishness. I might be a little grey, but my sight and memory are baby fresh."

She wasn't dressed like any of the employees. Danny finished making his selections, then he walked to the table. Jackie looked at him, Nana and her started laughing.

"What? What's so funny?" Danny asked as he took his seat.

"Nosey, just like his father. If he isn't Eric's twin," Jackie said, looking at Danny's face.

"You know my dad?" He thought to himself, *is this Kenya?*

"Yes, too well. I'm Jackie, Kenya's sister."

Danny looked at Nana. Then, he stood up and extended his hand. "Nice to meet you."

Jackie looked at his hand as she moved in and hugged him.

"I wish you would try to shake my hand! You're practically family. Your grandma just told me that you're getting married, congrats. Do you have a caterer?"

"Yes, we already gave them the deposit and signed the contract." Danny sat back down.

"That's okay, I had to ask. I would still love to be a witness of your special day."

She pulled a business card out her back pocket and wrote her cell phone number on the back. Then, she passed it to Danny. "Miss Pat, it was nice to see you. I'm going to stop by and see you now that I know where you are. We gotta catch up. You still like Pink Champale?"

"You know it," Nana said.

"Good. Enjoy y'all meal, and I will be waiting for that invite," Jackie walked off.

The waitress brought their food out and placed it on the table. "Do you need anything else?"

"No, we good honey," Nana said.

Nana prayed over their food, then they started eating.

"What was y'all laughing about when I walked up?" Danny asked.

"Nothing," Nana said with a smirk.

Danny side-eyed her, knowing she wasn't telling the truth. When he took her home, Nana walked straight to the kitchen. Danny walked around the living room, looking at the pictures on the wall that he had seen millions of times. She fixed him two to-go plates of food, placing them in a grocery bag and walking into the living room. He took the bags from her and kissed her on the cheek.

"You're the best, Nana. Love you, Thanks for the food."

"Love you too, baby."

Danny opened the door, walked out, and went to close it behind him, but Nana grabbed the knob and stopped it from closing. Danny turned around to face the door.

"Make sure you call Jackie to see what you can find out about Kenya," Nana said, and then she shut the door in his face.

Danny stood there a second with his eyebrow raised before walking to the elevator.

Back at the house, Bruce and Eric were watching the game in the Boom Boom Room. Bruce's team was the Packers; they'd won Thursday, and he had no problem telling Eric every few minutes. Eric was getting frustrated. 30 seconds before half time, the Bucs were up by six points. Monica had already texted him a picture of Bentley the Butler, rubbing in their bet. By half time, the Bucs were still at 16 points, and the Giants were at ten. Eric got up, disappointed, to get some beers.

"I don't know why you surprised. You all can't put two winning seasons back to back. Just face it," Bruce said.

"Whatever. You keep talking like that, and I'm going to start charging you for your beers."

The front doorbell rang.

"That better be Dee. I don't mind waiting, but watching your sorry team is killing me."

Eric gave Bruce the middle finger. Then, he grabbed his cell phone off the bar and called Dee.

"Hello," Dee answered.

"Come in the side door, it's open. We downstairs."

"Cool." Dee ended the call.

Eric handed Bruce a Heineken. Dee came in the side door and walked down the steps. Dee gave them both dap.

"What's going on that you couldn't speak over the phone? Do

we have someone trying to sue us for some damage we done on their property?" Dee said, looking at them.

(The Crew had a landscaping business that they'd started 20 years ago—The Landscaping Crew. The four of them began the business to have something for their children. They thought it would be great to see, out of all their kids, who would keep the business going.)

"No. I called you over here because you and Bruce need to talk. I'm going to leave y'all down here. Don't tear up the Boom Boom Room," Eric said.

"You don't gotta leave. Matter of fact, I rather you be here," Bruce said.

Dee looked at Bruce, then at Eric, not knowing what was going on. Eric sat down while they both stood.

"Do you have some animosity towards me?" Bruce asked Dee.

Dee didn't say anything. He just frowned in disbelief of what he'd just heard come out of Bruce's mouth.

Bruce tried again. "Or, did I do something to you that I'm not aware of?"

"No, and no. Where is this coming from?"

"I'm just trying to understand why you have been coming at me sideways about my marriage. The key word is 'my!' That's my marriage, my business..."

"You right. But when did I come at you about your business or your marriage?"

"You can't be serious. You've got real comfortable telling me what I should be doing in my marriage. The last time was when I came to your promotion celebration with shorty. I've been letting you slide because you just got saved. I went through the same thing when my sister got saved. Trust me, I get it. I know I could be doing better in my marriage, as well as other areas in my life. But this judging and taking shots stops today," Bruce clapped his hand aggressively with his words.

"Wow. You really in your feelings, but I'm going to let you live. I'm not saying anything about you and your marriage after today. We have been boys too long to let something like this come between us."

"That's what I'm thinking, that's why it's been bothering me."

"Help me understand one thing, thought. Why stay married if you are running around with so many other chicks? Do you think you should be single?"

"That's a hard one. I guess... the same reason you were cheating on your first wife."

"Exactly. I'm trying to keep you from losing everything like I did. My ego and I was trying to sex the world. I wish someone would have kept it real with me. I love you, and I just want better for you and Angel."

"I wish it was that simple. Me and Angel relationship has been over for years. If it wasn't for the kids, I would have *been* left. It might sound crazy, but my side pieces help me deal with my wife and her ways. If it wasn't for them, I'd probably be in a straight jacket right now."

"I can give you my marriage counselor number."

"No thanks. I got six more years before my youngest pass that child support threshold. And I'm out."

"Say no more. Sorry for judging your situation without talking to you about it. We good?" Dee asked.

They dapped up each other. "To the soil."

CHAPTER 12

Jackie set her phone on her kitchen table at home as it rang on speakerphone. After the fifth ring, she picked it up, ready to hang up.

"Hey, little sis," Kenya finally answered her phone, and Jackie set hers back down.

"Hey. Guess who came into the shop today?" Jackie asked.

"Barack, Nas, Porzingis… You know I don't play the guessing game. Just tell me," Kenya said sassily.

"Okay, no fun Nina… Calm down. Mrs. Pat and her grandson. She looks as young as ever."

"What's the odds on that, seeing her after all these years? Did she remember you?"

"Definitely. She asked about you. She wants you to come to her grandson's wedding. She believed that her grandson brought her into the restaurant to see me. He saw the prom picture of you and Eric at her place. He thinks she doesn't know what he's doing."

"What is he doing?"

"Ain't it obvious? He's trying to hook you and Eric up!"

"Have you been hitting the bottle? Because you sound crazy."

"Do I? We'll see, when her grandson Danny reaches out to me. I asked to go to his wedding if he has any open spots. He's going to check with his fiancé."

"Why did you do that?"

"Mrs. Pat told me to."

"Both of y'all have lost your mind. I haven't spoken to Eric in over 25 years. And that was when he moved back to New York from Georgia. If he wanted to reach out to me, he knows how to get me."

"To my understanding, he hasn't got a clue to what his son is doing. Danny is doing this on his own."

"Well, I hope it works out, but I'm not gonna involve myself. What did Zackary say about you doing this?"

"I haven't told him yet. Once Danny reaches out to me, I'll see what he's up to. And I'll call you back after I book your flight."

"Whatever." Jackie could hear the smile in Kenya's voice.

"I called to give you the heads up while it's still fresh on my mind. Let me hop in the shower, we going to the movies. Love you, girl."

"Love you, too."

Kenya ended the call, then stood there for a second in deep thought.

She walked to her kitchen and hit the light switch behind the refrigerator, opening the door next to the fridge and walking into the garage. She scanned the boxes stacked in the corner to locate an old box. She stacked a few boxes into a new pile to get the box labeled 'Awards.' She sat on the pile as she opened the awards box. Searching through it, she pulled out a manila folder, labeled 'news clips' in Sharpie. She unwrapped the string and opened the folder, pulling a few Georgia Tech basketball newspaper clippings out before she pulled out the picture. Their prom photo.

She reminisced on them dancing at the prom. Eric was looking into her eyes, and their love was pure. They danced to 'Slow Hand' by The Pointer Sisters. She smiled fondly, then flipped the picture over and read the back.

I had a great time at your prom.
Your beauty was breathtaking tonight.
Jayne Kennedy beautiful.
Love You, Eric

It would be nice to see him again, Kenya thought to herself, still smiling at the picture.

CHAPTER 13

Fifty days from the wedding. Danny was packing up his briefcase after finishing his last class of the week. He scanned the desk to make sure he didn't forget anything, patted his pocket for his cell phone, and pulled it out. "Call Jackie mobile," Danny said to his phone. The phone dialed Jackie's number. After only one ring, he ended the call and put his phone in his pocket as he walked out of the classroom. He had been attempting to call Jackie the last few days, but hadn't followed through. Yolanda had offered to make the call, but he refused her help. That was his best attempt thus far.

As he opened the front door of the school to walk to his car, his phone started ringing again. He pulled the phone out of his pocket to see that it was Jackie. After the third ring, he answered it.

"Hello?" Danny answered.

"Someone from this number just called my phone," Jackie said.

"This is Danny, Eric's son? Sorry, I hung up, but I got another call as I was calling you."

"You're good, sweetheart. Unless you're calling me with bad news about me coming to your wedding."

"Not at all. I got you down with a plus one."

"Thanks. I've been waiting for this phone call. I will see you there. Thanks again."

"Don't hang up. Do you have a minute?"

"Yes, I'm free at the moment."

"This might sound... a little out of left field, since I just met you the other day. Your sister Kenya..."

"What about Kenya?" Jackie said, sounding puzzled.

"Is she married?"

"Yeah, you went left," Jackie answered. "But, she's no longer married."

"Good! I mean... not good for her... well, let me explain. I'm trying to find my dad a date or a love connection for my wedding. He hasn't had a serious relationship for nearly thirty years since my mother's death."

"I'm sorry to hear that."

"Thanks. As I visited my Nana, I stumbled on a picture of my dad and Kenya. My nana told me a little about my dad's love for her. I might be reaching or even out of my mind, but I believe that stumbling on that picture wasn't a coincidence. Can she be your plus one?"

"She can, because my husband doesn't do weddings. I will try my hardest to get her to come."

"I will fly her in, pay for her hotel and rental car. All her expenses will be taken care of."

"Wow. I'm impressed. You're going hard for your dad on your special day."

Danny laughed. "I got to, he sacrificed his wants and needs to raise me. I know that's what most parents do, he just did it without any second-guessing. Hopefully, Kenya has a spark that needs to be lit, too."

"You really are Eric's child. You're confident that if she comes up here, love will handle the rest. You don't even know her dating status."

"My nana always said, 'either you're married or single. There's no grey area.' Plus, I believe in love, faith, and opportunity. You convince her, and I will handle the rest."

"Okay, Captain Stubbing."

"Captain who?"

"Before your time. Let me call Kenya now."

"Great. Bye." Danny ended the call, feeling relieved as he walked to his car.

Jackie called Kenya, but Kenya didn't answer. She texted instead.

Jackie: Call me when you get a second

CHAPTER 14

49 days from the wedding

"Hurry up! The driver is waiting for us!" Danny yelled up the steps.

Eric walked down the steps to see the front door left open. He grabbed his keys out of the bowl on the dining room table. Eric locked the door, then got in the car with Danny. The driver started heading to Chelsea Piers.

"You're funny, dad," Danny said.

"Why you say that?"

"You're the one who planned this, and yet *you're* running behind."

"I'm running late to your standards. To The Crew, I'm early, mark my words. Bowlmor Lanes doesn't close until 2 in the morning."

"Are you sure you and The Senior Crew can hang out that late?"

"Whatever. You'll find out shortly. When I'm laying down, those go Bundy strikes." He crossed his forearms, making an X.

"You might win the first game, but that's it."

"I hear you, son."

They sat in silence for about five minutes, looking out their respective windows, until Danny asked the question that he hoped would get the conversation rolling.

"Can we finish the conversation that we had the other night?"

"I knew this was coming. What you wanna know?"

"How did you propose to Moms?"

"Wow!" Eric paused with his hand over his mouth, looking down, trying to think hard. After about thirty seconds, he moved his hand away again and started telling Danny about The Day. That was what Danielle and Eric had called it.

"It was award night at Georgia Tech. I was getting dressed--it was a formal event. Dee was in the bathroom. Your mother walked in and was looking stunning. Her curls were hanging perfectly. She had on this gold gown that took my breath away. It was sexy and classy at the same time. Sleeveless, V-neck gown that showed too much for me, but at the time, I was very protective of your momma. She sat on my bed and started looking through this magazine that was on my nightstand dresser.

"I waited for Dee to leave the room when I asked her to pass me the cuff links out of the top drawer. When she opened the drawer, my heart started racing. I've been going over this day so many times in my head, but I felt my heart trying to come through my tux. She walked to me with the cuff links box. I held my sleeve out for her to put on the cuff links. She looked at me with the side eye, you know? Then, she opened the box to see the engagement ring. She froze, holding the ring in her right hand and the box in the other. I dropped to one knee reached up to pull her hand to her side. She wouldn't relax her hands enough for me to pull it down. I pulled a little harder, and I was able to dislodge the ring from her hand. I took the box out her left hand, then threw it on the floor. Holding her left hand, I looked up at her as nervous as I could be. I took a deep breath, and before I could finish exhaling, tears started rolling down her cheeks.

"'When I first met you, I knew you were going to be mine. I even envisioned you being my wife before we ever shared a kiss. Over the years, my love has only grown stronger for you. Everything in my life that is good, you either led me there, assisted me, or have given it to me. I hope that I have filled your life with joy as you have for me. I can go on and on but what I'm trying to say is... will you marry me?' Of course, she said 'yes.' Then she dropped on her knees, and we kissed. When we stood up, I placed the ring on her finger. I yelled it official, like a referee whistle. We laughed and hugged. Dee and your mother's girlfriend Paula came in with a bottle of champagne and glasses."

"Wow. I could only imagine how she felt. You were romantic even at a young age."

"Yeah. The Crew used to call me Loverboy. I wrote The Crew love letters for girls they were trying to get with."

"The ironic thing is more you open up, the more it's like meeting you for the first time, Dad."

"You know me, son. I think when your mother died, a certain part of me might have died with her. Or, should I say, been packed away? That's enough talking about your mother. We are going to get our drink on and talk about your future, not my past."

"You right, but can you answer one more question? I promise it's not about Moms."

"Yeah, shoot."

"The last time you were talking, you said something about 'love color.' I tried to Google that, but some foreign singing group came up. I know that's not what you mean. Is it?"

"Not at all. It's something that I made up for me to stop comparing different relationships. I believe that every person brings their color to the relationship. For instance, I always saw my color as blue. Therefore, every relationship I enter, I bring that color with me. Now, let's say I get into a relationship with a person, and her color is yellow. The more we come together as one, the more we'll make the prettiest green you ever saw. The less of our color you see individually, the greater we came together as one. On the flip side of that, if we break up, I leave with my blue. Then, when I get with someone else, we will make our own color. If she's red, we will make purple. No two relationships will make the same color, even if the people have the same colors as a prior relationship. We might be created the same, but never exactly. You get it?"

Danny nodded thoughtfully. "Do I... that was deep, Dad. You need to get that published. I don't know what made you think like that, on that level, but I'm going to use that."

"My biological dad made me think on that level with all his mess, but that's another story."

"I hear you."

My dad really is opening up. I've heard him reference his father only a few times my whole life. It was always in a negative way. This time he said his biological and he's the only dad he ever had in his life. My nana never had him around any other men, Danny thought to himself as they made it to the city.

Kenya sat on her couch watching TV as she texted back and forward with her daughter. Her daughter Kelsea lived back on the east coast, in Richmond, Virginia. She was an assistant girls' basketball coach at VCU.

Kels: Love you mom. I will ttyl

Kenya: Love you too.

After Kenya pressed send, she scrolled through some of her other texts. She saw the last text that she'd sent Jackie. She never got back to her the other day. She dialed Jackie's number. On the first ring, Jackie answered.

"I guess you are just getting out that meeting," Jackie said, trying to be funny.

"I'm sorry, I was so drained after that meeting. Then it slipped my mind even to hit you back. My bad, girl."

"I got that call about the wedding. Just like I said, he wants you to be in attendance."

"Did he say that, or you're just assuming? You know how you do, Miss Cleo always knows," Kenya smiled referring to Cleo the psychic.

"Stop playing. He said it himself, and he also said he would pay for all your expenses."

"Are you serious?" Kenya was stunned.

"Yes! From your flight, hotel, and car rental. He wants you to be there."

"Wow."

"I know, right? He's very confident that if he gets you there, Eric will be happy to see you. He reminds me of Eric."

"Not saying I'm going to come yet. But when is the wedding?"

"The Saturday after Thanksgiving on the 25th."

"Let me see if Jacob is bringing the family to Cali for the holidays. His wife's family lives about an hour from here. If he's not coming, I will pay my way. I can kill two birds with one stone. I can visit Kelsea and the kids in VA, then shoot to the City for the wedding."

"Okay. I will tell him you're coming. Love you. Bye." Jackie ended the call before Kenya could say anything more.

Kenya looked at her phone and smiled. She got up off the couch, then walked in front of the fireplace. She turned back to face the couch, looking into the mirror over the couch. She sucked in her stomach and poked her butt out, standing on her tippy toes. The duck lip faces she was making were priceless. After profiling, she skipped into her bedroom with the biggest, teenage girl-esque smile.

"You up, Nephew. And you're in last place. Let me find out the The Elderly Crew is smashing you. Yeah, E told us what you said. Who's old now? Huh?" Bruce jeered as he gave Eric a high five.

Danny looked at them as he picked up his bowling ball off the rack. He shook his head as he set up to bowl—three steps, then his curved release. The ball spun from the right side of the lane to the left. Danny felt a strike coming.

The ball hit the lead pin. Danny turned to face them, as if he knew it was a strike. Bruce, Eric and Maleek all shrugged their shoulders at him. Surprised, Danny turned around to see he left a split--the last two pins on each side hadn't fallen. As Danny waited for his ball to come back up the rack, Dee walked up. Dee gave everyone dap and took off his jacket off, set it on the chairs, then walked to the bar. Danny knocked one of his pins down. He picked up his mug and took a celebratory drink. Dee returned with a mixed drink.

"I paid for two more pitchers and fifty mixed wings. Damn!" Dee said, shocked, when he glanced at the score. "I see somebody got their wedding on their mind, not winning." Dee looked at Danny.

"I'm good. I always start slow, but the strikes are on the way," Danny assured.

"Speaking of strikes. Have you thought hard about this marriage? Did you cross your t's and dot your i's, nephew?" Bruce asked.

Danny looked at Bruce, and then he looked at his dad. He knew his dad was up to something, inviting him out with The Crew. Danny smiled when he answered Bruce.

"Yes. I thought long and hard. I'm ready, and she's ready."

"That's good. With you out the way, I'll take your black book," Maleek said. Everyone laughed, except Danny.

"You crazy," Danny said.

"No, I'm serious! A black book is for emergencies, break in case of fire. Or a bad argument, whichever comes first."

"All my contacts are on my phone, plus they stored on my Google account. We not in the stone ages no more."

"Okay, Mr. Technology. When you get married and one of those chicks decide to call you while you're laying in the bed with your wife, the stone she hit you with ain't going to be from no stone age. You feel me?"

"I didn't think about that. Good looking."

"Remember, not only married people have good advice. Delete, block, or change their names in your phone. Think ahead, and be prepared, because marriage is serious," Maleek said.

"I got you."

"Remember everything that we say tonight and take heed. Put God ahead of your life, and let Him govern your marriage," Dee chimed in. "As long as you all are evenly yoked, you can withstand any storm. Trust and believe in your heavenly Father."

"Listen to your Uncle Dee, because if anyone can blend God into every situation holding Ciroc and cranberry, it's him," Eric said with a chuckle. They all laughed at Dee, while he twisted his lips.

They played five or six games. Drink after drink, The Crew got to see Danny in rare form. There were so many plates of wings on the table, yet they wouldn't let the waitress take the plates. They kept telling her they were still eating off them. They liked to play this little game, to see how long it took before the waiter or waitress got frustrated. Danny still hadn't won a game, and it was after 1 A.M. The spot would close in less than an hour.

"Tell the waitress to get another round of Patron," Danny said as he waited for his ball to come back on the rack.

Maleek waved a waitress down and told her to get the waitress that waiting on lane 40. She returned to the bar.

"Yo! Did I tell y'all what happened when I had a bad Viagra experience? The waitress reminded me of the young chick I bagged in D.C.," Maleek said.

"Nah," Dee said.

"What D.C. chick?" Eric asked.

"No, but I gotta hear this," Bruce said.

"Danny, come over here, you need to hear this," Maleek said, all hyped up.

Danny walked over and sat down with the rest of them. Maleek stood up and started telling his story.

"Check it. I was in D.C. promoting one of my artists. He was doing six shows in the DMV area. I was at this spot at the bar and met this girl. A bad redbone, long hair all hers. She had on this romper that wasn't tight but was fitting her so sexy. You know I don't play any games, so I hit her with my favorite line. 'You coming home with me, or I'm riding with you? I said, all seductive looking, looking straight in her eyes."

"'Excuse me? She'd said. 'My bad. My name is Maleek. I'm in town on business promoting this artist. When I saw you, something in my mind told me we need to spend some time with each other. We don't have to go to my hotel or your place. But something in my soul is telling me that I need to get to know you, and vice versa.'

"Then, she leaned back and stared at me for a second. 'You serious?' She said, looking me up and down. 'So serious. When the energy is right, I follow my heart. Maybe I'm reading you wrong, but your eyes are telling me to pay out our tabs and let's find a place to eat. You hungry? Because I know I am. I'd said."

"To make a long story short, we left her car and went to eat at Bourbon Steak at the Four Seasons Hotel. She didn't know at the time, but that was the hotel I was staying. We chatted over dinner. Her name was Leslie, and she was from Cali. She wrote a column at one of the papers in D.C. She was bougie, valley girl, mixed with a little urban flavor, but not ghetto. She started rubbing her foot up my leg, then went to my crotch. I looked at her with a *don't start this* face, and she looks back like, *let's starts this*. When she went to the bathroom, I pulled out a Viagra and broke it. I took one half with a sip of water."

"I knew she had a few glasses of wine, but when she came back from the bath, she looked different. She whispered, 'I'm ready,' and she showed me her panties balled up in her hand! 'Check, please,' I'd shouted to a waiter that wasn't mine. I snuck and took the other half of the pill as the waiter took my card to cash me out."

"Riding the elevator to the room, she sucked my tongue like she was giving me oral. When I opened the room door, she kicked off her heels and sat Indian-style on the couch. Her dress was rolled up high on her thighs. I could see *everything*. She reached in her purse and pulled out a small jewelry box. When she opened it, I could smell the loud she had in there. She started rolling a joint. I'm looking around to see where she could smoke that at. The windows wouldn't open, and I didn't have a balcony. I was like, 'Ma, you might have to go downstairs and smoke that, maybe in the parking deck. This room is a non-smoking room. You already saw how they were looking at us when we were eating."

"'That's cool, I respect that,' she said. I felt relieved. She put the joint up and pulled out a bag of mushrooms. 'Come here and take one with me," she said as she held two in her hand.

"'I don't do shrooms,"I'd said, looking at her.

"'Don't or won't? This is natural. Google it. You can't get addicted to mushrooms, you need to worry about getting addicted to *this*," she'd said, and then she rolled her dress up even more. I bit my lip looking at her va-jay-jay. Then, I flopped on the couch beside her. I took the shroom out her hand, and we tapped the shrooms as if we were making a toast. We ate them. She smiled, then got up and turned on some slow music on her phone. She danced to music as she was one with the music. I felt like Neno Brown watching G-Money girl."

"She took off all her clothes and jumped in the bed. I got up and got a condom. We were getting it in for twenty minutes or so before I started feeling funny. I thought I might be a late reaction from the shroom. I'm hitting it from behind; then, I started having a sneezing episode. My tongue on the side started itching, like I was having an allergic reaction. I tried to keep it together, trying not to stop our session. Then the last sneeze happened, and my right hand got stiff. It was stiffer than a broom, I couldn't bend it."

"I was scared to death, praying and everything. My heart was racing, but I couldn't stop it was like I was possessed. She turned her head and told me to slap her butt and talk dirty. I start slapping her left side with my left hand and talking dirty. Then she said, 'The other side, baby.' I tried with my right hand, but it was too stiff. It was stretched straight out like a crossing guard stopping traffic. I had to slap her right side with my left hand. I caught a glance of me doing that in the mirror. I looked like a handicapped Cowboy at a rodeo on a horse. I pulled it off and she fell asleep. I couldn't sleep, though, cause my arm was stiff for two hours after my penis went down. I haven't used a Viagra or shrooms after that night. True story," Maleek said, ending his tale.

"Wow. I've heard of a lot of bad Viagra stories. But yours takes the cake. You had an arm-on, not a hard-on. Wow. You were hitting her with that 'STOP, in the name of love' sex." Bruce laughed as he raised his arm up, doing a 'stop' motion while humping at the same time.

They all started laughing then. Danny laughed so hard that he started to gag.

"Hand down, man down," Dee said. Then, he took Danny to the bathroom.

They saw Eric threw some napkins onto the throw-up, and heard Bruce going to the bar to tell them they needed the check and someone to clean up the mess.

Danny rinsed his mouth out and took off his shirt. He threw his shirt in the trash, pulled out his tank top from where it was tucked in his pants, and fixed himself in the mirror.

"Thanks, Unk, for giving me that card. I talked to Jackie. Hopefully, she can convince Kenya to come to the wedding," Danny said, slurring his words.

"First of all, I didn't give you no card. Furthermore, this isn't a conversation we need to be having, now or never. You got it?" Dee looked at Danny with a serious expression.

"Yes. I got it... mum's the word," Danny said slowly as he put his finger over his lips.

"C'mon. With your drunk tail. Remind me never to drink with you."

CHAPTER 15

48 days to the wedding

Eric reached over on his nightstand, trying to locate his cell phone with his eyes closed. He finally found it and pulled it to his face. He opened his eyes to see that it was 8:15 A.M.

"Danny! Danny!" Eric yelled from the bed.

He didn't get any response. Moving slowly as he dragged himself out of bed, he grabbed his pajama pants off the recliner, put them on, and slid on his bedroom shoes. On the way downstairs, he knocked on Danny's door.

"Yeah?" Danny called, sounding pitiful.

"Get up and come downstairs. I'm making breakfast."

"I'll be down there in a minute."

"Now, son."

"Okay."

Eric smiled as he headed to the kitchen. He knew Danny was feeling bad and it tickled him. He hadn't seen him like that since he was a teenager. Eric was hard on him, and rightfully so, but he was very proud of the man that Danny had become. He took out eggs, turkey bacon, and pancake mix, and placed them on the counter. Eric opened the freezer and pulled out a ziplock bag with a frozen, light-greenish concoction. He put a pot on the stove and turned it on high. Danny walked in as Eric turned the burner on and sat at the table.

"You good, son?" He said extremely loudly, messing with him.

Danny just looked at him, his face said a thousand words. Eric laughed to himself while mixing up the pancake batter. He pulled the griddle out of the cubby and placed it on the counter. He wiped it off with a napkin, then turned it to 275 degrees.

"Put that zip lock into that boiling water."

Danny got up and picked up the ziplock bag. Before he placed it into the water, he smelled the inside.

"Whatever this is, I hope it's for you. This not for me, right?" Danny placed the bag in the water.

"It's for me..."

"Good," Danny said with relief.

"And you. I call this 'Snap Back.' A couple of sips of this and a good breakfast, you'll feel like a million bucks, ready to run a marathon." He sprayed the griddle with olive oil, placing the bacon on half the griddle and pouring pancakes on the other half.

Danny frowned, thinking that he might have to take some of that, after all. He heard his phone ringing, though, and went upstairs to get it. By the time Danny got to the phone, it had already stopped ringing. He'd missed a call from Yolanda. He called her back as he walked back down the steps. *Ring, ring.*

"Hello?" Yolanda answered her phone.

"Good morning, baby," Danny said, taking a seat at the table.

"Good morning. I had to check on you because you didn't hit me last night. I knew you were with your dad, so I didn't call you when I woke up to use the bathroom. If you thought I was crazy, that call wouldn't have been sweet. I woke up at 3, and I checked my phone to see that you didn't text me before you went to bed. You never even responded to my text when I text you good night, last night..." Yolanda was saying.

"Not to cut you off, but you're right. I should have let you know when I made it in safe. I was dead wrong, and very inconsiderate of you worrying yourself to death. I'll try my hardest not to let that happen again."

Eric looked at Danny and gave him the thumbs up. Then, he pointed to the stove, trying to show Danny that the Snap Back was ready.

"Are you still there?" Danny asked Yolanda.

"Yes... I'm just a little shocked at your response. I prepared myself for all your excuses."

"You don't have to worry about any more excuses. No one's perfect, but if I don't check my flaws, how can I get better? I'm trying to go into this marriage proactive, trying to be the husband you can love forever. Hold on, let me pour up this sewage my dad wants me to drink," he said, placing the phone on the table.

After Danny poured himself a cup, he picked the phone back up. Eric placed their plates on the table. Then, he got two cups and the orange juice out of the refrigerator.

"Hello," Danny said to the phone as he sat down.

"I'm sorry," Yolanda said.

"Sorry for what?"

"Just, not recognizing your growth and how you're trying to be that kind of husband. I need to step up my wife-ness, instead of focusing on you, huh?"

"We good, baby. We're going to grow together and make the perfect love color. We'll talk about that later, me and my dad are having breakfast. Love you."

"Love you, too. Tell Mr. Eric I said hey. Talk to you later."

"Will do, bye." Danny ended the call.

"Yolanda said hey, Dad."

"Tell her I said hey when you talk back to her. I see you learning, son. It takes two to tango, and one to throw up the white flag. Just don't use it too often, or she is going to realize it's game."

"I got you," Danny said, smashing the bacon.

They ate their food as they laughed about last night, until Danny's text alert sounded on his phone. Danny opened the text.

Jackie: All is good, Kenya will be there. She said she would pay for her way but thanks for the offer. We will see you there.

Danny: Thanks for your help and I can't wait for that day to get here.

Danny pressed send on the text as he tried not to scream or smile too hard.

"Is that a nudie text smile?" Eric asked.

"No, something came through for the wedding."

"Okay."

Eric got up and put the plates in the sink. As he cleaned off the griddle, Danny cleaned off the counter. Danny placed the eggs in the refrigerator; then, he stared at Eric with his hand on the door. He caught Danny staring at him.

"Is everything okay, son?"

"Everything is great. I was thinking about these last few weeks. Our talks have been priceless."

"You can say that again. I've used the company therapist twice, and neither one of those talks have been this fulfilling."

"I get it. Now it's my time to open up to you about something that has haunted me all these years. I need you to sit down, and don't interrupt me."

"Here we go again," Eric rolled his eyes as he sat at the table.

"I know we've never talked about Mom's death. For her to die on my fifth birthday was devastating. I remember that day like it was yesterday. I heard you and Moms talking loudly. I was outside in the backyard. I looked through the patio door and saw you holding my Spiderman costume. I ran in the house to you and grabbed the costume from you."

"I went up to my room and got dressed. When I came downstairs, I asked to see the cake. You told me after you took a shower you were going to get it. I'd frowned and started crying, because usually when you told me that, it didn't happen. You told me, 'top crying; we don't do that here.' I kept crying until Moms grabbed her purse and said, 'I'll be right back with the cake.' I said thank you and skipped back outside, going through the party bags."

"I forgot all about the cake once the guests arrived and started having fun. From the clown to all the gifts on the table, it was the start of a great birthday party. Until I ran into the house to show you the dog the clown made with the balloons. To see you crying, holding Moms purse standing with two police officers with the door open. I asked what was wrong. You turned to me and fell to your knees and hugged me tightly.

I kept asking where Mom was, until you finally told me that she was in a car accident. She would have never got killed by that drunk driver if she wasn't getting my cake. If I had just... just waited for you to take a shower, she would still be here." Tears started rolling down Danny's cheeks.

"That's not true. And I'm sorry that you have been living with that pain that you didn't cause," Eric said. "I was supposed to pick up the cake after work. The loud noise that you heard when you were in the backyard was... your mother was fussing me out for buying the costume instead of picking up the cake. She'd picked up your costume already. I got it mixed up, son. I blame myself. If I had remembered to pick up the cake, your mother and my soulmate would still be here. Knowing that, all these years, I haven't forgiven myself. Then, for that to happen a week before we got married was overwhelming." Eric swallowed. "I should have married your mother a long time ago. Me being stuck in my ways, letting what my dad told me about marriage make me hesitant."

"Those are the two biggest regrets I've ever made in my life. If I knew you were feeling this way, thinking that you caused this. I would have *been* told you about that day. The counselor in Georgia when that happened told me that I would know when it was time to discuss her death with you. He also told me to wait until you got past her death, because telling you early could have you hating me while mourning your momma. I convinced myself never to tell you. I never wanted that day to come between us. I hope me keeping that from you doesn't make you hate me? I hope you can forgive me." Eric's eyes got glassy.

"I could never hate you, Dad. I love you."

"I love you, too, son."

Eric walked over to Danny, and they hugged each other as they had that day. They both cried during the embrace. The tears weren't sad tears, but tears of joy—tears of release, tears of closure.

CHAPTER 16

Fourteen days to the wedding

Danny and Brandon were looking at the numbers on the elevator as it went up, stopping on the penthouse floor. They got off the elevator holding two bags apiece. Danny put his bag out of his right hand onto the floor by the door of the hotel room. He got the key card out of his pocket to open the door. Brandon turned the knob and walked into the penthouse.

"When you told me you had a suite at The Dominick, I would have never thought it would look like this! This is bananas, I'm about to I.G. this to death," Brandon said as he took the bags of liquor to the kitchen.

Danny followed him to the kitchen with his two bags.

"This view is ridiculous, I feel like Ghost off *Power*. Wait until the strippers see what you are working with. How much did this run you?"

"Nothing, my dad booked it for me. When he found out I wasn't having a bachelor party, he started making some phone calls. Then, the hotel called me and asked me which two days that I wanted to reserve. It worked out that the same week Yolanda is in Cancun, they had an available penthouse."

"That's what's up. I'm glad you didn't listen to me and do it at the Boom Boom Room."

Danny grinned as he placed the empty bags in the trash. He had known Brandon all his life. Brandon was Bruce's oldest child. When Eric and Danielle would bring him from Georgia to New York, he would play with Brandon. That was every summer until they moved back up here. Usually, when Danny got in trouble, Brandon wasn't too far away. Yolanda would catch a jet back if she knew Brandon was helping with his bachelor party.

"Come on, Bee. I need to make one more run," Danny said.

"It's two beds on opposite side of the suite. One gotta be mine!"

"I hear you."

"You hear me, but you don't feel me."

Danny had a little smirk on his face as they walked to the elevator.

Yolanda and Sheremah were sitting in the spa chairs, tilted back, with apricot masks on their face and cucumbers on their eyes. They were enjoying some of the amenities at Breathless Riviera Cancun Resort and Spa. Their friends Alesha and Destiny were having a late lunch with a couple guys they'd met last night. The waitress came back into the spa with their drinks. She set down the glasses, and then she left.

"One more drink and I'm going to need a nap before we go out. These drinks are stronger than they were last night," Yolanda said as she took another sip from the straw.

"It ain't even that strong, you've just been out the loop. I remember when we went to Charleston and we got super drunk. Now, *those* drinks were too strong," Sheremah said.

"No, those drinks weren't this strong. We got super drunk because I let Destiny talk us into hitting that weed bong, hookah, whatever you want to call that. That's why we got that drunk. I learned after that night not to follow her on anything. I love all my girls, but Destiny got some stuff with her."

"Yeah, but you gotta take the good with the bad with her. I love that she books the best affordable trip ever, and she knows how to have fun. Plus, she's the best when you need to snap out of a broken heart. Lord knows."

"Amen. You can say that again. I cried on her shoulders many a nights."

"You and me both."

They laughed, thinking about how many time Destiny had saved them. *My girls!* Yolanda thought to herself. She and Sheremah's grandma lived in the 40 Projects. They'd known each other for so long that people might think they were cousins. They met Alesha and Destiny at I.S. 8 when they were in junior high. They had been tight ever since. They were all so different, and yet their bond was more familial than most families. Destiny and Alesha were very outgoing, while Yolanda and Sheremah were more reserved.

Destiny and Alesha walked into the spa.

"Y'all going to sit here all day with that butter on y'all face. Where the facial lady at? Excuse me! Excuse me," Destiny said, making a scene trying to get the ladies' attention.

"There she goes, with that boogie down etiquette," Yolanda said with her best Rosie Perez voice. Sheremah and Alesha laughed.

"Whatever!" Destiny rolled her eyes.

Yolanda always got on Destiny because she moved to Queens from the Bronx when she was 12. The aesthetician came back into the room and started cleaning up the ladies' faces. Destiny looked at Yolanda with her eyebrow raised as if to let her know, *I made that happen*. Then, she and Alesha left again. After they were all cleaned up, Sheremah and Yolanda walked to the outside pool area with their drinks. They didn't see the other girls out there, so they took their robes off and sat in the pool chairs in their bathing suits.

"Call them and see where they're at," Yolanda said to Sheremah.

Sheremah found her phone, but put it down after a moment.

"I called, but she sent it to voicemail on the first ring."

"That's cool. She'll hit you back."

Brrr, Brrr. Sheremah's cell phone vibrated--she got a text back from Destiny. She read the text aloud so Yolanda could hear.

Destiny: Pull your salsa dress out your bag and if you don't have one buy one. I've bought some salsa lessons off Groupon and it's going down

"I knew it was something. Did you text her back?" Yolanda asked.

"I'm doing it now."

Sheremah: 10-4 Captain

Sheremah showed Yolanda what she texted back. They both smiled, because they knew that was going to get under Destiny's skin. She immediately sent a middle finger emoji back. They smiled, taking sips of their drinks. Sheremah waved to the waitress and signaled for two more.

CHAPTER 17

Later that night, Yolanda and Sheremah walked in their hotel room with a handful of bags. They went to buy a dress to go dancing in, but they ended up buying everything that wasn't nailed down. Yolanda emptied all her bags onto her bed. She looked over all the purchases.

"Do you ever have buyers remorse?" Yolanda asked Sheremah.

"Not at all. You probably should ask if my credit card company has remorse for upping my credit limit."

"You too much."

They took showers then started trying on all the different dresses. They knew they'd overdid it when they couldn't figure out if they tried them all on or if they'd skipped a few. After 45 minutes, they both stood in separate mirrors while putting their makeup on. Yolanda let the lady at one of the shops pick out the dress she had on. The dress was red with a high-low ruffle style cut. The top and sleeves were lacy, and the bottom of the dress hugged every curve God gave her. Sheremah had on a canary yellow dress, sleeveless, with short hand sleeves that matched the dress.

They were running behind; Destiny told them to be in the lobby of the hotel at 8 P.M., sharp. When they finished fixing up, they grabbed their purses and headed to the elevator. Once the elevator opened at the lobby, they got off and walked to the lobby.

They didn't see Destiny or Alesha anywhere. Sheremah pulled out her phone and called Destiny. Destiny didn't answer, sending the call to voicemail.

"I'm getting tired of her not answering my calls."

Before Sheremah could put her phone back in her purse, someone tapped her on her shoulder. When she turned around, she jumped as if she was startled. The noise she made as she jumped made Yolanda turn around. There stood Destiny and Alesha in salsa competition dresses. They even had high updo wigs that matched their outfits. Destiny's dress was lime green, and Alesha's was aqua blue.

"Wow. Y'all went all out! And words can't describe how far out I'm talking about," Yolanda said.

"You know my motto. When you're in Rome, do what the Romans do. I even got us a limo for the night, let's make it count." Destiny said, and then she started walking outside to the limo.

Alesha started walking behind her until she noticed that Yolanda and Sheremah haven't budged. "Are y'all in or out?" Alesha asked.

They looked at each other then before saying, "We're in." Alesha turned around quickly, and her dress flared out like an umbrella. She worked that dress to the limo.

"It's something funny going on, I can feel it," Yolanda said to Sheremah.

"Just pray and come on, bride-to-be."

Yolanda cut her eyes at Sheremah as they walked to the limo. The limo had three ice buckets with two bottles of wine in each. Destiny opened a bottle of Moscato, passing it to the girls. Once she'd fixed her drink, she made a toast.

"To my girl, Yolanda. I love you, and I'm so proud of you as you jump the broom with Danny. I knew that we would all have to come to this place in life where we would become someone's wife. For you to be the first, it could only be by God's design or his sense of humor. Nah, I'm just playing. But for real, Danny couldn't have picked a better life mate than you. I love you, girl, and wish that you get everything your heart desires. Cheers, amen, and turn up," Destiny said.

They all said amen as they tapped wine glasses. They drank and poured more drinks until the limo stopped. They downed their glasses, and they got out of the limo. The chauffeur held their hands as they stepped onto the sidewalk. Destiny walked to the instructor once they were inside. They talked for a second, and then he addressed the group.

"Hello. My name is Ramon, and I will be your instructor for the night. I will start out by showing you a few moves as a group, then I will lead you with a basic routine, one at a time. In the punch bowl is Sangria, so help yourself," Ramon said.

Ramon started showing them how to use their hips as he counted. 1, 2, 3, 4, 5, 6, 7, 8... The girls watched as they fixed another glass of wine. Yolanda watched his every move. Then, they all followed him as he taught them as a group. He noticed Yolanda was getting it a little faster than the other girls. After thirty minutes or so, he went into the back and brought back a female instructor.

"For no extra charge, I'm going to have my dance partner, Gloria, help the bride as I help the rest of you. Therefore, when I get to you," (he pointed at Yolanda), you will be ready for a more advanced routine. ¿Sí?" Ramon said.

He started dancing with Destiny as the others watched. Gloria helped Yolanda with her hip movement and her spins.

Danny was standing in the corner of the penthouse, looking out the window-slash-wall. Most of the walls were glass, from the floor to the ceiling. The movement of the car lights was hypnotizing; as his bachelor party carried on, he found himself stuck. Looking out across the city scape, he thought about how his life will never be the same in two weeks. *It's definitely happening.*

"Danny. *Danny,*" Brandon said as he tapped the window in front of him.

Danny hadn't even realized he was there until Brandon tapped the glass. Everything snapped into focus,. He had been hearing the noise of the music, but wasn't understanding the words. In the background, Jim Jones "Ballin'" was playing. He turned to face Brandon.

"The strippers are asking for you. They want to thank you and give you a private dance in the bedroom."

"I'm good on the dance, but I will talk to them."

"There you go, always being picky. I got two more waves of strippers coming through. I got the best for last, she doesn't dance with other dancers. She's the Show Stopper. True story."

"You got *more* coming?" Danny asked as he made his way over to the strippers.

Brandon didn't say anything. He raised his hands in the air, full of singles and a devilish smile. Danny thanked the strippers for coming out and politely turned down the private dance. They went back in the other bedroom to change clothes. He walked in the kitchen area, only to run into Thomas.

"When you get here?" Danny asked Thomas as he gave him dap.

"A couple of minutes before the stripper wrapped it up. When they started raking up the money off the floor, I stepped in the bathroom to call my wife back. I hope she stops texting me," Thomas said.

"Good luck. What the f--" Danny started to say as he caught a glimpse of the three new strippers Brandon was leading into the bedroom to change.

"Damn. Is it me, or are they triplets?" Thomas said, eyes wide open.

“I don’t know... Bee didn’t tell me anything about this wave of strippers. He told me about the Show Stopper, that’s it.”

“Hold up. You’re having waves of strippers, *and* there’s a show stopper coming?”

“Yes. And I didn’t want any of this. This is Bee and my dad’s idea. I wanted to go shopping for the house and get some drinks at a bar or something. This is a lot.”

“You damn right it’s a lot. This is people loving you a lot. Snap out of it and enjoy it a lot. Don’t rush to be a family man--take it from a married man. Don’t get me wrong, I wouldn’t trade my family for anything in the world, but if I knew I could have waited a few more years to have what I have, without a doubt, I would have waited. On that note, let’s get more drinks and use these singles.” Thomas pulled out a new handful of singles from the bank.

As Danny poured the drinks he smiled, knowing Thomas was right. He was a little uptight because he’d told Yolanda that he didn’t want any strippers, only to have all this now. He hadn’t lied, but he still felt a little guilty. Danny handed Thomas his drink as Brandon walked over to them.

“The dancers want you to sit in the seat in the main room.”

“I told you... you know what--what chair I need to get in?” Danny said, downing his drink.

Thomas and Brandon grinned at each other, knowingly. It was about to go down.

“That’s my Dan--NYC, baby. Who’s world is it?” Brandon shouted.

“The world is mine!” Danny shouted back as he followed Brandon.

After Danny sat, Brandon took out a blindfold and got to work. He couldn’t see a thing. The room started to erupt with whistles and claps. Danny's heart was beating so fast, and he tried his hardest to squint through the blindfold somehow. He felt the girls circling him, felt their hands reach out to touch him. He followed them with his head, but still couldn't see anything. They all stopped, and they pulled his shirt and tank top off. Then, they tugged the blindfold off. One woman had on a black dominatrix skirt, boots, gloves, mask, and a whip in her hand. He could tell she had nothing on under the skirt. The other two had on leopard skin boots, belts, collars, and lacey gloves. They might as well have been naked.

"I'm Bast, The Cat Goddess. This is Catina and Catilya. Enjoy the show, and tip big," the dancer in black all but purred.

She whipped one of the dancers on the back. The dancer dropped to her knees and crawled over to Danny. She was rubbing her head on his inner leg, making them open even wider. Then, Bast whipped the other one, who dropped and did the same. They moaned as they seductively rubbed their body on his, just like cats. Bast walked behind Danny, placing her whip on his chest. She pulled the whip slowly to his shoulder, and the girls followed the whip. They slithered up his body until they both sat on each knee, one on each side. Finally, she lowered the whip to his crouch. They purred as they fondled the whip on Danny's lap with their hands. A shower of singles started falling from everywhere. It was raining money--literally.

Danny leaned his head back and whispered to Bast. "I'm good. Let them work the room."

She smacked her own hand with the whip, and they stopped. The girls followed Bast, doing a routine of the floor that started from a split stance. Danny got up and grabbed his shirts. As he pulled them on, he watched the three get their money. Brandon threw what must have been a hundred or more singles in the air, before walking over to Danny.

"Oh, yeah. They are triplets, by the way. I know when their father found out he was having three girls, he probably died.

And if he didn't then, he damn sure would now, if he seen this. Tomorrow, I'm taking my daughter out to lunch. You heard," Brandon said as they watched the performance.

Ramon went in the back room to take a break after finishing up with the other girls. Gloria had already finished up with Yolanda thirty minutes ago. Yolanda had watched Ramon instructing Sheremah, since she was the last one he'd danced with. She couldn't wait for her turn, moving her hips and counting the step as she watched.

Ramon returned to the room in all black, a red bandana tied around his neck and a black sombrero on his head. The girls got up from their chairs as Ramon walked to Yolanda. He reached out his hand, and she grabbed it. She stood up and he spun her into him. He held the lower part of her back as he looked into her eyes. He spun her back out, still holding her hand. He threw the sombrero towards the girls. When they started dancing, the other girls watched them with smiles on their faces.

Ramon looked like something out of a girl toy magazine with perfect hair, dark eyes and rugged-yet-trimmed facial hair, giving him some kind of mystique. Then, there was his body, chiseled out of stone. The girls couldn't tell in his first outfit, but he'd let it all out in this one. His pants were so tight around the thighs, they could see the definition in his legs. The bottom of the pants were loose, and flared out as he danced. Yolanda looked amazing doing the routine with him. The girls every now and then would clap, showing their appreciation. They did four dance routines. Gloria had clearly been a great teacher for Yolanda.

"Let me take a water break. I will be right back," Ramon said as he untied the bandana around his neck. He placed the bandana around Yolanda's neck, and then he walked off.

"Is it just me, or is he flirting with you, hard?" Destiny said with her eyebrow raised.

"*Whatever*. He did the same thing when he was dancing with y'all," Yolanda said as she walked to the table with the punch bowl.

She started fixing a drink, trying to not look back at the girls. Taking a sip of the drink, she thought about her face pressed to his hairy chest. She couldn't stand hairy men, but his hair had been soft and released the fragrance of his cologne. As she stood there, refusing to turn to face the girls, she felt Ramon press his body against her from behind. He reached around her and took her glass out of her hand. He put the glass down on the table, then turned her towards him. He only had on a g-string and his dance shoes. She tried to pull away from him, but with little force. Behind him the grinning girls already had their money in their hands, ready for the show--even Sheremah.

"Follow me," Roman walked backward, holding her hand.

The lights dimmed as she followed him to the middle of the dance floor. He grabbed her by the waist and started dirty dancing. She blushed, and was so embarrassed that she couldn't enjoy herself. The girls surrounded them throwing money and putting it in his underwear. Gloria came out in her own g-string and dance shoes. Gloria danced behind Yolanda. They sandwiched her, to the point that she either had to enjoy it or stop it altogether. She could no longer back up with Gloria behind her.

"Relax. This is your night, have fun and let go," Gloria whispered in Yolanda's ear, and then she kissed the back of Yolanda's neck.

That kiss had sent chills down her spine. She closed her eyes as she moved to the music. The other girls smiled so hard, knowing that Miss Congeniality had finally left the building. After two songs' worth of being sandwiched by Gloria and Ramon they danced with everyone in the room. The party finally got turned up and Yolanda was in rare form.

Brandon walked back into the room from walking the triplets to the elevator. Danny noticed only then that he only really knew four guys that were present, out of forty or so. Brandon, Thomas, Corey, and Reggie, from work. Anyone else wouldn't be able to tell that Reggie didn't know anyone at the party but Danny. Everyone patted him on the back as Danny walked through, and he overheard a couple of guys say that this was the best twenty dollars they'd ever spent. Danny thought to himself, *only Brandon would be charging people at my bachelor party.*

"Yo, thirty minutes til the Show Stopper gets here," Brandon called.

"You loving this, ain't you?" Danny asked Brandon.

"You already know. Plus, to know that you're about to be locked down, I'm trying to send you out with a bang. Even if we could stop now, the night has already been epic. I've been listening to the crowd, and they are *loving* it."

"I heard them, too, and they said they paid twenty beans to get in here."

"Not everybody paid twenty! Just the ones I like. Most of them paid forty or fifty. These strippers ain't free, and those bottles don't grow on trees. I love you, but I aint holding like that."

"Just don't charge the people I invited. If you did, give them their money back."

"I should have, seeing how much money they're throwing."

"Whatever. If you come up short, I'll cover the difference."

"No dice, I will make it be enough. You just have fun." Brandon gave him dap and walked off, making a round of the room and giving people singles for larger bills. Danny went to the kitchen to find Corey and Thomas fixing drinks. Corey--aka 'Cool'--a man of few words.

"What up, Cool!" Danny said to Corey.

"Chillin'."

"You enjoying yourself?"

"Most definitely." Corey nodded his head up and walked into the main room. Thomas and Danny smiled to each other as they watched him walk away.

"He hasn't changed. I remember when your dad took us to I.S. 8 to play in that basketball tournament. I thought Corey wasn't talking to me on the bench because I'm white, but that's just him," Thomas said.

"Now and then he might string a few words together. He might be quiet, but he always comes when you call him. He's very loyal."

"I know that's right."

Brandon turned the music down then, and he tapped his glass with a knife. "Everyone come in here!"

They all walked into the main room.

"The grand finale is in the building. Put your phones up, absolutely no pictures or recording. Get your money ready--it's about to go... down," Brandon said, turning the music back up.

Brandon left, going into the hallway. Five minutes later, he walked in the room. Behind him followed a 6'5, black as tar bouncer-slash-bodyguard and a pretty, brown-skinned chick. She had a chinchilla fur jacket and the fattest butt. Behind her was the Show Stopper, who needed no introduction--she was breathtaking. As she walked, her hair seemed to blow in the air, even though there weren't any fans blowing--she had a radiance coming from her. Every step she took in her three-quarter fur coat was full of confidence. She went into the bedroom to change, and the bouncer posted outside her door. The other woman turned the music down and addressed the room.

"The Show Stopper will be out in ten minutes. If anyone disrespects her, you *will* have a problem with Killer, her bodyguard. I'm Fancy, her manager. I will be passing out my card for booking. Enjoy the show," Fancy said, turning to join her dancer in the bedroom.

"What is she?" Thomas asked.

"A stripper," Danny said, looking at him as if he was crazy.

"No, no, I'm talking about her ethnicity. Is she black? Mixed, asian, alien, or an angel?"

"I don't know, but she looks a little exotic. She got that Kim Kardashian tan or complexion, but thick like a sister. If her hair is hers, she might be mixed or have good genes. No matter her race, she's gorgeous."

"You can say that again."

Fancy walked out of the room without her jacket, looking fine. She handed Brandon a CD, and he placed it into the player. When the music started playing, the Show Stopper walked into the main room. She had on a two-piece white g-string outfit and super tall high heels. More clothes than the other dancers had had, but way more beautiful. She started in the middle of the floor, blowing kisses at the room. She lifted her leg straight up into the air as if she was a ballerina, held it for a second. Then, she dropped into a split, and the room went crazy.

Money flew from everywhere. Song after song, she was raking it in. She still hadn't taken off her top, and yet no one had even complained.

Danny watched her as if he were hypnotized, until Brandon and Fancy pulled him to the side.

"Here's a hundred dollar bill," Fancy said, placing it into his hand. "When she puts her legs in the air laying on her back, wait for her to spread her legs wide. I need you to put the hundred on her hot box with your teeth, then step back. Can you do that?"

Danny looked at Brandon, and his eyes said, *say yeah*. He looked back to Fancy and nodded. He went back to watching the Show Stopper's every move. She moved so seductively, and Danny moved to the music as if he were dancing with her. She rolled onto her back, then she raised her legs to her head. She was holding her lower back so her butt would be off the floor. As she opened her legs into a split, Danny got on his knees and placed the hundred between his teeth. He placed the bill squarely down as instructed. He stood up, and she winked at him as the hundred flew off her crotch--somehow she'd blown it with her hot box. The hundred flipped through the air in slow motion. The room and Danny couldn't believe what they'd seen. One guy flipped a handful of twenty-dollar bills towards her.

Danny went into the kitchen to get a bottle of water; he'd seen enough. He grabbed a water out of the refrigerator, then closed the door, only to be startled by Corey standing right next to him.

"You trying to give me a heart attack?" He grumbled at Corey.

"No. I want to know if she's tricking. And if she is, how much. I never paid for sex, but I never saw anyone blow money with their coochie. I gotta have that, even if my girl finds out, she *gotta* understand, or she needs to step up her game."

"I'll ask Brandon for you."

"Good lookin'." Corey walked back in the main room.

Danny cracked the bottle of water and turned it up. He was smiling while drinking the water, thinking about what Corey had said. *If Corey knew like I knew, he would be asking about anyone named the Show Stopper. Plus, seeing all the tricks she displayed during her routine, I wish I would try to get some of that,* Danny thought to himself. He finished the water and tossed the bottle in the trash. Danny started picking up beer bottles and pouring the leftover beer into the sink. Brandon walked into the kitchen.

"You good?" Brandon asked.

"Yeah. I'm straight, just waiting for this to be over so I can get some rest. I'm burned out on the low." He picked up the rest of the bottles and trash.

"I feel you. Today has been a long day. Stop cleaning up, I got the cleanup crew coming soon as the last dancers leave. Trust me, I got everything. You need to enjoy your night, which has been epic thus far."

"I can't. If I stop moving, I'm going to sleep wherever I stand."

"I've been then before."

"Do you know if she's trickin?"

"I don't know, but I can ask. You always switching up on me, but I like this switch up."

"Oh. Oh no, not for me, for Cool. He asked me, so I'm asking you."

"Whatever, I don't judge. Everyone is entitled to wild out for the night. Just make sure it a three for one."

"What's that?"

"Three condoms for one thot, all on at the same damn time. Extra, extra protection. You heard!" Brandon walked out the kitchen.

Danny stayed in the kitchen for another twenty minutes cleaning up. He heard the music turn low, and Fancy started talking. He walked back into the main room. Danny caught the end of what she was saying. Something about taking a break, and then she turned the music back up. The Show Stopper had already gone into the other room. The fellas were still talking about how she blew that money up. He started cleaning up in the main room. Thomas was so drunk he was sitting on the floor with his back to the wall. He was mumbling to himself, but Danny couldn't make out what Thomas was saying with the music playing. *I'm going to drag him tomorrow. He knows he's a light drinker*, Danny thought, shaking his head exasperatedly.

The Show Stopper had changed clothes. She had on black boots and a g-string. Black lipstick and a lacey, see-through negligee. Fancy stood behind her, holding a mesh bag full of sex toys and accessories. The Show Stopper walked over to Danny and grabbed his hand, leading him to the bedroom. He looked back, and Brandon had the biggest smile on his face. She opened the door and pushed him into the room. She took the bag from Fancy, and then she closed and locked the door.

CHAPTER 18

"I'm not interested in sleeping with you," Danny said before she could speak.

"Relax, I know. But they don't know," the Show Stopper said, and then she put her bag on the nightstand.

"Huh?"

"Everyone out there wondering what we're doing in here. The tips will get bigger, and the offers will come. Sexual offers, that is."

"That's smart. Real smart."

"Yeah, I might be a dancer, but I'm no dummy. Now, you need to go in the bathroom and strip. Come back out here just a towel around your waist. Usually, I charge $1000 for sex, $500 for a hand job, and $250 for a massage. I'm going to give you a massage for free--your party paid for it with their tips."

"I don't want a massage. I'm good, thank you."

"I didn't ask you!"

Danny found himself walking to the bathroom with a confused look on his face. He stopped at the door of the bathroom and looked back at her. Her back was turned to him as she looked out the window. He went in the bathroom, took off all his clothes, grabbed a towel and wrapped it around his waist. He took his wallet and cell phone out of his pocket, then placed his pants on the sink. Danny walked back in the room to slow music and three candles lit on both night stands. She was sitting on her knees on the bed. She was no longer wearing her heels or her negligee. All she had on was her black thong. He placed the items out his hand in the drawer of the night stand, and she smacked the bed. Danny sat on the edge of the bed like a scared virgin. She came up behind him and started massaging his shoulders. Her hand had him melting. They were tough squeezes with a pin-point release of tension. She laid him down on his stomach, then she sat on his butt as she massaged Danny.

"When is the wedding date?" She asked while massaging his lower back.

"In two weeks," Danny moaned from the massage.

"That's good. I hate it when the bachelors have their party days the night before the wedding. It's just tacky, if you ask me."

"Uh huh," he mumbled.

She massaged him with her knuckles, elbows, and thighs. She closed her legs to squeeze his hip as she sat on Danny's butt. He could feel her warmth through the towel. Danny was almost tempted to roll over a few times. It felt so good that he fell asleep with her massaging him.

Yolanda laid in her bed, scrolling through her phone. Looking at a picture of her and Danny, she smiled to herself. Sheremah walking into the room.

"I thought you would have been asleep. I guess you wasn't as drunk as you say you were," Sheremah said as she put her pocket book on the sofa.

"Well. I guess not. I left before I indulged more than I wanted to. If I wasn't in love with Danny and about to get married, I would have stayed."

"You don't have to explain. If I was in your shoes, I probably wouldn't have even come out here. And if I did, it *definitely* would've been with Destiny."

"Wow. Destiny must have shown out when I left."

"Showed out ain't the word. I can't tell you what she did, but I can say this. She wanted us to watch. That girl is a mess, trust and believe."

"That's funny, I'm glad I left... Do you think Danny's up? We're an hour behind, so it's 3:15 there."

"I don't know. It won't hurt to text him, but I wouldn't call."

"You right. I hope he texts me back. I want to hear his voice."

Yolanda: *I love you, my KING*

She sent him a text and waited for a response. Five, ten, fifteen minutes later, she gave up waiting. She plugged in her cell phone and went to bed.

CHAPTER 19

"Baby. Wake up and walk me out. Wake up," a female's voice said to Eric, trying to wake him up.

She pulled the covers off him, and he jumped up. He shot her the evil eye, but she didn't mind the least bit. She found her bra between the sheet and covers once she pulled them back.

"There you go," she said as she picked up her bra and put in her purse.

"Why must we do this every time, Samone?" Eric asked, half asleep.

"Yes. You are going to get up and walk me to the door like a gentleman. My momma said, 'If a man can lay with you, he should have the decency to respect you. Chivalry is only dead if you don't demand it to live in people.'" Samone raised her eye-brow, looking at him.

"I'm getting up, so you can shut up, it's too early. I just don't understand why, 'cause you can lock the door behind yourself. Time has changed from when your momma's been out here."

"You wish I would let myself out. Hurry up--I'll be upstairs, and don't you talk about my momma." Samone walked upstairs with an attitude.

Eric sat up on the edge of the bed, stretching his neck. He slipped on his house shoes, then headed upstairs. When he got to the living room, Samone was standing by the door with her arms folded. Eric opened the door and hugged her. She kissed him on the cheek and walked to her car. He watched her get in the car before he closed and locked the door.

Eric walked back into the kitchen and grabbed a new box of chocolate Entenmann's donuts off the top of the refrigerator. The doorbell rang as he was halfway back up the stairs. He headed up again, thinking to himself, *What did this girl leave now?* At this point, he had a whole shoebox of things she'd left over at his place. He opened the door to discover it was his neighbor Bridget. Eric tried to stay behind the door, as he was only in his underwear still.

"Sorry to bother you, but have you heard from Danny since his party last night?" Bridget asked.

"No, but should I have?"

"I don't know... It's just that Thomas' wife called me early this morning looking for him. He didn't come home from the party, and he hasn't been answering his phone. Can you please call Danny?"

"My phone is downstairs, but I will call him. Let me put some clothes on, then you can come in while I call."

Eric left the door open and headed to the Boom Boom Room. Before he made through the kitchen, Bridget had already walked in. He knew he should have closed the door. Eric felt her eyes from behind, burning a hole in his boxer briefs as he tried to hurry up the stairs.

"I like what you've done to the place!" She yelled after him from the living room.

He placed the box of donuts, still in hand, on the bed, then put on a sweat suit and grabbed his phone. He dialed Danny's number as he walked back to the living room.

◆ ◆ ◆

Danny heard his phone going off in the nightstand drawer. He was wrapped up in the covers that he fell asleep on. He rolled out of the covers as he opened the drawer, and, to his surprise, he was naked. He pulled the phone out, answering when he saw that it was his dad.

"Hello?"

"Hello, son. Is Thomas there with you?"

"I don't know--I knocked out on them, you know I can't hang. Let me put something on and I will call you right back."

"Do that, son. Bridget is over here and she's worried. Call me right back."

"I got you, Dad."

Danny wasn't trying to freak out on the phone with his dad, but he'd woken up naked, after all. As he got dressed, he tried to think if he'd done anything with the stripper. Not too sure what all happened last night, he walked to Brandon's room. No one was in the main room as he made it to the other bedroom. He pushed the door open, already partially opened. Brandon was lying in the bed, spooning with two females.

"Wake up, Bee. Wake up!"

"What's good?" Brandon yawned, peering at him.

"Nothing. Did you make sure Thomas made it home? You get him a cab, Lyft or something?"

"No. That fool still here somewhere, unless he sobered up after all that throwing up he did in the bathroom. You need to look in the kitchen, that's the last place I saw him." Brandon sat up in the bed, stretching.

"Damn, Bee. I thought you could handle the guests."

"I handled *my* guests. That's your man. I promise you, I think he did more than drink. For real."

Danny closed the door completely and walked through the penthouse. He finally spotted Thomas lying on the cold tile floor of the kitchen. Danny tried to sit Thomas up, but he slid back down, and hitting his face on the floor. He left him there and returned to his room to sit on his bed. He dialed his dad. The phone started ringing.

"Hello."

"Yeah. He's over here. I've never seen him this drunk. I tried to sit him up, but he's still dead weight right now. Tell Miss Bridget that I'll bring him home once he sobers up."

"Okay, son, thanks."

"No problem." Danny ended the call.

"Thomas is there, but he wasted to the point of no return. Danny said he would bring him home once he sobers up, but he can't even stand him up right now."

"Thank God he's safe. I hope his wife doesn't kill him when he gets home. I must call her. Knowing her, she's going to flip. I can hear her now." Bridget affected an impression, pitching her voice. "'What's the address to where he's at?' Don't tell me, Eric, because I don't want to know. Thanks for calling Danny. Talk to you later."

"No problem."

Eric opened the door to let Bridget out. She left, and he closed the door behind her. He texted Danny, and then he finally went upstairs.

Eric: *Make sure you have that place cleaned up. I'm coming up there to watch football. See you around 1*

Danny walked back into his room after he dragged Thomas to the couch. He'd almost thrown his back struggling with Thomas' weight. He sat on the edge of his bed, trying to remember what happened last night. He remembered that The Show Stopper ran down her prices for him. He reached into the drawer and pulled out his wallet-- only to find every dollar gone. He groaned, got up, and headed to Brandon's room.

"Bee! Come here for a second! Come here, now!" Danny yelled.

"Coming, yo! Calm down."

Brandon had wrapped a towel around his waist as he opened the door. Danny was waiting outside the room, shaking his head with disgust.

"Where's the fire?" Brandon asked.

"You got jokes, but all my money went. I had ten one-hundred-dollar bills in my wallet when I placed it in my nightstand drawer. Now, I got nothing. You need to call Fancy and get my money."

"I'll call her, but you sure you didn't pay for the girl's services?"

"You serious? I *told* you, I don't get down like that. All she did was give me a massage, and I fell asleep. That's all I remember, and she offered that. I didn't request anything."

"You know I don't judge, but when she came out of the room to finish her last set, she left your room's door wide open, and you were butt-naked, no socks or nothing. All I saw was butt cheeks and elbows. True story."

"Well, when I fell asleep, I know I had a towel around my waist. I wasn't that drunk, I know I didn't do anything. Plus, I know what I had in my wallet."

"I hear you. But, before I call Fancy, let's make sure you didn't drop it or misplace it." Brandon walked into Danny's room.

"You check! I'm done," Danny followed Brandon, arms crossed.

As Brandon started his search, Danny picked up his cell phone and read through his texts. He read the one from Yolanda and his dad; he texted his dad back first.

Danny: *Ok, Dad, see you when you get here.*

He hesitated to text Yolanda back. He couldn't think of the right words--especially after she'd addressed him as a King. He watched Brandon look around the room instead, meeting his gaze with a facial expression saying, *it's not here*. Brandon looked in the drawer, reaching his hand inside. He pulled out a note and read it aloud.

Dear Danny,

I'm sorry that I pulled your towel off.

I had to set the stage for the rest of the room that I put you to bed.

Never leave your wallet in an open area in a hotel full of people. I put your money under the mattress. Thanks for letting me entertain you and your guest. Good luck with your marriage.

Thanks again,

Marcia, The Show Stopper

Brandon stared at Danny. Danny lifted the mattress and grabbed his money. He counted it, and it was all there. Brandon tossed the note at Danny and walked out of the room. He flopped onto the bed, still holding his money and his phone. Danny's phone rang in his hand. The name on his screen read 'Yolanda.'

"Good morning, baby."

"Good morning, love. You didn't get my text?"

"I got it this morning. I was knocked out. I was trying to get Thomas together before I called you. Bridget went to the house bothering my dad about Thomas' whereabouts. I know he pissed, but that's a long story. How's my Queen?"

"I'm doing great. It was a long night. These fools call themselves throwing me a bachelorette party."

"You serious? That's crazy... Wow!" He said, sounding happy.

"Why you say it like that?" She replied, puzzled.

"Nah. It's funny because the same thing happened here. Brandon pulled some strings with these strippers and everything."

She clucked her tongue. "So, you were around strippers."

"Baby. You know I don't do strippers. So, relax... Did you not have strippers at yours?"

"Yes, but..."

"But nothing. That's our first and last bachelor and bachelorette party. It's over now--let's focus on the wedding and spending our lives with each other. That's what I'm looking forward to."

"Me too. I can't wait."

"You just come back in one piece so that we can tie the knot."

"Will do," she laughed.

They talked on the phone for an hour more, kissing their phones and saying how much they missed each other.

CHAPTER 20

Danny walked back into the penthouse, only to hear a lot of screaming at the television. He thought to himself, the Giants must be losing.

"Son. Bring that salmon dip out the refrigerator and those Scoops off the counter!" Eric yelled from the main room.

Danny shook his head with a little smirk as he walked to the kitchen. He grabbed the items, then brought them to the main room. He placed them on the coffee table quickly, trying not to get in the way of anyone's view of the television. He went back into the kitchen and grabbed a beer. Danny stood there for a second, watching the game over their shoulders until he ultimately sat down next to Dee.

"What's good, nephew?" Dee asked.

"Everything, I can't complain. I had the best time of my life last night. Now it's just getting through these last two weeks in one piece. This process is the real deal. I see why some people go to the justice of the peace to get married."

"I been there twice, so you know I feel your pain. They say the wedding is for the bride and the honeymoon is for the groom. Once you make it through the wedding, cash in all your chips in on the honeymoon night. That might be the first and last night she'll do whatever you ask."

"You think?"

"No. I *know*. You ever seen that movie, Groundhog Day with Bill Murray in it?"

"I don't think so, but it sounds familiar."

"Well, anyway. It's a movie about this guy who keeps waking up at the same time every day. And when he wakes up, he must relive the same day over and over. I always secretly thought, if I had to live any day over and over, it would be my honeymoon, hands down. I could live the time we left the reception to the next morning over and over."

"Why that specific time frame? Or did it matter?"

"Damn right it matters. The ceremony was special, and confessing our love to one another in front of witnesses was priceless. But when we left them, riding that loving-commitment high? That still gives me chills. You almost yearn to be alone, to be intimate for the first time after being married. I don't know if that's how everybody felt when they got married, but I know I did. The whole time during the reception, I would catch myself looking at my wife, smiling. Smiling in anticipation of how I'm going to love on her once we left."

"Wow... I love when I hear other peoples' experiences, especially when they're good," Danny said, before he drifted off with his thoughts about his wedding.

"Touchdown! I needed that on my football sheet. Now, nail this extra point for the over points to be good," Eric said as they lined up for a two-point conversion.

The Giants made the conversion, and Eric jumped up, clapping and cheering, "Hell yeah!" Danny paid him no mind. Eric looked at Dee, then looked back to Danny, who was in another world.

"It's tied up, son!" Eric yelled at Danny.

"It is?" Danny was surprised. He opened an eye to see the score, but a commercial was on.

"No. We down by ten with a minute to play, and it's the Forty

Niners' ball. What are you thinking about?"

"My bad, Dad. I got a lot on my mind with this wedding and everything."

"I get that, son. That reminds me--I have your wedding gift in your room. Let's get it now, this game is over."

"I thought this suite was your present?"

"It is, but there's more."

Danny walked to his room, and Eric followed him. He grabbed the envelope that Eric had set on his bed when he'd first gotten there. Danny opened the envelope and started reading the documents. Page after page, he read them thoroughly. Eric couldn't understand his facial expressions as he read the documents.

"Are you sure, Dad? You want to give me the house in Georgia?"

"Absolutely. Your mother and I planned our lives out way before you ever stepped into the world. We always said our first child would get our first home while we were still alive. Me and her planned to move to Florida or Hawaii." Eric swallowed, trying not to sound too emotional. "We wanted to retire in a place where the weather is warm year-round and the beaches are beautiful. I've been thinking about this day ever since you told me you were considering marrying Yolanda. I was going to wait until the day of your wedding but then I thought, if my lawyer could have all the paperwork signed and notarized, I could present it to you and your wife on your wedding day."

Danny smiled softly, still staring at the papers in his hands. "Thanks, Dad."

"Don't thank me, thank your mother. She might not be here physically, but her spirit lives with us every day. I'm just happy that I've been up holding to a lot of things that she put forward. In the midst of her death, her hands on this family were felt."

"What you mean by that?"

"When your mother died, I didn't go back to work for a year. We had a hundred-thousand-dollar life insurance policy on both of us, which held me and you down that first year. I was so broken-hearted, it took me longer to pull it together than I'd thought. Words can't even express how thankful I am that she suggested that we got those policies. But at the time, I was skeptical. Us being in our twenties at the time, I just knew death was a long way from us. We could have placed that money into a retirement saving. But, like most of the time, I still sided with her, knowing that she had an old spirit. Like a mother's intuition, you know? Then your Momma May deposited a check for three-hundred-thousand dollars in my account."

"Wow."

"Exactly. Your mother had another policy that she was paying, but it was in your Momma May's name. I used that money to pay off the house in Georgia, which is just one of my rental properties. You can do whatever you want with the house, it's yours. The tenants are moving out on the twenty-eighth of December. If you want to use the same property management company let me know. Just sign all the places that are blank and let me complete one of the promises I made to your mother."

Danny walked out of the room with the paperwork, coming back with a pen. He signed the paperwork, put it back in the envelope, and passed it to Eric. Eric took the envelope, and a feeling of joy shot through his body.

"Are you okay?"

"I couldn't be better, son. Give me a moment, and I'll be back in there to watch the next game."

Danny nodded as he left the room. Eric looked at the envelope in his hands, and then he dropped his head into his hand. The envelope was pressed to his forehead. He took a deep breath as his eyes got watery, then he exhaled. Eric got up, hit the light switch off, and walked back in the main room, feeling like a heavy weight had been released from his shoulders.

CHAPTER 21

One day before the wedding. Kenya opened the door, and the bellhop rolled her bags into the room on a cart. He placed her luggage by the window on the floor. As he rolled the cart toward her to leave the room, she stopped him, pressing a tip into his hands. He thanked her, and then she closed and locked the door behind him. She walked to the window to see the view, dropping her pocketbook on the bed. *This is beautiful*, she thought to herself, looking over the outside pool.

Looking out at the city, she started to reminisce about when she and Eric had taken a train to the city to see the Christmas Tree at the Rockefeller Center. That was the first day that they'd held hands in public. Eric had always thought that insecure men held their ladies' hands. Even at a young age, he wouldn't follow the crowd, making his lane. He had been very protective of her that night, and they were in awe of the lights that illuminated the tree. The more crowded the streets got, the tighter he'd held her hand and pulled her closer.

Ring, ring. Her phone rang from her purse. She snapped out of her childlike smile and got her phone out of her purse.

"Hello?" Kenya answered her cell phone.

"When were you going to call me and let me know that you made it to the city, young lady?" Jackie asked mockingly.

“You funny, but I just touched down. I mean literally. I just checked into the room.”

“I hear you. But let me find out when you were in Richmond, you turned down two dinner invites. What’s that about?”

“I just wasn’t in the mood. I came to see Kels and catch up with my grandkids. It was creepy how everywhere I went, the men were acting real thirsty. I must have had a ‘divorced’ sign on my forehead that I wasn’t aware of. That’s how bad it was.”

“You don’t have to tell me. I’m married, and I still go through the same thing. For us to be over fifty and still get all the looks that we do is just being blessed with our mother’s genes. I wish you would live a little. A free meal and a little conversation never hurt anyone.”

“Okay. Says the lady who sent me the email of the different website dating serial killers. I don’t even know if they caught that guy yet. Plus, I make my own money. I’m not chasing a free meal just to wind up becoming the meal.”

“I can’t agree with you,” Jackie said with a slight snicker.

“I don’t know why. You already know how I’m wired.”

“Are you going to come to the house? Or will I see you tomorrow?”

“Tomorrow. I’m burned out from this ride--plus the grandkids wouldn’t give me a free second to myself. I’m in the same hotel where the wedding is located. If you feel like coming to the city later, let me know. I can’t wait to show you this view! I got the Skyline View King room, and it’s *amazing.*”

“I’m sure it’s amazing. You ain't even slick.”

“What are you talking about now?”

“So, you conveniently got a room in the same hotel as the wedding. For easy access. Legs to the ceiling.”

“Whatever. Don’t confuse me with you. Let me get off this phone so that I can get a spa treatment. Hit me if you decide to come out here."

"I will. Talk to you later."

Kenya went through her luggage, looking for her sweatsuit. She found it, and she went to the bathroom to change.

Eric was sitting in a chair in the lobby waiting for Danny. He got up from the chair and headed to the elevator. He pressed the button, as both elevators were coming down. A group of women walked up behind him as he waited. They all smiled at him as they continued talking about not being late for the Broadway play they were all going to see. The elevator opened, and three of them jumped in before him, but the others waited for him to get on.

"Y'all good. I can wait on the next one, enjoy your play."

"Get in here," one of the ladies said as she locked arms with him.

The lady pulled Eric on the elevator, and the other women followed. It was a real tight fit, but they didn't seem to mind.

Kenya stepped out of the elevator into the lobby, heading to the front desk. She didn't realize that she just missed Eric.

He unlocked room and flopped onto the bed, face first. His phone vibrated in his pocket. Eric rolled over and pulled it out of his pocket. He had a text from Danny.

Danny: *Sorry to the wedding party. We are going to cancel today's walkthrough. The brunch is still going on. Yolanda and I might be running late, excuse us but feel free to eat all you want. Thanks for understanding.*

Eric: If you need me, I will be in my room.

Danny*: Thanks, Dad.*

Eric: NP

Eric grabbed the remote from under the pillow and turned the television on. He flipped through the channels until he stopped at *House Party*. Eric watched that until he dozed off.

Danny walked Yolanda to her room. He didn't go in; he merely talked to her at the door as she stood in the room.

"I wish Mr. Taylor would have should up at the brunch. Most of the wedding party came late, but he didn't even show up. I have a funny feeling about that," Yolanda sighed.

"Don't worry your little head with my dad. When I texted him earlier, he said to hit him if I needed him. I decided to let him relax. I know that he's doing all this for us--this isn't his cup of tea. The Couples' sensed his discomfort at the eighth or ninth rehearsal. I thought it would be best to let him rest the day before," Danny tried to calm her nerves.

"I understand. Just check on him before you go to your room to make sure he's okay?"

"Will do. Is there anything else that you need me to do as your fiancé? Because tomorrow, we will be Mr. and Mrs. Taylor. You can officially change your social media status."

"I don't need anything else with your corny tail."

"Okay, my love, I will see you at the altar," Danny said backing away from her door, kissing his hands and blowing towards her. She caught every kiss he blew with a smile until she closed the door.

Danny went straight to his dad's room. He knocked three times on the door. No one answered. He knocked again, and then he placed his ear to the door, trying to see if he could hear anything. Eric opened the door then, and Danny stumbled into the room.

“My bad, Dad.” Danny gathered himself.

“You good. I see you haven’t learned anything from listening to my door.” Eric closed the door behind Danny.

They both laughed; when Danny was younger, he had once listened to Eric and Sharlene roleplaying. They’d had on superheroes’ costumes and everything. She kept saying, ‘You're going to choke me again.’ He’d heard the moans and feared his dad was killing her. In all fairness, he had been--but not in the way Danny had thought.

“I should have learned my lesson. When I busted in your room to save Sharlene might have been one of my biggest mistakes. I never looked at her or Wonder Woman the same again.”

“Damn. I forgot about that costume. I miss the fun we had together.”

“Whatever happened to y'all?”

“She got in her feelings and wanted more than what I was offering. Or, at least, what I wanted to give her. She might have got married four years later. Bruce ran into her a few years back in the subway, and he said she looks like a completely different person.”

“What he meant by that?”

“I heard her husband got killed in front of her.”

“Wow. I know that had to scare her deeply... I couldn’t imagine something like that happening. That’s crazy.”

“Too crazy. But I know you didn’t come to talk about my past. What’s good, son?”

“Nothing. Yolanda was just worried about you not showing up for the brunch that ran over into dinner. She made me check on you.”

"I'm good, as you can see. I needed that rest."

"Okay, great."

Danny picked up Eric's tux that was draped over the desk chair. He hung the tux in the closet.

"See you in the morning." Danny let himself out and went back to his room.

Kenya cut the light off as she came out of the bathroom from taking a shower. She walked past the bed to the window and noticed the full moon. She made her way to her refrigerator and snatched a miniature bottle of moscato with a twist-off cap. Kenya slid the recliner to the window and sat down with her wine and her blue silk pajamas, hypnotized by the moon's beauty. Sipping her wine and enjoying the view, she thought she saw a shooting star. Not too sure, she got up and placed her hand on the window as she looked close

--

Three floors up, Eric watched a star streak across the sky. He was about to close the curtain, but he thought about what Danielle used to say when she saw a shooting star. *Make a wish and do it fast, claim your blessing before it's passed.* Eric could almost hear saying that. He closed the curtain with a smile on his face. He didn't make a wish, but in his heart, he wished he was marrying his Danielle tomorrow. Eric got in the bed and laid there for a moment, staring at the ceiling until he went to sleep.

CHAPTER 22

Three hours to the wedding

Yolanda's suite was packed with almost twenty people. She was sitting on the bed with her robe on, like a queen bee. Everyone was moving with an agenda that constructed around her. As the wedding planners walked out, the hairdresser walked in and started setting up his station. She watched him as he pulled out what must have been ten different curling irons and lined them up. Mrs. Bank caught her staring at the hairdresser as if something was wrong with him.

"Mini!" Mrs. Banks shouted, trying to get her attention.

Mrs. Banks, Yolanda's mother; everyone called her Mrs. B. She was about 5'6 and as jazzy as she wanted to be. Mr. and Mrs. B had been married for over forty years. Mr. B was about 6'2 and cooler than the other side of the pillow. He was a man of many words, and Mrs. B couldn't stand it. They were certainly an odd couple, but it worked for them nonetheless.

"Mini!" She repeated as she tapped Yolanda on her shoulder.

Yolanda jumped. "You scared me, Momma. I didn't even see you come into the room."

"I know. I haven't seen that look on your face in years. Is everything okay, baby?"

"Yes. Just thinking... I love your dress. What happened to the white and gold one?"

Mrs. Banks had on a silver, off-the-shoulder embroidered gown. She spun around to show off her full dress.

"I'm still wearing white and gold, just not the one that you saw. No one has seen it. No... one..."

"Okay, Momma. Do the damn thing! Where's Daddy?"

"He's coming. Unless God answered my prayers."

"Momma, don't say that."

"I'm just playing, fix your face. It's your day, and I'm going to be on my best behavior."

"Good."

"I think Princess is ready for you," Mrs. Banks said as she pointed at the hairdresser.

"That's Peter, Momma. And what happened to your best behavior?"

"I said that about your dad, not him. Hmmm," Mrs. B hummed as she cut her eyes at Peter.

Yolanda sighed as she walked and sat in the chair. Peter tilted her head straight and stepped back, looking at her. She thought to herself, *Momma might be right.* He had on more bracelets on both arms than an African Princess. She smiled to herself as he got started.

Kenya walked into her room from working out in the hotel's gym. She took off her yoga outfit and jumped into the shower. Holding her head back with her eyes closed, the water beat on her pelvis bone. The shower head and water pressure were both very soothing. She turned around and let the water hit her back as she dropped her chin to her chest.

After a few minutes, Kenya grabbed her soap and loofah, then began bathing. She started thinking about the last time she saw Eric. It was a couple of years after he moved back to New York. She was visiting her father, who was sick at the time. It had been over two decades, but she remembered it as if it were yesterday. Driving from her father's house, she'd spotted Eric playing ball at I.S. 8 Park. She parked the car, then started walking to the court where he was playing. He had the ball at the free throw line, beneath Kenya had snuck up on him as he was talking trash to Dee. She kicked the ball out from under his foot. Eric slipped a bit, then turned around, ready to go off.

"Who the fu..." Eric stopped as he realized it was Kenya.

"Hey, E.T. give me a hug," Kenya said, then she opened her arms, waiting for him to hug her.

Eric slowly moved in. He gave her that sort of hug your bible school teacher gives. Maleek and Dee waved at Kenya, and then they walked off. *She smells so good,* Eric noticed as he let go from hugging her.

"What brings you to New York, Mrs. Cali girl? I see your tan."

"You still got jokes. I look the same, thank you--but for real. I came to see my dad. He got sick, and Jackie's not the best care-giver."

"I'm sorry to hear that. Your dad's a good dude. Except for that time he caught us in the bed. My heart was racing when I was getting dressed. Then, I had to walk down the steps while he was standing in the middle of them. It seemed like it was five hundred steps from the second floor to the first. I just knew when I got close, he was going to punch me or kick me down the steps."

"You silly. He's not even like that. He told that story to my husband. Why? I don't know. Him and his sense of humor. He's feeling better now."

"That's good. How's the married life?"

"It has its ups and downs, but I can't complain. He gave me two beautiful kids and a lovely home."

"I hope that it gets good for you one day."

"I didn't say it was *bad.*"

"Yeah, but you also didn't say it was good. Just do everything you can to make it the best."

"You right about that. Did you get the card that I gave to your mother when your fiancé died?"

He smiled, a bit bitterly."Yes. That meant a lot to me."

"How are you doing with that? I know that had to be tough."

"To be honest with you, a day hasn't gone by that I don't feel empty. Alone, even. If it wasn't for my son, Danny, I don't know where I would be right now."

"I'm glad you got him." She nodded as she spoke. "Are you going to be busy later?"

"Yeah. The Crew is going to check out the Knicks." He'd looked back, and only then realized they weren't there.

"Well, I'll be at my father's house for two more days. The number is the same at the house. Use it."

"I just might do that."

Bam! Bam! Bam!

Kenya snapped out of her reminiscing. She looked down, and the only place where she was lathered up was right below her belly button. She rinsed off and grabbed a towel to see who was at the door. Looking through the peephole, she saw Jackie's big face. She opened the door.

"Damn. I was about to leave. I've been knocking for fifteen minutes. Luckily, I heard your phone ringing through the door when I called you. You got me looking like a jealous lover, the way I was banging on your door." Jackie walked in with a garment bag.

"I didn't hear you, I was in the shower." Kenya closed the door.

"I guess you're like me."

"What does that mean?"

"I like to please myself to get rid of the butterflies. You're nervous to see Eric. Or, should I say, your Teddy Bear."

"Whatever, that's you."

Kenya went back into the bathroom to finish her shower. She thought for a second, *Should I...? Nah!*

Eric was sitting on the edge of the bed, watching *College GameDay* on ESPN. He was semi-nervous, as if he was the one getting married. He looked at his tux and started thinking, *I hope that they don't have any surprises. Every time someone thinks that they know someone that's my type, it always goes bad. Hell, I don't even* know *my type. Yolanda is a lovely young lady, but her favorite aunt looks like my favorite uncle. I don't know what they were thinking. Then, Candice--her aunt had the nerve to say she's not looking for a serious thing, just wants a friend with benefits.*

He had smiled, with an internal frown, when she'd said that, not trying to hurt her feelings. But he'd thought to himself, *I'd rather pay for Obama Care before I accept her benefits*. She wasn't unattractive; she'd even had a nice shape. The mustache had been what threw him off. Eric had faked a stomach ache instead, and left Yolanda's family get together. A little after he got settled at the house, Danny had called.

"Hello, son."

"Yeah. I'm just checking on you. How's your stomach?"

"It's better. I think I needed to come home."

"Cool. Candice hasn't stopped talking about you ever since you left."

"Well, she can stop."

"Why? She doesn't want anything serious. So, you're trying to tell me

that you wouldn't hit."

"I wouldn't hit that with your car... You didn't see her mustache?"

After Danny laughed, he'd answered. *"It's light, Dad. It's not even that bad."*

"It's bad. The whole time she was talking, I was thinking about an episode of Tom and Jerry. Where the one mouse kept snatching Tom's whiskers off to use on his guitar? She was weirding me out."

"You silly. You kind of put me in a bind."

"How?"

"They told me to call you and see if it was okay for me to give her your number. What am I supposed to tell them?"

"Tell them I'm allergic to mustaches... Just tell them I'm trying to see if this one relationship works out before I start anything else. Tell them that."

Danny had hung up after that. *When he came home, I let them have it. He never tried to hook me up with anyone again.* Eric smiled to himself, thinking about that crazy encounter.

What time is it? He wondered, unsure how long he'd been sitting there.

He grabbed the remote from behind him and pressed the guide button. "*Damn!*" He jumped up and got into the shower.

In Danny's room, Brandon was sitting on the sofa with his feet on the coffee table, and Thomas was sitting in the chair next to the window. Danny came out of the bathroom with his toothbrush in the holder in his hand. He placed the holder on the desk, then sat on the bed.

"This your last time, or forever hold your peace," Brandon said to Danny.

"For what?"

"For me to call the Show Stopper--Miss Sunshine?--and get you some of that exotic sex."

"You crazy. And you better say that real low. Yolanda has supernatural hearing. Plus, the only sunshine I want is in the sky. You trying to have me messed up like that dude on *Harlem Nights*."

"Word. He was sprung. Let me get out here so I can get dressed. Even though I'm not in the wedding."

"When I asked you, you said 'no,' so save that."

"You right. I'm going to see you in a few," Brandon said as he let himself out.

Danny went into his safe in the closet and grabbed the rings. He sat on the bed and opened the box.

"*Wow!* You should have a security guard with you or something, man. That ring is shining," Thomas said to Danny.

"This is my mother's ring. A few added carats, specially designed. Yolanda doesn't know because we picked out wish rings a few years ago. I took some pictures with my phone when she looked at another set. It's amazing what these jewelers can do."

"You're about to make me cry with that sweet story, but I know the real you."

"Huh?"

"I remember when you recycled a Valentine's card someone gave you."

"I did do that, but I was, like, thirteen," Danny chuckled.

"I know. I had to change the mood before you start crying. I know how much you must love her, to trust her with your mother's ring like that." He patted Danny's shoulder. "On that note, I'm out. I've seen too many videos of men crying on their wedding day. See you in a minute."

Danny looked at the ring until he saw his mother's smile, shining like a twinkle in the ring. He placed the rings on the bed, walking to the closet to get his tux.

CHAPTER 23

One hour to the wedding

Mr. Couple came into the room and told Danny the guests have already started showing up. The Couple's had told the guests that if they weren't in the door before 12:30, they would not be able to enter. Eric went and peeked from the side door, and saw that everything was beautiful. They'd picked some lovely wedding colors--the white flowers and gold decorations gave him chills. It almost seemed like a king's wedding--straight royalty. When he walked back into the room, he could practically see the butterflies in Danny's chest from his face alone; he looked a little pale. Eric whispered into Thomas' ear, since he was the only groomsman.

"Talk to him to get his mind off the wedding. He's looking spooked."

Thomas nodded and immediately sparked up a conversation. Danny smiled, and Eric felt a little relieved. The last thing he needed was for Danny to need him for comfort. Eric was sure he was more nervous than Danny. He would have never thought that he would be attending--never mind actually being in--a wedding. He was trying to be a good sport about this for his son, but he still felt awkward, out of place. Eric walked to the mirror and posed in his tux, trying to keep moving to stay relaxed.

◆ ◆ ◆

Down the hall, Yolanda was having a fit. The make-up artist had had a seizure and was taken out by ambulance. Her assistant had never applied any makeup on anyone.

As Jackie and Kenya were getting off the elevator, they overheard someone on their phone, reporting what had happened to the make-up artist.

"You know, you could help," Jackie said to Kenya.

"Help with what?"

"Help with the bride's makeup. Could you imagine this happening on your wedding day? You might question if you're making the right decision."

"Why do you always do this to me?"

"Huh?"

"You know. You always make me feel guilty about something to reel me in. My God."

"Is that a yes?"

"Yes, but I'm not going to ask them. You can."

Jackie grinned as she walked to the room where the bride was, and Kenya stayed in the foyer. A moment later, Jackie leaned out of the room and waved her in. When Kenya walked into the room, Yolanda had tears streaming down her face.

"Sweetheart, there's no reason to cry. We don't need your eyes to be puffy on your special day. Get me a robe and let me work my magic," Kenya said.

Yolanda wiped her eyes and noticed how beautiful Kenya was--her dress was stunning. She had on a blue velvet off-the-shoulder gown. It fitted her like it was made just for her. It even had a train that dragged along the floor, and a slit over the left thigh. Kenya pulled the robe over her dress and started looking over the makeup on the counter.

“Who are you?” Yolanda asked.

“I’m an old friend of the groom’s father,” Kenya said simply, and began to work her magic.

Less than fifteen minutes later, she was done, and Yolanda looked ravishing. She couldn’t stop thanking Kenya. It was after 12:30 by then, and so they called Mrs. Couple into the room to have them let Jackie and Kenya in the ceremony. Yolanda told Mrs. Couple to seat them on Danny’s family’s side next to Nana, Danny’s grandmother. Meanwhile, the rest of Yolanda’s team got her gown and started the dressing process.

At one o’clock sharp, the ceremony started. The ushers marched the parents in. The wedding party followed, and then the flower girls. They placed their flowers carefully on the floor instead of throwing them. It was going just as rehearsed, Eric standing to the left of Danny, and Thomas to the left of him. Thomas and Eric had on white tuxes with gold vests, gold bow ties, and white shoes. Danny, in contrast, had on gold shoes, white pants, and a white shirt with a European collar. His coat was white and gold honeycomb fabric. Eric nodded at Danny as they stood there to let him know he was looking sharp. Danny smiled back. Across the altar, Sheremah was the maid of honor, and Cherri, Yolanda’s niece, was a bridesmaid. They both had on matching sleeveless dresses, gold on the top and white on the bottom.

As soon as John Legend’s “All Of Me” started playing, everyone stood up and faced the door. The flowers that the girls placed on the floor suddenly lit up gold--bright gold. The doors opened inward, and there she was, standing with Mr. B. The sight of her took the air out the room. Mr. B marched her down the aisle with locked arms. The song was synced as if it were made for this moment as her train followed behind her. They stopped once they reached the wedding party.

Yolanda’s dress was like something out of a fairy tale. She looked like a mermaid princess--simply magical. The pastor asked who was giving the bride away; Mr. B answered, and then he sat down next to his wife. Mrs. B grabbed his hand and placed it on her lap as she held it. He looked at her, still looking stunned.

Danny was about to explode with all the emotions he was feeling, seeing Yolanda for the first time in her gown. She stood there in white and gold, crystal beaded. The pastor said a few words. Then, he instructed Danny to hold Yolanda's hand. He did so as they both faced the pastor.

Looking at Danny's face, Eric realized he was making the right decision. Eric took a deep breath, then exhaled, feeling joy watching his son undergo the biggest commitment a person can take. He looked in the direction of Nana to see if she was enjoying this as much as he was. As he looked in her direction, the photographer's light made it hard to see his mother. Eric squinted to get a better view, and he froze, almost stopped breathing.

He saw Danielle sitting next to his mother.

Eric could hear the Pastor doing the ceremony, but couldn't make out what he was saying. He squinted once again, and his eyes focused; the person next to Nana was bending down. When she came up, she passed his mother her glasses that had fallen, and, to his surprise, it was Kenya sitting beside Nana. She was looking beautiful, and he was totally shocked to see her. Eric stared at her so hard that his mother caught his eye, gesturing at him to look forward, then she pointed at Danny and Yolanda. He felt like a kid that got caught looking up a grown-up's dress or down their bra.

The ceremony continued, but he still couldn't hear a thing. The last time that sensation had happened was when he had had that season-ending injury in college. Luckily, he was able to play it off from all the rehearsing they did leading up to the wedding. No one was the wiser, because Eric still smiled on cue. Every so often, he would look in the direction of Kenya. The next time, she smiled and waved. He nodded back, but in his head, he licked her nose, and she tasted good.

Eric's hearing was starting to come back--and just in time, too. He got to hear the pastor tell Danny, "You may now kiss the bride." They kissed, closed-mouthed, but very deeply. The room erupted into claps and cheers. The newly-wedded couple turned around and jumped over the broom. Then, they walked out, holding hands as bubbles came from every direction. The wedding party stayed as most of the guests went upstairs to the banquet hall where the reception was taking place. While the photographer was taking more pictures, Eric's mind kept rambling with questions. *Why did my mother invite Kenya? Did she come from California? Or is she back here?*

Eric had so many questions going through his mind that the poses were a blur. Finally, the picture taking was over, except for the bride and groom.

Mrs. Couple escorted the wedding party to the banquet hall, as they would be announcing the party as they entered the reception hall. Everyone entered the elevator and went up.

Meanwhile, the newlyweds were practically glowing in their pictures. The photographer was loving shooting a little too much for Danny's taste, though.

"Don't you think we have taken enough pictures?" Danny whispered in Yolanda's ear as he stood behind her in yet another pose.

"I don't know, but I'm ready to get upstairs with everyone," she replied under her breath.

"I think that's enough here. Save some for the reception," Danny said to the photographer.

"Okay. I need to get a few shots of the wedding set. Then, one pose with your fingers locked together, chest-high as you'll look each other in the eyes... trust me, it's a priceless effect!"

They looked at each other knowingly, but they did what he instructured. Mrs. Couple watched them wrap up the photo shoot, and began to usher them to the reception.

CHAPTER 24

The wedding party was sitting at their table, waiting for Danny and Yolanda to enter so that the party could begin. Thomas kept pointing at different females that he said kept looking at him and Eric. Eric could tell Thomas was ready to act up, since his wife and kids were in Pittsburgh.

As Eric looked around over the scenery, he was impressed. During the rehearsals, he thought the Couples Wedding Planners were a joke. But now, seeing how they'd pulled all this off, they were worth every penny. The tables were beautiful. The white and the gold sparkled from the lights of the chandeliers. Even the band had on white and gold. Eric didn't know what song they were playing, but they got the whole room swaying. Thomas tapped Eric on the shoulder and pointed to the far-left table.

"She wanted me to get your attention. She's nice looking," Thomas said.

Eric looked over to see who Thomas was talking about, and saw it was Candice yet again. Even from that far, he could practically see her mustache waving at him. He looked away fast so she wouldn't see him. The conductor of the band grabbed the mic as they played the music low--the music of Jodeci, "Love You 4 Life."

"Attention, everyone. Will you please stand and show your love for Mr. and Mrs. Danny Taylor?" The conductor said.

The room stood as the door opened. Yolanda was holding Danny's left hand as they walked in with a two-step groove to the music. She waved her own left hand, as if she was the Queen of England. Danny stepped in cadence with her, pumping his fist like he was getting the dog pound wound up. The cell phones came out, recording and taking pictures. Mr. and Mrs. Couple frowned--they specifically had, in bold letters on the ceremony and reception do's and don'ts, written: "No rice throwing and no cell phone photos or recording."

Eric, however, smiled. He had never seen Danny this happy, and he was proud of his son.

When they made it to the table, he pulled his new wife's seat out, and she sat down. Eric hugged him tight before they sat down. The conductor then passed Danny the microphone.

"I want to thank everyone for coming out to celebrate our special day. This day was inevitable. The first time I had a conversation with you, I knew I was talking to my wife. I love you, baby, with all my heart," Danny said, then he kissed her. "Before I bless the food, the caterers would like for y'all to come up by the tables. They will direct the traffic." He took a breath and bowed his head. "Heavenly Father, I come to you as humble as I know how. Thank you for your mercy and all your blessings, even though I'm not worthy. Thank you for my wife, my family, and friends. Thank you for the food that we're about to receive, and the hands that prepared it. Thank you, Lord, for this day and the days to come. In Jesus' name. Amen."

Danny cut the mic off, then handed it back to the music conductor. When he sat down, Yolanda kissed him again. Joy and admiration came over Eric's heart. He looked at Danny, still somewhat in awe of the man he had become. To hear Danny pray like that reminded Eric of Nana making him pray over his meals as a young boy. Over the years, he'd become less religious--some might say not even spiritual. He was glad that Nana had instilled that in Danny.

Everyone started coming to the wedding party's table to greet the newlyweds. The head caterer came to the table to see what everyone in the party wanted before they called the other tables. After he got the orders, the crowd surrounded the table again. The caterers brought the food out and started calling out for the tables. As people took their seats again, Dee and Bruce walked up the table.

"You think you slick. Now I know why you went against your no wedding rule," Bruce said.

"Negro! What are you talking about?" Eric asked.

"Kenya, Kenya, Kenya. Oh, did I say Kenya?"

"The funny thing is, I didn't even know she was coming."

"Are you serious?"

"As a heart attack. When I saw her sitting next to my mother, I almost had a panic attack. And I never had one of those."

"It might be fate," Dee said.

Bruce and Eric looked at Dee as if he were suddenly talking Chinese.

"I don't believe in fate, but I believe in opportunities. And yours is walking out the door," Bruce said.

Eric turned around to see Kenya and Jackie leaving the banquet hall. He jumped up without another word and ran towards them. Danny looked to see where his dad was going. He smiled as he noticed Eric chasing Kenya.

Eric caught up to her in the hallway. He tapped her on the shoulder. She turned around as Jackie kept walking to the elevator.

"Were you going to leave without speaking to me?"

"No, silly. I was going to walk my sister out, she's the one leaving. I'll be right back. I promise." They locked eyes, then she followed Jackie out.

He watched her 5'9 sexy strut in her blue dress until they got on the elevator. Maleek stepped out of the elevator beside theirs, throwing his hands up in the air like a referee signaling for a field goal.

"What you doing out here? Is it dead in there?" Maleek asked as he gave Eric dap.

"It's as alive as a wedding reception should be. And you just missed Kenya. She got on the other elevator."

"Wow. You knew Kenya was coming?"

"Not at all. It must be my mother's doing. I need to speak to that woman."

They walked into the hall together. Maleek went over to The Crew's table where Dee and Bruce were eating. Eric sat next to his mother. He kissed her on the cheek.

"What you want? After a kiss, there's always something, so spit it out." She looked at him with her head tilted.

"Did you invite Kenya?"

"No."

He looked at her for a second and waited for her to come clean. Then, he realized she was telling the truth. He was baffled.

"So... Who did?"

"I don't know. You're asking the wrong person. Ask her."

A plate was set down beside Eric on the table. When he looked up, it was Kenya again.

"Can I get a hug, stranger?" She asked as she stood over him.

Eric looked at his mother as he stood up. He gave her a big hug, and noted that she smelled amazing. He tried not to hold her too long, but their embrace was electric to him. If the room were pitch black, that hug would have lit it, clear as day. As they released, Eric gazed into her eyes briefly. In that moment, he experienced a calm that he once yearned for ever since Danielle passed. They sat down, and she opened her napkin and placed it on her lap. Then, she started going in on her food. He forgot that they were in a crowded room, not to mention a wedding reception. Watching her eat made him reminisce. He couldn't hide the smile that appeared on his face.

"I see your appetite hasn't changed," Eric said jokingly as Kenya ate with no regard to the rest of the table.

"I see you still haven't got a job at *Saturday Night Live*."

They both laughed. Danny had sent a server to bring Eric's food to Nana's table. As they ate, they made a little small talk. Nana had long since gotten up and was mingling with Danny's other grandparents. Eric and Kenya finished their food and walked to the open bar. Standing in line, she leaned closer and whispered in his ear.

"Do you know what today is?"

Eric thought to himself, *November 26*. He knew her birthday was in August. He didn't say anything, just stood there with his eyebrow raised, trying to think.

Kenya pulled him out of line by his hand. "Let me show you." She led him out of the hall and to the elevator, pressing the button. The elevator opened, and a couple exited. She pushed Eric onto the elevator, and then she got on and pressed the button for what he assumed was her floor. Eric stood behind her, somewhat shamelessly looking at her butt. *Hmmm! I'm loving her grown weight... We are not kids anymore, h*e thought to himself as he bit his lip.

CHAPTER 25

The elevator opened, and Eric followed Kenya to her room. When she got to the door, she searched for the key card in her clutch bag. He tried to act cool, but his heart was beating twenty miles an hour. An older couple walked by as Kenya was searching. The woman said that they were the most beautiful couple that she'd seen in years. She also told them to enjoy their night. Eric didn't correct the woman, he simply smiled. Kenya pulled the card out her purse and showed it to Eric as she rolled her eyes. He smiled at her, because he had seen her nose flair from aggravation as she'd searched. She swiped the card, and then she finally opened the door. Eric stood in the doorway, waiting for her to get what she was trying to show him. She grabbed a big pocketbook on the desk. Then, she looked back at him.

"Will you get in here and close the door?"

As he did so, she pulled an envelope out of her bag. Then, she sat on the bed and placed the bag behind her. Eric made his way further into the room. Kenya tapped on the bed for him to sit down. He did, and she handed him the envelope.

"Open it. I hope this refreshes your memory."

Eric took the envelope and looked at her with a confused look on his face. He shook the envelope, and something slid back and forward. He got very curious at that point, opening the envelope and pulling out an old friendship bracelet. "Wow," Eric gasped as he examined the bracelet. It was still in great shape.

I remember making that in arts and crafts class right before Thanksgiving break. I even got into an altercation over the bracelet. James snatched it from me as I was admiring it. I chased him all over that class, Eric smiled as the memory came to him.

"E.T., phone home," Kenya said, laughing, trying to get his attention.

"My bad. This brought back a lot of memories, from the blue and purple plastic stings intertwined. Blue is my favorite color and purple yours. And the white letter beads saying, 'MY LOVE.' This is crazy."

"Yeah. That's why I brought it. Just knowing I was going to see you on the Saturday after Thanksgiving. The universe has a way of telling you something."

"That's right. I did give that to you that Saturday. Man... Do you remember that Saturday?"

"Do I... I"ll never forget how my father yelled up the stairs and told me there was someone at the door me. As I came to the door he told me, 'Don't leave off the steps.' We sat there on those steps for hours talking about everything under the sun. Then you told me to close my eyes and you put out my hand. I did it, then you placed something in my hand. I opened my eyes to see the friendship bracelet you gave me. I said thanks and hugged you." Eric smiled as he saw it as Kenya told the story.

"I was a little confused because we'd been going together for six months. Everybody knew except for my dad--even my mother knew. Then, you said in your cute way, 'While making this bracelet, I thought about what I learned in science class. That one stick, even if sturdy, can be easily broken. But if you take a lot of sticks and put them together, it's going to take a great force to break them. I thought about us when Mr. Whitaker gave that lesson. Therefore, I took our favorite colors and bonded them to make our bond strong. Then the words "My Love." Today, I want you to know I love you. I try to play tough guy, but I realize, I truly love you. And by you accepting this bracelet, I'm giving you my heart. And as long you have this bracelet, you will forever have... "My Love."

"I could have dropped dead when I heard you say that. I put on the bracelet and went out to the side of the house. I kissed you, and you were so scared to kiss me back you couldn't stop looking at the curtains in the windows on the side of the house. I know we kissed so many times, but this time was different. I believe that was the first time we kissed being in love."

"You right. And that was the first time we made love."

"I know, and I was so nervous. We waited five whole hours on the porch for my parents to go to sleep. I told you to meet me in the back yard in two minutes. The look on your face when I told you that was priceless. I knew you didn't have a clue of what I was preparing to do. You had experience, but I was still a virgin in the flesh, but we'd been together in my dreams various times. I went into the house and got a blanket. I opened the back door and led you down the stairs. The basement wasn't furnished. The floor was hard cement, not an inch of carpet or flooring. I laid the cover on the floor, and I laid down on my back. You climbed on top of me, and we kissed so hard, like we were trying to take each other's breath. You undressed yourself and me gently as I watched. When you stuck it in, my stomach tightened from the pain. It didn't feel like my dreams that left my panties wet. Minutes in, the pain became pleasure, and I saw you with a different set of eyes. Then, when we finished you laid beside me; you gave me a kiss that followed behind you licking my nose. I'd said, 'Ew! What's wrong with you?' and we both laughed. That was the first time you licked my nose, but not the last. That cover is still in my father's basement in a box I kept hidden."

"Yeah. You do reminder? I smiled and cried at the same time about that day for a week."

"You cried because you were in love for the first time?"

"That, too. But I cried because my pants kept aggravating the rug burns I got from the covers and hard floor. I just *know* I used all the cocoa butter in the house that week."

"You silly."

"No, I'm serious," he said, smiling as he looked at the bracelet.

Kenya got up and walked to the refrigerator. She pulled out a bottle of wine and a big red velvet cupcake in a clear plastic container. She handed Eric the cupcake, and then she placed the wine on the table and opened it with the corkscrew. She walked to her closet, mumbling to herself. He watched her every move as his heartbeat sped up. Eric was hoping that she wouldn't be able to hear the way his chest was pounding. She walked back from the closet with two wine glasses, a lighter, and a candle. She tossed the lighter and candle on the bed next to him.

"Open the container and put the candle in the cupcake," she instructed as she poured two glasses of wine.

Eric opened the container and did what she said. He pushed the candle too far, enough that he had to pull it out a little. She handed him one of the glasses of wine as she sat next to him. Kenya grabbed the lighter and lit the candle as she held the cupcake.

"Today is our anniversary. Thirty-eight years ago, we made love that changed our relationship forever. And, you also gave me your heart. Before we blow out the candle, we need to make a wish."

Eric closed his eyes, not only to wish, but because, in that moment, they were too close for his comfort. He was trying hard not to throw the wine and jump on top of her. When he opened his eyes, she still had hers closed. When she finally opened her eyes, she took a deep breath. Then, they blew out the candle. She tossed the candle aside and pushed the cupcake to his mouth. Eric took a bite, and Kenya bit the other side. Eric stood up enough to place the cupcake on the desk. When he turned around, she was standing right behind him.

“What did you wish for?” She asked him.

“Wouldn’t you like to know?”

“You right--don’t tell me, so that it can come true. Let’s make a toast.”

“To what?”

“First loves all around the world.”

“To first loves.” They tapped glasses.

They took a drink as their eyes locked. Eric wiped the wine from his lips with his left hand, without unlocking eyes with Kenya. She moved in, and he couldn’t back up because the desk was behind him. He realized then that, even so, he didn’t want to back up. She licked the wine off his bottom lip, and they started kissing. They kissed so passionately that he felt as if they were back at the side of her parent's house. That kiss woke up something inside of Eric that had been asleep. It felt amazing. Too amazing. He pushed her away and asked her.

“You sure you want to open this back up?”

“Only one way to find out.” Then, she took his glass and placed both of them on the desk.

She walked over to the curtains and started closing them. Eric came up behind her and started kissing her on her neck. He pushed the curtain back open. She turned around with a surprised look on her face. He kissed her as he kicked off his shoes and pants. Eric did all that without skipping a beat as they kissed. He backed away to pull off the rest of his clothes. She tried to get out of the way of the window, but he wouldn’t let her. Eric shook his head slow and seductive as he bit his bottom lip, and Kenya grinned back. He’d taken everything off but his socks, and he kissed her and spun her around.

He unzipped her dress, and they struggled to pull it over her head as she tried to stop it from messing up her hair. Eric tossed her dress on the recliner. He kissed her from her neck, back, to her thighs as he took off her panties. He took a knee as he rubbed her up. Eric was in awe of the smoothness of her caramel skin and grown figure. He tapped her legs open, and she spread them, as her hands were on the window. He could feel her looking down on him.

Eric massaged her vagina from behind. He could feel it throbbing as she clenched her cheeks. He grabbed her thigh and turned her back around. He placed his tongue in her as he caressed her waist. She grabbed his head as she sucked her lips in. He kept going to see how much she could take. Then, he stood up and stuck himself inside her. Kenya moaned as she held his shoulders. Eric didn't know when the last time was that he wanted to see someone's face while being intimate with them. He picked her up while still inside her and laid her on the bed, where they continued until they fell asleep.

CHAPTER 26

Mr. Couple walked up to Danny and whispered to him in his ear, telling him that it was time for the best man to make his toast.

"Okay. Give me a second, let me get my dad."

Danny texted his dad. The phone vibrated, but there was no answer.

Danny: *Dad we are waiting for you to give the toast.*

He waited five minutes--still no response. Then, he called his dad again.

Brrrrr. Brrrrrr. Eric phone was vibrating on the bed. His phone was still on vibrate from the wedding.

"Baby! Your phone keeps vibrating--it might be important," Kenya said to Eric as they laid on the floor, on top of the comforter with the sheets covering them.

Eric reached up on the bed, feeling around to locate his phone, but had no luck. Kenya got up, tossed the phone to him as she walked to the bathroom. He stared at her as she walked away. It was incredible that, even though they hadn't been together all those years, that she was still the type of woman he was attracted to. Eric looked at the phone to see that he had a text and three missed calls from Danny. He quickly called him back.

Ring, ring, ring.

“Where are you, Dad?”

“I’m in the room. Is it possible that Thomas could do the toast?”

“He could, but is everything okay?”

“Yes, son, I’m a little... indisposed right now. Just do that, and I will explain when you get back from your honeymoon.”

“I got you. I can’t wait to hear this.” Danny smiled as he ended the call. He saw when Kenya and his dad left the hall.

Eric put the phone back on the bed. He grabbed the remote and turned the television on. Still sitting up on the floor, he started flipping through the channels. Kenya came out of the bathroom and sat on the bed in front of him. Eric tried not to stare at her, as part of her was eye level to his face. He stopped on the college scoreboard, then placed the remote next to her thigh. He placed his hand on Kenya's knee and started rubbing it. Eric noticed the look on her face. It was quite alarming. He got on his knees between her legs.

“Are you okay?” Eric asked, concerned, as he looked into her eyes. She looked spacey.

Kenya focused her eyes on him and put her hands on his hands atop her knees. “I’m good. It’s just... I have so many emotions running through my body. Plus, I have so many questions going through my head.”

Eric stood up and sat next to her on the bed. He put his right arm around her as he thought to himself, *This is usually when I peel out. I have no tolerance when a woman starts getting in her feelings too early.*

He surprised even himself, thought, as he asked, “What kind of feeling and questions?”

“I don’t know how to say it... but, when we first kissed, it was weird. Not in a bad way, but like a very familiar and safe place.

I already knew that our chemistry was always our strong suit. However, who would have ever thought that it would be this strong after all these years apart? I might be rambling or all over the place... but I can't stop thinking. What if?"

"What if, what?"

"What if we had never broke up? Don't get me wrong, I wouldn't change my two kids for anything in this world. But while you slept, I laid next to you with my eyes closed, and my thoughts were coming a thousand miles per second."

"Believe me, it's mutual. I just don't want to spoil the moment. I'm going to enjoy you and this moment as long as I can. Or, should I say, as long as you let me? I can beat myself down with my thoughts later."

"You right." She faced him and they kissed.

"Lay on your stomach. I want to give you something."

"You don't think that you've already given me enough?"

"Just do it, beautiful."

She looked at him with a half-smile before she laid on her stomach. Eric sat on the edge of the bed and started massaging her shoulders. Kenya's shoulders were so tense, you couldn't imagine. He stood up next to her to get a better angle to apply intense pressure. She oohed and aahed with every squeeze over her shoulders.

"When does your flight leave out?"

"Tomorrow at 8 P.M." She said as she moaned from the massage.

"Do you have to leave tomorrow?"

"Not really..."

"How about you leave on Tuesday? My mind has been ticking just like yours, and it dawned on me. That was our first-time having wine together. I could think about a lot of first times we could have in three days."

"Like what?"

"Change your flight and find out."

She rolled over to look him in his eyes. "You're serious?"

"As a heart attack. I'm just waiting on you before I call my secretary to move my schedule around."

She sat up and grabbed her phone, looking up the number to dial the airline. He picked up his tux from around the room. Eric got redressed, and Kenya watched his every move as she spoke to customer service.

"Hold on one second," she said to the customer service rep. "Where are you going?"

"To my room to pack. We're going to Atlantic City. Maybe my luck will help me cash out."

"Don't make me wait another 30 more years."

"Never that." He leaned down to kiss her.

Eric went to his room thinking about the letter Danny read to him in the kitchen. That sparked him to take the shot and put the game in over time. Kenya continued to change her flight dates while smiling, thinking about their trip.

CHAPTER 27

They drove to Atlantic City. The whole ride there, they held hands, Kenya sometimes rubbing his knee. Between her sensual touch and the R&B station she found, Eric was tempted to pull the car over several times and finish what they'd started in New York. He hadn't felt like this in years. Too many years, if you asked him.

They pulled up to the Golden Nugget Hotel and Casino. The bell-hop grabbed their bags and let the valet park the car.

"Wait here while I get the key to the room," Eric said to Kenya.

She sat with the bags while Eric went to the front desk. The clerk was having a hard time finding his reservation, since Eric only booked the reservation a matter of hours ago. The clerk went to get someone out of the office. This was starting to aggravate Eric. He looked back at Kenya, and she was on her cell phone. When she saw him looking at her, he forced a small smile--he wasn't exactly in a smiling mood, dealing with the idiot behind the desk. Eric turned back around, and the clerk came back with a piece of paper. He didn't know what was on the paper, but he typed the information into the computer. The manager finally found the reservation, and also gave them a complimentary gift basket for the trouble. Eric walked back to Kenya and grabbed the cart the bags were on, heading to the elevators.

When they got to the room, she took the key card from him and opened the door. Kenya went into the room and walked to the window; their room had a great view. It was only 6 PM, but it felt so much later. She flopped down, face first, on the bed, and then she rolled over and kicked her shoes off. Eric looked at her while biting his lip. *Should we stay in for the night? Or do what I've been plotting on the way here?*

"What are you thinking?" She asked.

"I have this restaurant in mind, it's a real nice spot. I gotta get something to wear. The outlets are not too far from here."

"Wear your tux so we don't have to run out. We can relax until it's time to get ready to go."

"Are you going to wear the dress you wore to the wedding?"

"No. I packed enough dresses to go out for a week."

"I know you did... but I'm not wearing this tux. You can chill while I run to the outlets. I'll be right back."

Eric grabbed the key card, walking to the door. Kenya jumped up, ran to the door, and pushed it closed as he opened it. He turned around ready to question her, not understanding what was wrong with her. She kissed him so hard that he dropped the key card, and he was soon trying to pull up her shirt. She pulled it down as she backed up.

"Go get your clothes, but don't make me wait too long." She kneeled to pick up the key card, never breaking eye contact. Eric wasn't sure how she knew exactly where the card was without looking. Kenya handed him the key, then stepped away. He took a deep breath and exhaled slowly, grinning as he went out the door.

Kenya sat on the bed with her back to the headboard. She turned the television on with the remote and flipped through the channels. She stopped at a channel showing *Ray,* starring Jamie Foxx. Kenya placed the remote beside her and grabbed her cell phone. She had two text messages from Jackie.

Jackie: I returned your rental car. They were very rude about me not being you. You probably can't rent from them any more because I showed out a little.

Jackie: Okay. It was a lot. They even called security. I'm good, I know that's what's on your mind. Enjoy Eric. Love you...

She started to text Jackie back, but thought better of it, deciding to call instead. *Ring... ring... ring...*

"Hello?" Jackie answered in a child's voice, as if she was in trouble.

"Thanks for turning the car in."

"No problem..." Jackie said, still sounding as if she was expecting Kenya to react as a mother would, rather than as a big sister.

"I want to say thanks before I fall off the map. Eric is trying to have me lose my mind. I haven't told him that I haven't been on a real date in over a year. Those two blind dates I did at that time were a disaster... Plus, I only did it because I lost a bet. I don't know who's worse--Charita, or you for getting me into some mess."

"Whatever. What's he's doing to make you lose your mind?"

"Everything. From the sex to this spontaneous trip to Atlantic City. He was always sweet when we were younger, or, should I say, when we were kids. But now his sweetness has really turned into romance. Even the look in his eyes is different..."

"Stop. Are you sprung already? Damn! That's why I told you to stay in circulation as it comes to dating. I realize he's your first love but remember, he's been single for a long time. Plus, Eric is Mr. Available when it comes to having a good time. I think his heart died when his fiancé died. That's what I heard from the ladies that come in the restaurant once they get a few drinks. They love how he is with his son, but he's unavailable when it comes to a serious relationship. Be careful. In other words, open your legs, but close your heart. Have a good time without making it more than it is. You got me?"

"I got you... I'm good, trust and believe. Now, that's enough of worrying about Kenya. Let's talk about you."

"What about me? I'm happily married."

"I'm not talking about your marriage. What did you do to have them call security?"

"I'll tell you later, my phone is about to die. Can you hear me? Can you--" Kenya heard the dial tone; Jackie had hung up the phone before Kenya could respond.

Kenya smiled as she tossed her phone to the foot of the bed. She turned the volume up on the television and scooted down until she laid flat on her back. *Open my legs and close my heart. Close my heart and open my legs*. She repeated those lines to herself over and over, until the point that she fell asleep.

Two hours later, Eric hopped in a cab coming back from the outlets. Looking at all the bags in his hands, he knew he'd overdone it. He could have used her arms to help, he thought to himself, as he struggled walking from store to store. Plus, trying to watch his bags and shop at the same time was difficult.

Ring... ring... ring...

"Hello?" Eric answered the phone. It was Dee.

"Can you talk?" Dee asked. The sound of the call told Eric he was speaking through his car's Bluetooth

"Yes. What's good?"

"Nothing. Just seeing how everything is going with you and Kenya."

"So far, so good. We out here in A.C. I'm coming back from the outlets. I left her back in the hotel."

"Okay, playa, I see you trying to get those panties," Bruce's voice said through the phone. Eric laughed.

"Why you didn't tell me Nasty Nelson was in the car? And, for your information, I *got* the panties back in New York. This just me catching up on another level. Something you wouldn't know, so close your ears while grown folks talk."

"Whatever. I'm older than both of y'all," Bruce said.

"Anyway. Dee, I'm feeling her right now. I mean, I'm really, really, *really* feeling her."

"Damn. I haven't heard you say that in a long time. I don't think I ever heard you say that. Do you think it's because it's Kenya, or because of the wedding atmosphere? A lot of people have fallen in love at a wedding. Love goes viral at weddings."

"I don't know. I could see that wedding stuff, but... I don't believe I fall into that category. Y'all haven't called me a sucker for love in damn near 40 years. That dude left the building ages ago."

"True. Embrace it, then, you ain't got nothing to lose! You know how I feel about love and marriage. I wouldn't exchange it for anything in the world, especially when it's good."

"I hear you. I'm going to hit y'all tomorrow, I just pulled up at the hotel."

"Cool. Embrace it!" Dee said again, then he ended the call.

"I give it two months before he starts feeling bad about the promise he made," Bruce said to Dee.

"I forgot about that. Hopefully, things will be different this time. I know Eric hates that he made that promise." Dee took a left on Merrick Blvd.

Eric paid the cab driver. The bellhop rolled a cart to the cab as he saw all the bags Eric had. He walked over to the front desk and ordered a car service for the next two days. After he finished at the front desk, Eric went back up to the room. He tipped the bellhop outside the room door. As he walked off, Eric listened through the door while using the key card to open it. Kenya had the television on blast. Eric pushed the cart in the room, only to see her there, knocked out. She was spread out all over the bed. He found the volume button on the television and turned it down, and Kenya woke up instantly.

"Hey, baby, I didn't hear you come in." She stretched as she laid there.

"I tried not to wake you." He walked over to her and leaned over her to kiss her. She sat up in the bed as Eric lifted up the bags from the cart.

"Wow! When you said you were going shopping, you meant that."

"Ha, ha, ha. They had a lot of Thanksgiving's sales. I even got you something. I hope you like it." Her eyes lit up when Eric said that. He located one of the Victoria's Secret bags and headed towards her.

"Let me guess. You got me some lingerie?"

"Nope. Just see what it is."

She took the bag with a puzzled look on her face as if she didn't believe him. She pulled out a silk purple scarf and two bottles of perfume. She rubbed the scarf against her cheek, then wrapped it around her neck. Afterwards, she read the perfume names out loud.

"'Heavenly' and 'Love.' Are you trying to send a subliminal message?"

"Okay. I see you're a little cray-cray... it's no message behind this, just being thoughtful. Even after all these years, I remember you wearing this perfume--it used to drive me crazy. I smelled too many fragrances at the outlet, but none came close.

I did like these two, though. Hopefully you don't have them."

"No. I don't have either one of these. Thanks, baby. They're both good, but I like 'Heavenly' more." She continued smelling the cap of the bottle.

"You're welcome. Let me hop in the shower first. I know how women are," Eric said as he put her other bag behind his Saks Fifth Avenue Off 5th bag.

"What's in that other Victoria's Secret bag?"

"Nothing. Something I picked up for myself. Don't go peeking, I'll put it on when we get back from eating." Eric went into the bathroom to take a shower.

She got up and looked at the bathroom door, which was cracked open. Then, she opened the bag quietly, trying to be sneaky. Looking in the bag, it looked like a black lacy situation. She pulled the contents out and saw that it was a floral black lace teddy. She held it up to her, and it was just her size. She walked to the cracked door, smiling.

"I can't wait to see you squeeze your muscular physique into this teddy." She held it out in her hand.

Eric pulled the shower curtain back to see her holding the teddy. "Damn! They mixed up the bags. I picked out a blue one, and it was a little longer than that one. If that's your size, you can keep it. I don't like returning merchandise," he said, with a fake look of disappointment.

"Yeah, I bet you don't like returning things." She walked off, laughing to herself.

CHAPTER 28

Eric was standing in front of the window, trying to use the reflection to see if he should wear the red bow tie or not. He couldn't see his shoes, but he knew he was looking sharp. He had on a white, slim-fit Polo dress shirt and a black Polo sweater vest, Oxford-style black shoes, Express slim-style slacks gently touching the shoe. Red and black striped socks for the "sit-down" effect. Even with all of that on, he was still debating wearing the bow tie. Eric couldn't wait for Kenya to come out of the bathroom so he could use the mirror instead.

He heard the commentator say, "Brace yourself for what we are about to show you." Eric turned around in time to see a college football player getting his ankle broken during a tackle. *Damn,* he thought to himself as they showed the replay. He sat there on the edge of the bed, thinking about when he blew out his knee in college. The bathroom door opened, and Kenya came out.

She walked up on him as he was watching ESPN. Eric didn't realize that she'd come out of the bathroom until she bumped his knee with the back of her thigh. He looked to his right to see her dress, unzipped. Eric stood up to zip the dress. As he grabbed her zipper, he was mesmerized by her body in the dress. She had on a purple, sleeveless fitted dress, with flattering panel detail in lace on the side. The lace pattern stretched from under her arm on the side to a point four inches below her waist. As he was zipping her up, he was wondering if she had any panties on, because he sure didn't see any.

"Grab your hair, love, before you get mad at me," Eric said as he got to the top of her dress. She held her hair up with a laugh. After he zipped it up, she walked back in the bathroom. He grabbed the bow tie and followed her in to check himself out; he was finally getting a chance to see himself in the mirror, and yet he watched her more than he did himself. The way she was doing her eyelashes was turning him on. He shook it off and asked her.

"Tie or no tie?"

"Definitely no tie. Just unbutton... let me do it." She turned around and fixed his collar. Then, she grabbed his shoulder, turning him so he could look in the mirror to see what she'd done. "It looks good, right?"

"You look beautiful... simply gorgeous."

"Thanks. You look very handsome yourself. But I was talking about your collar, not me."

"My bad. My collar is good, but you look beautiful."

She smiled, rolling her eyes as she pushed him out of the bathroom. She clearly knew he was leaning in for a kiss. Eric smiled as he grabbed his three-quarter-length pea coat and hat.

"Not to rush you, but I don't want to be late for this reservation."

"But you are rushing me," Kenya said as she came out of the bathroom and went straight to the closet. She stepped into some heels and pulled out her full-length white mink coat. She walked over to the bed, opened her large purse and pulled out her Michael Kors card holder. Then, she grabbed her purple clutch bag off the table desk.

Eric took the key card off the chair by the window and they finally headed out. They put on their coats as they stood in the elevator. When the doors opened the light caught them by surprise. Walking through the lobby, Eric felt something special was ahead of them. They walked to the valet, and it was very cold. *I should have bought some of the gloves, scarf, and hat sets I saw them selling everywhere*, Eric thought to himself. He whispered to the valet attendant and pointed to the middle limo, of three parked in a row. The valet buzzed the driver, who got out of the driver seat and opened the back door. He grabbed Kenya's hand and walked her to the limo. She cut her eyes at him, then smiled as she got into the limo. Eric sat next to her, and the driver closed the door behind him. The driver then got back in the driver's seat and rolled the privacy glass down.

"I will be your driver for the evening. My name is Gregg Hartman. You can call me Gregg. The bar is stocked with scotch and bourbon, so help yourself. We should be arriving at Café 2825 in ten minutes. If you need me for anything, press the button located on the doors and bar," Gregg said before he shut the partition again.

"How did you get a reservation for that place? Every time me and Jackie come up here, we can't get reservations. They're always booked, weeks at a time... Hold up! Am I your replacement date? Did you have all this for someone else?"

Eric looked at Kenya with a smile as he poured them each a drink. She crossed her arms, waiting for him to respond. "Relax, Matlock. No, I didn't. The owner of the restaurant is a client of the accounting firm I work for. It's not always what you know, most of the time it's who you know." He handed her the glass of bourbon. Then, he sat back next to her with his glass. "I want to make a toast. Here's to our first weekend getaway, our first limo ride. Hell! Here's to our first real date, but not our last." They tapped glasses and took a sip. She stared at him with a look on her face that he'd never experienced from her.

"What? What's that look on your face?"

"I'm sorry. I didn't know I had a look on my face. It might be the alcohol," she said, taking another sip.

"Oh, really, the alcohol? You took a sip and a half. What is it?"

"Just trying to enjoy the moment. It feels so good, but..."

"But? What's the but?"

"I'm being careful... You got to understand. I hoped that this would happen once I decided to come to the wedding. And trust me, it has been an *amazing* day thus far, more than my imagination could ever make up. With all that being said, I'm still a little leery."

"Leery about what?"

"About what? I know we haven't been in contact for years, but I've heard a lot about you since we were kids. Plus--"

"Let me stop you--"

"I wasn't finished."

"You don't have to say no more. Once I say what I'm about to say, you can finish if you still need to. First of all, I couldn't care less about what you have heard about me. Let's get that clear. I'm not saying that it's the truth or a lie, but understand that it wasn't with you. And that's not us, never has been and never will. Secondly, don't let what you think you know be a roadblock that stops you from enjoying yourself. Roadblocks keep you safe, but they don't keep the flow going on moving forward. And that flow or momentum can make or break a relationship. Don't I know it, I've been living with that roadblock for the last twenty-plus years, until... until I laid eyes on you sitting next to my mother.

"The whole time the ceremony was going on, I felt something moving inside of me. It was like the black cloud that was hovering over my heart was blown away. That might sound a little over the top, but that's how I felt. True story. This is not a game, or me trying to play with your emotions or heart. This is me, moving *with* my heart. I don't know what to expect these next couple of days. But I know I'm going to follow my heart and enjoy myself to the fullest. I don't know about you, but it feels amazing to be spending time with someone that I truly love being with."

"It does feel amazing."

"So, let's make a toast to letting whatever play out, play out. We're in Atlantic City! We came here to win and have a good time."

They toasted for winning and having a good time. The chauffeur opened the door, and they got out and walked into the restaurant, Kenya not saying a single word.

CHAPTER 29

They were sitting at the table sipping on Dom Perignon and eating calamari, talking about the old days, waiting for their food to come out. They laughed about how Jackie would try to peek on them once they got the heart to make love in Kenya's bedroom. Eric just knew Jackie made $20 a week in hush money. Then, there was the time when the condom had burst, and he'd kept going. That had never happened to him before, so he didn't recognize when the feeling changed from plastic to nothing. That might have been the last time they used a condom. They'd taken a lot of risks back then, but you couldn't have told either of them that they weren't going to be together forever. The stories kept coming by the dozens. The waiter walked up with their food, right in the middle of all the laughter.

"Veal chop Milanese with spinach and roasted potatoes, for you, sir. Lobster and shrimp Francese with shoestring zucchini and pasta marinara, for my lady," the waiter said as placed the food on the table. He poured more champagne into their low glasses. "I'm going to leave this dessert menu here. I would recommend our famous homemade coconut cheesecake." He kissed his fingertips as he said, "It's delicious. Enjoy your meals. I will be back to check on you in a few."

"Thank you," Eric said to the waiter, placing a napkin on his lap, getting ready to go in. Kenya closed her eyes and prayed over her food silently. When she opened her eyes, she caught him watching her. He looked away and started eating. The food was terrific, which made sense, seeing the high demand. When Eric went over the prices on the menu, he thought at first it was a front. Now, he saw that the chef demanded those type figures to come through the door.

They didn't talk much once the food got there. It was like they were making love to the forks. Eric caught himself moaning as he stuffed his mouth, sounding like a fat boy at an all-you-can-eat restaurant. Kenya requested two cheesecakes to go when the waiter brought the check to the table. They finished the bottle of wine waiting for the waiter to bring Eric's card back. Kenya went to the bathroom, passing the waiter bringing the receipt. Eric grabbed his card and the cheesecake, then walked to get their coats. He told the valet to tell their chauffeur they were on their way out. Kenya walked over to him, and Eric helped her put her coat on before they walked to the limo. Gregg was standing with the door open, and he had Marvin Gaye playing on the radio.

"What's next?" She asked with a smile as she shrugged off her coat.

"Why you say it like that?"

"I can see your mind turning. You got something up your sleeve."

"Not up my sleeves, in my coat pocket," Eric said, pulling out two cigar containers out of the inside pocket of his coat. He passed one to her. She stared at the containers while he opened the sunroof.

"Is this a joke? You know I don't smoke."

"Neither do I. But I had two hours by myself while you were in the hotel. I thought way more than I shopped. And you know I'm a big *Godfather* fan. It's customary to have a cigar to celebrate a special moment. They do it to celebrate a birth, the death of enemies, business success and marriage... We don't have to inhale, but let's make this night memorable."

"I don't know, Eric. I don't know..."

"Put your hair down and live a little. Just hold the smoke in your mouth for a second, then blow it out. It's that easy."

"You did this before?"

"Never. I'm just repeating what the guy told me at the cigar shop. He also said it would enhance the taste of the alcohol."

"Oh, really?" She side-eyed him.

"Let's try it, and if we don't like it, we can toss them. Trust me."

"The last time I listened when you said 'trust me,' I lost my sandal running from the police when we snuck into Liberty Pool that night with the whole neighborhood. I don't know what I was thinking. My father thought I was at my friend's house. If I had got caught, he would have killed me."

"Wow. I forgot about that night. But, you gotta admit, we had the most fun that night. Even scared to death, you were so beautiful to me."

"You right. That was one of my best nights with you."

"Does that mean you're going to trust me?"

"Yes. Hurry up before I change my mind."

Eric stood up in the sunroof, holding the cigar. The wind was cutting too hard when he faced the direction they were driving. He turned around and let the wind hit his back, telling Kenya to fix them some drinks in the meantime, which she did. Eric got the cigar out of the container and tossed the container back into the limo. She kicked off her heels and stood up with him, placing her face against his chest. She held him with one hand and her drink with the other. He lit the cigar with a lighter as they were stopped at a light. Eric puffed twice and blew the smoke out. It was nasty, but at the same time somehow enjoyable. Kenya turned around and rubbed his thigh as she took a sip.

He took another puff and held it. She took the cigar out his hand and took a puff. Kenya passed it back to Eric, and all he could think was, *Bonnie and Clyde*. She blew out the smoke and started coughing. He'd figured she might inhale some. Eric patted Kenya on her back as they laughed.

Riding through the town standing in the sunroof was nice. Eric had been to Atlantic City plenty of times, but the view looked different from here. Kenya ducked back into the limo to get his drink. He held his head back, trying to blow out a circle with this thick cigar smoke. As he did, Eric felt her unzip his zipper. He looked down at Kenya as she dropped his pants. She massaged him while reaching for her clutch. Kenya popped a cough drop and leaned in to take him into her mouth. It felt so good that Eric tossed the cigar and held on the top of the limo as if he were on a rollercoaster. With his eyes closed and the wind whipping against his cheeks, he felt like he was about to scream, it felt so good. Eric opened his eyes then, only to see they were stopped at a light, and a police car was behind them. He almost knocked Kenya down trying to push her off him, then he slumped down in the limo.

"You didn't like it," she said, holding the cough drop that she took out her mouth.

"I loved it, but the police are right behind us," he said, slumping down in the seat.

She started laughing as he blushed. He was so embarrassed. They watched as the cops turned off from behind them. She rolled her dress up to her waist and straddled him. Kenya placed Eric inside of her and started moving gently. Not only was it sensual, but it was also exciting. His adrenaline rushed as the cars passed on both sides as they were engaged all the while. She changed her motion as the songs changed on the radio.

"We're at the Helicopter Charter," Gregg said through the intercom.

"Plans have changed. Take us back to the hotel," Eric said, trying not to moan too loud as she didn't stop.

"Okay, sir. Back to the hotel we go."

CHAPTER 30

Tuesday afternoon. Eric grooved to the Sugar Hill Gang's "Rapper's Delight" as he drove Kenya to the airport. He noticed her playing with the strings of the bracelet he'd given her years ago. That song was about as old as the bracelet. Eric drove around, trying to find her terminal; he smiled to himself, thinking about the weekend. It had been nothing short of epic.

"Take this left to United Airlines," she said.

Eric took a left, then he cut his eyes at her. Kenya had been quiet ever since they left Jackie's restaurant. He asked her once if she was okay, and she'd said yes. She said that she was zoned out to the music. He didn't think anything of it, because she loved music, and that particular oldies station kept the jams going back to back all day. Kenya knew songs that always surprised Eric.

He finally pulled up at her terminal but couldn't park in front of it. There wasn't any space. Instead, he parked at the other airline next to hers. Eric shut the car off, took off his seat belt, and opened his door.

"Close the door. I'm good, plus I don't want you to get a ticket. You already know how these airport police are. That's why I usually catch a cab." She faced him as she took off her seat belt.

Eric looked at her for a second to see if she was serious. He closed his door and asked her, "Are you sure everything is alright?"

"Yes. But I do have something on my mind."

He knew this was coming. The Life of Eric *is about to unfold. Every time things are going good... BAM! Someone overthinks the situation,* Eric thought to himself. "What's on your mind?" A nervous turning was going on in his stomach.

"We talked about our past with each other, and our careers and family. I have two kids, you have one. I have grandchildren, and you have none. We both not married at this time but.... I'm not seeing anyone and haven't for a long time. It will be two years in January since I been involved with someone. In other words, you broke the seal on that treasure. Hmmm! You did that..." She paused for a moment as Eric smiled. "I don't know what you have going on and I really don't care. I enjoyed myself more than you will ever know. Trust me, I will smile all the way to California thanks to you. You just spent the last three days with a grown woman. Grown to the point that I don't do foolishness or drama. You don't have to lie to me or tell me what you think I want to hear. So, let's be honest with each other. You were my friend before you became my first love, and I value that friendship. Even if we're not involved, we shouldn't let these many years ever pass again without speaking."

Eric nodded as Kenya spoke. "I feel the same."

Kenya smiled. "That's good you agree. So, if we decide to--or not to--build on this weekend, either way, I will be fine. I'm just being blunt. I'm not trying to scare you away, but I don't want you to assume how I feel. Now, pop the trunk and let me get my bag."

Eric popped the trunk. She reached over and gave him a hug and a light kiss from her seat. Then, she got out of the car and grabbed her bag. She shut the trunk and walked over to his window. He rolled it down.

"Take this. I want it back when you give me your heart again, okay? Not a moment sooner." Kenya gave Eric the bracelet back. Then, she bent over and gave him a passionate kiss, ending with three pecks. She wiped her lip gloss from his lips with her thumb, and then she walked around the front of the car and to her terminal. Eric watched her sexy walk until she was out of his view. He sat there for a second, not fully realizing what just happened. She'd controlled that whole exchange, and, secretly, he admired her for that. It was very different and a turn-on. He smiled as he pulled off, sill holding the bracelet.

Eric headed straight to the house after he dropped her off. He had to make two trips from the car to the house, with all his luggage and shopping bags. He looked over all the clothes that he'd placed on the bed, thinking again that he overdid it. As he started hanging up the clothes, he noticed an envelope under a shirt he picked up. He dropped the shirt back onto the bed and picked up the envelope. It was a card; he ripped the envelope open and pulled the card out. When he unfolded the card, a picture fell onto the floor. Eric bent down got the picture that was face down, covered in writing on the back. He read the back while taking a seat on the bed.

Dear Eric,

I had a magical weekend with you. From the dinners, limo, spa, helicopter ride and even watching Monday Night Football at the bar. Every moment I shared with you was electric. Our chemistry is off the radar. We made a weekend of firsts and here are the pictures that prove it. I just hope it's not our last.

Your First Love,

Kenya

Eric smiled after reading the back of the picture, and then he flipped it over. She'd already sent him these pictures to his phone when they were driving back to New York. She had taken four of the pictures and made a collage. Eric had never seen an actual picture collage of him. Kenya had put the picture that she had the waiter take at Café 2825, the limo, and the helicopter ride. Also, she had added the most ridiculous and sweet selfie picture they took at the spa. They'd crossed their eyes and twisted their lips in that picture. He couldn't stop smiling at that picture. Out of the whole weekend, the spa was when they'd had the most fun. Eric didn't know when the last time he was with someone that got him in every way. Kenya dug his humor. He placed the picture on his nightstand, propped up against the lamp. The card was simple; it had a big smile on the cover, and on the inside, it read, 'Thanks for everything.' She didn't write in the card, but she'd kissed it, leaving a red lipstick impression. Eric kissed her lips, and then he finished putting up his clothes.

After he finished unpacking and putting everything away, he took a shower and laid across the bed with his towel wrapped around his waist. He was sound asleep shortly.

Six hours later, Eric's cell phone woke him up. It was his mother.

"Hello?"

"Hey, baby. Have you heard from Danny?"

"No. He's still on his honeymoon. He should be back in the states on Saturday."

"I keep forgetting that he's in Africa. Do you think his Facetime works over there?"

"Yes, if he has wi-fi. Hold up... When did you get an iPhone? I just got you that new Galaxy 3 months ago."

"Danny got it for me. He thought it would be nice to see each other even when he can't stop by."

"So, where's the Galaxy--forget it. Try to Facetime him. Okay, Ma. Love you."

"I'll try. Love you, too, sweetie."

Eric hung up the phone, only then realizing how many hours had gone by. He put on some pajamas, heading downstairs while holding his phone. He cracked Danny's room's door as he walked down the hall. When Eric got to the kitchen, he placed the phone onto the table. He fixed a bowl of cereal and sat at the table, he should have heard from Kenya by now, at least in a text saying she made it.

Eric finished his cereal, rinsed the bowl in the sink, and placed it in the dishwasher. Just then, his phone started ringing. He smiled, thinking it was Kenya, but it was his secretary, Tina. Eric sent her to voicemail. He texted Kenya as he walked up the steps.

Me: I'm just checking on you to see if you made it home safe.

Almost immediately, her name lit up his phone as it rang.

"Hello there."

"I'm sorry about that. While I was texting you, Jackie called in. I thought I sent the text. I'm glad you texted me, or I would have never known. Anyway, what are you doing?"

"Nothing. Getting ready to relax in my bed and flip through the television. What about you?"

"Sitting on the couch looking at our picture. Did you open the card?"

"Yes. You need to stop leading me on. I know a sport fisher when I see one."

"Whatever."

"Nah, but for real. Every time I look at the picture, it makes me start thinking about the weekend. I'm glad you decided to do that."

"Yeah. When I went to CVS, I made them. You're not the only person with tricks up their sleeves."

"I see."

They talked on the phone for a good three hours. Eric laid in bed with his phone on speaker, as it was on the charger. He didn't let go of the picture for the whole time they talked.

CHAPTER 31

Saturday, one week after the wedding. Danny and Yolanda got out of the cab. The driver placed their luggage on the curve outside their home. Danny gave him a generous tip before he drove off. They stood there for a second, holding hands and looking at the house.

"Stay here, baby," he said as he rolled the two big luggage bags to the garage.

He opened the garage by punching the code in the keypad. Then, he made another trip to get the rest of the bags. He placed them all in the garage, then closed the garage door. He walked over to her, grabbed her hands and looked into her eyes.

"Are you ready to enter our home, our castle?" Danny asked.

"Only with you, my king. Only with you."

They kissed, then they walked to the front door, still holding hands. Danny put the key in the door and opened it. The door swung open, and Yolanda smiled as she got a glimpse of their house for the first time. Danny placed the keys in his pocket, bent down, and picked her up. He took a step in the door with his left foot. Then, he leaned her up in his right arm, so she wouldn't hit her head on the doorway as he stepped his right foot into the house. He used her foot to close the door, then he placed her on her feet.

"Wow! It's beautiful here. The pictures of the house empty had me excited, but..."

"But, what?"

"I have chills the size of raindrops." She held her arm up, showing him.

Yolanda proceeded to walk into every room downstairs, amazed how he'd decorated everything. They picked out so many things online to decorate the house, but she hadn't known what he decided to go with. She walked up the steps as he got the bags out the garage. The bedroom was just the way she'd envisioned it. She flopped onto the bed, looking up at the top of the canopy. The Villa Valencia canopy bed had always been her dream bed. She marveled at all the designs engraved in the wood, and she smiled from ear to ear as she scanned the room from the bed. From the dressers, bedside tables, wall mirror, writing desk, and chair, everything was beautiful. Danny stood in the hall right outside the room, watching her fondly. He left the bags in the hall as he walked in the room.

"Is this as far as you made it?" He teased.

"Yes. And I love it."

"I'd hope you would. I know some of the other rooms you're going to change a little or even completely. However it goes, take your time. You can start with the bathrooms, because I didn't touch any of them."

"Thanks, baby. And I like how you got me a work area in here. That desk is so elegant. I know the ideas are going to flow from there."

"That's not your workstation. You have the other big bedroom--or should I say, your second office..." He said as he sat on the bed, looking at her.

She sat up and kissed him. Then, she pulled him down and started pulling off his clothes.

"You don't want to see the rest of the house before we...?" He was saying, but she quickly covered his mouth with her hand. Rather than answering, she kissed his neck and started nibbling on his ear lobe.

◆ ◆ ◆

Later that night, Eric was parked outside of Bruce's house in Queens, waiting for him to come out. "I wish this dude would hurry up. Me and Dee entered this pool tournament at Déjà Vu, and it starts at 10," Eric said on the phone to Kenya.

"I didn't know you played pool. I have a pool table at the house right now. My ex-husband left it when we split up. I haven't played in a while. I've just been using that table to fold my laundry."

"Wow! I can't believe that you're disrespecting that table like that. Better his than mines... I guess when I come out there, you'll have to clean the table off. Maybe we can play a few games of strip 8-Ball."

"You always trying to get me naked. And I also heard what you said."

"What are you talking about?" Eric smiled, waiting to hear what it was.

"'When you come out here...' You think you're so slick. Instead of you asking or telling me. You'd rather throw it in random conversation to see how I respond. You're worse than a rapper, with your indirect lines." Eric laughed, and she continued. "Although, it would make my day for you to come out here. I was thinking the other day to see what you were doing for Christmas. The last few years, I've been going to Virginia to see my grandchildren for winter break. My job shuts down on the 22nd of December to the 8th of January. It doesn't have to be around that time, but I have a lot of free time on my hands around Christmas. Just putting that out there."

"I was joking when I said that, but since it would make your day.... I guess. Nah, but for real, I can make that happen. I'll look at flights tomorrow. We will talk, for sure. That sounds like a plan."

"I'm going to look for flights tonight. You know I don't play no games."

Eric laughed again. Just then, Bruce tapped on his car door for him to unlock it. Eric didn't even see him come out of the house, he'd been so distracted. He unlocked the door, and Bruce got in. "Bruce just got in the car. I'm going to text you after the tournament. Hopefully, you'll still be up."

"Just Facetime me, I should be up."

"Say no more. Talk to you later. Bye." Eric ended the call and placed his phone on the dash by the navigation screen.

"Did I hear her say 'Facetime me?'" Bruce asked, grinning.

"Damn. Let me find out I'm driving a Federal Agent around." Eric started driving.

"Whatever. I didn't realize my Galaxy phone done switched over to cry phone. Ain't that what you call it? Hold up... the airport is that way," Bruce said, looking confused.

"I know where the airport is. I got to pick up Dee. We signed up for that pool tournament at Déjà Vu. And yeah, I got me an iPhone. I'm damn near addicted to Facetime, on the low. It works out, because Kenya real far. I wish it didn't kill your battery so easy, though."

"I hear you, Lover Boy. Heh. I haven't called you that in a while. I thought that was tapping up one of your oldies. But let me find out you done got struck by the wedding love bug?"

"Whatever! Nobody got struck by anything. This is different. Kenya and I have history--plus, I'm not getting any younger..."

"Hold up! When did you become this old man... talking about 'I'm not getting any younger.' Did I get in the car with my man Eric Taylor, notorious for hitting and running? Hitting and splitting, need I say more?"

"Oh, you got jokes, huh? I'm not that bad. Am I?"

"Just that you have to ask is enough. But it's cool, everybody has their own thing. I'm a habitual cheater, and you're a habitual runner. You run away from serious relationships like criminals run from the police. Or like when Forrest Gump got--"

"I *got* it. You don't have to give me a monologue," Eric huffed. He parked in front of Dee's place and honked the horn.

"Now you in your feelings... It ain't no fun when the rabbit got the gun. You can dish it out, but you can't take it. I'm done... before you put me on the side of the road."

Eric unlocked the car doors, and Dee got in the back seat. Eric drove Bruce to the rental car place without saying a word--Bruce had really struck a nerve.

Eric and Dee had made it just in time before the tournament started after dropping Bruce off. Eric made it to the quarter-finals round before losing on a careless mistake. He'd scratched on the eight ball. The cue followed the eight ball after dropped it into the corner pocket. His opponent had five balls left on the table. Eric watched Dee win the whole tournament from the sidelines. On the way to drop Dee off at home, he couldn't stop thinking about what Bruce said about him. He'd let Bruce get under his skin.

"Let me ask you a question?" He asked Dee.

"Go ahead."

"Do you think I'm scared to have a serious relationship?"

"I wouldn't say scared. I would probably use the word 'terrified,' or 'fearful.'"

"'Fearful?' Wow. I'd rather be scared than fearful, but I get it. I know I've been hard on these females. I would have never thought The Crew been talking about me and my love life."

Dee shrugged. "You taking this too far. We've had this same conversation while you were present. We haven't talked about it in a while, but we understand. You made a promise to Danielle, and you've been paying for it ever since."

"Hold up. I'm fine with the way my life has been. Raising Danny, my career, our business--plus the rental properties I own. What can I ask for more than that?"

"Honestly? A life partner, a better half. Someone that you want around on your good days *and* your bad days. Life is too short to be living it alone."

"You watch too many Lifetime movies. I haven't been lonely in over twenty years. You sound crazy," Eric said with a chuckle.

"You know what? I might be a little out of my mind because I know I played out my mind tonight!. The champ is here! Let me out right here. I want to walk the rest of the way holding my trophy."

Eric pulled over close to the curb. Dee gave him dap, and he got out of the car, but before he closed the door, he left Eric with a few final words.

"Food for thought. You said you haven't been lonely in over twenty years. But when was the last time you've been whole? Or truly happy? Let that marinate, I will get at you tomorrow." Dee closed the door and turned to walk the rest of the two blocks home. Eric went straight home and jumped in the shower.

After his shower, he Facetimed Kenya for an hour and a half. It was one of their shorter conversations. She'd found him some flights which were excellent. Even after all that, when he hung up the phone, Eric kept thinking about what Dee said, from him being fearful to him not being whole. *You would think they would have taken it easy on me since they know the promise I made. As a matter of fact, where is that contract?* He thought to himself.

Eric got up from the bed and went to his safe in his closet. He entered the code, opened the safe, and grabbed the file label 'Wifey.' Sitting back down on the bed, Eric took a deep breath and exhaled before he opened the file. When he pulled out the contents of the folder, all he could do was smile. He stared at her school ID, as well as her driver's license. She looked so young and innocent in her school picture.

After a while, he pulled out the contract and read it.

May 17, 1989

I, Eric Taylor, promise not to marry anyone except for Danielle Danson.

I Danielle Danson promise not to marry anyone except for Eric Taylor.

By signing this, we both agree to these terms.

Danielle Danson   Eric Taylor

Eternal Soul Mate Contract

Eric smiled to himself as he read 'Eternal Soul Mate Contract.' *She always had a way with words.*

Finished, Eric placed the letter back in the safe, locked it, and went to bed. He laid there, trying to get rested enough to fall asleep, but couldn't. He tossed and turned for two hours until he finally went to sleep.

CHAPTER 32

December 22, 2017

It was the third time Eric saw Danny in person, but the first time he was without his wife. Danny was driving him to JFK Airport. Eric was on his way to Cali for two weeks. He has never taken a vacation this long without Danny or Danielle. Nervous, he kept tapping his knee, to the point it was noticeable.

"Are you okay, Dad?"

"Yeah and no. I'm happy to be going out there to spend time with Kenya. But at the same time, two weeks is a very, very long time. Don't get me wrong. I enjoyed our trip to A.C., we had a ball. I hope that in these two weeks, we don't get tired of each other."

"Do you have your own money and car?"

"Huh? What are you talking about?" Eric turned to look at Danny while he drove.

"That's what you use to tell me when I go on a date. Have your own money and transportation. If you don't like how everything is going, you can always leave."

"Facts," he said, smiling at Danny as his son tried to school him. "Oh, yeah. By the way, I haven't forgotten how you went behind my back and orchestrated all of this, getting Kenya to attend your wedding and all."

"My bad, Dad, I--"

"Calm down. I want to say thanks. You knew what I needed, even if I didn't. You have your Nana's heart, and her poker face. I suspected something, but not of this magnitude."

Danny blew out a sigh of relief. "You're welcome. Now I can start coming around more often."

"You been avoiding me?"

"A little bit." Danny smiled as he stopped at the light.

"That's funny. I remember when you broke Mrs. Charles' Volvo windshield with a rock, and she made you call and tell me what happened. When I came home from work, you were hiding, trying not to wear this whipping. I yelled and looked for you for over thirty minutes. When I finally found you hiding under the bed, I pulled you from under there. You got snagged by a loose spring, and I had to drive you the emergency room. Taking you to the hospital saved you from the worst beating you ever had in your young life."

"Those fourteen stitches didn't save me--it only delayed it briefly." Danny winced at the memory. "I think my worst beating was when I got caught sneaking those two exchange students in the Boom Boom Room. Thomas and I had a ball, but it wasn't worth that beating you gave me."

"I forgot all about that."

"I didn't, and I never will. Thomas' dad was still alive when that happened, and he got it worse than I did. We still talk about that day, the good and the bad." Danny pulled up to the drop-off for Eric's airline. He parked the car and helped get the bags out of the trunk. Eric pulled the handle out on the big bag so he could roll it on its wheels. Danny gave him dap and a hug.

"Be safe, Dad. I love you."

"I love you, too. Thanks for the ride."

"No problem. Tell Kenya I said I would love to sing at y'all's wedding if you need me." Danny ducked into the car before Eric could even react. He twisted his lip as he walked into the terminal.

After Eric went through airport security, he sat at the gate, thinking about Danny's words. T*hat boy is getting bold ever since he moved out.* He sat there, scrolling through his phone and trying to find a picture Kenya sent him. *Damn!* He didn't realize they texted that much; he gave up before finding the picture.

He dialed Michelle's number--the only girl that was part of The Crew, though only as an honorary member. They'd messed around briefly when they were all college, before he'd met Danielle. She was that chick--smart, ambitious, and funny as hell. She still lived in Atlanta, but she was born and raised in Matthews, North Carolina.

Ring! Ring!

"What's up, babe?" Michelle answered the phone, live as always.

"Nothing. Just had you on my mind. Plus, I wanted to run something by you. I'll call you back tomorrow--I can barely hear you with all that noise in your background." He listened carefully to see if Michelle had heard what he'd said.

"Hold on, let me walk to the balcony outside. I'm at this day party my friend is throwing. Give me a second."

"Shorty, let me holla at you Shorty. Shorty, I know you hear me," some guy was yelling at Michelle.

"Hello. Did you hear that guy being rude? I kept the phone to my ear thinking that they would let me breathe for a *second.* And the craziest thing is, I'm taller than him. When I go back in there, I have half a mind to call him 'shorty' and ask him if he was talking to me."

"Wow. I see you haven't changed a bit."

"Not at all. He doesn't know who he's dealing with," she said, and Eric could practically hear her rolling her eyes.

"And keep it that way. Don't say anything to that man. Please!"

"I might consider that because it's you, but forget that lame. I already gave him too much of my energy. What you want to run by me, E.T.?" She asked, jazzy and funny at the same time.

"You might not remember when you questioned me about that picture I had of that girl from back home... But, anyway, we got it in a month ago when she came to New York. Mind you, we've only seen each other twice in the last 30 years before we got it in."

"Wow! I think I remember that chick in the picture--go ahead, finish."

"To make a long story short... She hi-jacked my mind."

"Huh? You must explain this to me. Please."

"It's hard to explain, but it's like, she's taken control of my thoughts. I can't get her out of my head for nothing. I'm thinking about her all the time." After he said that, he paused for a while, and Michelle didn't say anything--not even a sound to let him know she'd heard what he said. "Are you still there?" He looked at the phone to check his bars.

"Yeah, I'm just... speechless. All the phone calls I got from you, telling me about different women. They never started or ended like this conversation. I told one of my girlfriends, you use me as a crazy barometer for these females, and it's true. I've been your second pair of eyes, your female perspective... But this time, I can't help you."

"Why? Because it's her, and you know we have a history?"

"No! Because you're in love and you don't even see it. You've been so removed from this place that you don't even recognize it. Hold on," she told Eric, and the audio went muffled for a moment. "Let me get a blue motorcycle," Michelle said to someone, and then her hand was off the microphone again. "Back to what I was saying--it's been a long time since you been in the place. Lord knows I've prayed for you to move on from Danielle, too many times. I finally stopped praying, because I realized you had to want it for yourself. You must let go of the past if you want any chance of having a future with this female. Or any female, for that matter."

Eric chuckled when he responded. "So, I'm living in the past?"

"Yes! I'm talking six Presidents and five versions of bell bottoms pants ago."

He laughed, more fully this time. " It must be 'Get On Eric Month.'"

"What are you talking about? You know what? Don't answer that. I'm your friend, not your hype man. I'm not always going to agree, but I'm always going to be there for you. Enjoy your flight to Cali--send my love to Kenya."

"How did you know where I was going, or who I was going to see?"

"Why? Just because we haven't talked in months doesn't mean I haven't talked to The Crew. Text me when you touch down. Smoochies."

Michelle ended the call before he could get another word in. Eric smiled incredulously while looking at the phone. He just knew Bruce had told her. Bruce loved it when he wasn't the target. Eric took a trip to the bathroom before they let them board the flight. He entered the plane to find some old lady sitting in his seat. Eric double-checked his ticket, looking at the row and seat number.

"I'm sorry, sweetie, I was trying to see if my son was loading our plane. He works for this airline," the woman said, getting out of his seat.

"You're good. You can sit there if you want to look out the window. I'm going to listen to my music and go to sleep."

"That's so sweet of you. Thank you." She looked back out the window.

Eric put his neck pillow's bag in the overhead compartment. Looking at the people around him to see if someone had a baby, he took his seat. Eric wrapped the pillow around his neck, plugged his ears with his headphones, and scrolled through the playlist, clicking one titled 'Old Jams.' "All I Need To Get By" came on. He smiled with his eyes closed as he played back in his head what Michelle had said about him being stuck in the past. If she heard his playlist, it would only serve to prove her point. Eric listened until he fell asleep.

CHAPTER 33

Eric grabbed his last bag off the conveyor belt, then headed out to find Kenya, who was waiting for him outside. The doors opened as he rolled his big bag outside, and the sun hit his face. When he left New York, it was cloudy and cold with snow on the ground. He was so far impressed by how light everyone in California was able to dress in December. Eric spotted Kenya leaning against the back door of her car with the trunk open. It was amazing to him, how he felt could see her beautiful eyes from that far, even though she had sunglasses on. When Eric got close enough to the car, Kenya gave him a big hug and a kiss.

"How was your flight?"

"It was good. I almost slept the whole flight, until this lady started snoring next to me. It took everything for me not to give her an elbow to the ribs," Eric recounted as he put his luggage in the trunk.

"I'm glad you didn't, silly. I would hate for your first day in Cali to be shared with the Esés, locked up."

They got in the car, kissed again, and drove to her place. Eric looked out at everything as Kenya pointed things out. He was a little nervous; because they talked and FaceTimed so much, he hoped that they would still have something to talk about in these two weeks. She pulled into the driveway of her house, and it was gorgeous. From the landscaping to the beautiful architecture of her ranch-style house. She pressed the garage door opener, and the doors rose to let them in. Kenya parked them in the garage and left it open.

"Welcome to my humble abode."

Eric looked at how big her garage was. There wasn't anything humble about this place. She popped the trunk, and he snatched his bags. He followed her up the steps into her kitchen. Eric was extremely impressed with how her place was decorated. She'd always been a neat freak when they were kids, and that clearly hadn't changed.

"Did you do all the decorating?" He placed his bags down and walked through the kitchen to the living room.

"Yes, that's what I've been doing for the last six years. Decorating while upping the value of the house, so when I get ready to sell, they'll have to show me the money. I need that. That's going to help me with my second retirement. Then, I can move closer to my daughter--either New York or Florida. I haven't made up my mind yet, but it won't be Virginia."

Eric laughed to himself, because she'd told him about her experience in Virginia the week of the wedding. "I get that, but what do you mean by your second retirement?" He looked out at her backyard through the glass sliding door in the living room.

"I retired from the Air Force years ago. I still work at the same Air Force Base--just in a civilian capacity. I'm leading a department in our space program. The last two years, I've been training my replacement so that I can step away with the program in good hands."

"I respect that you're doing it the right way. Most people wouldn't care who's doing the job once they're gone," Eric mused as he noticed her garden. "What kind of flowers are these?" He turned around from looking at her garden. Eric only then realized Kenya was right behind him, standing in her panties and bra. They started kissing, and she walked him back towards the couch. He stood up, taking his clothes off, while she sat up on the sofa, sliding her panties off. They went right to it without saying a word.

Eric woke up to India Arie playing on her surround sound system. He pulled his arm from under Kenya's neck slowly, trying not to wake her. She rolled over on her stomach and stayed asleep. He walked to the bathroom attached to her bedroom, naked. While pissing, Eric thought to himself, *Two months ago, we hadn't seen, or even talked to each other, for that matter. It's amazing how things can happen overnight, and you wish that day would never end.* He flushed the toilet, walked back into the bedroom and wrapped up with the towel Kenya had given him. He walked to the kitchen to get his forgotten bags.

Eric tripped over his boxer briefs in the living room. He put them back on and draped the towel around his shoulders. She had their AC collage photo tacked up on the front of her refrigerator. He smiled at the picture, as it reminded him of that weekend. Eric opened the refrigerator door to be nosey. Kenya had the food in colored containers, stacked neatly, as if ready for inventory. He opened the vegetable drawer and grabbed an apple. He sat on a stool at her island in the kitchen, eating the apple.

Eric soon heard footsteps, getting closer. He smiled when he saw Kenya enter the kitchen, and she returned it. Every time he saw her smile, it did something to him. Kenya walked to the refrigerator and stood there for a second with the door open. His tank top fit her like a glove, and was long enough that it stopped a few centimeters beneath her butt. Where the tank top ended, the sexy, pecan tan legs began, and they went on for miles. She grabbed a yellow container, closed the door, and turned around, catching him staring at her legs. Kenya stuck her tongue at Eric as she walked over to him. She pushed her stool right next to his and sat down. Her thigh pressed against his--that's how close she was. She opened her container and started eating some white grapes.

Eric got up and tossed the apple core in the trash. He didn't realize he was that hungry. He got his bags and started carrying them to her guest room.

"You gonna stop leaving me in random rooms by myself?" Kenya called after him with a seductive tone.

Eric looked back at her, and she looked like the girl all those years ago that couldn't leave the front yard. Innocent and ready at the same time. He was never going to get a chance to put his bags away.

"Random? Really? I'm going to come over there, but keep your hands to yourself. We got two weeks of being touchy-feely, right?"

"Cut it out. I know how to be good, more than you would ever know. Just sit next to me. I will be finished in a second. I'm gonna hurry up."

Eric strolled to her with a smirk on his face. He sat next to her, though not as close as he was the first time. She scooted over to make sure her legs touched his again. They both behaved as Kenya ate her grapes, but their temperature was rising. "Always In My Head" by India Arie came on, and suddenly everything changed. They both bopped to the melody. She played with two grapes, still on the stem, with her tongue. Eric closed his eyes, still dancing to the music, because he knew where this was heading. She touched his thigh, and then she caressed his crotch.

Eric stood up and placed the towel around his neck on the island. He picked her up and sat her on the towel.

"I thought you didn't want to do anything? We *do* have two weeks, after all," she teased, looking for his response.

Eric dropped his briefs, pulled Kenya to the end of the island and placed his passion inside of her. She held on with one hand as she placed a grape between her teeth. He looked at her as he stroked, not understanding why she was still eating grapes. Then, she bit down on the grape. Without her saying a word, Eric leaned his head up and licked the grape juice that ran down Kenya's chin. They kissed, intoxicated with love. She looked different from that point on. His calves started burning from him trying to give her every inch of him on his tip-toes. He slid her off the table, turned her around, and bent her over the stool. He held her waist as he gave her all he had. Every so many strokes, she would reach back and squeeze the base of him. It was tight, but not to the point that it stopped his rhythm. That did something to him.

Eric felt Kenya's body jerking, pulsing as she had an orgasm. It felt so good that he reached his own. She felt him turning into an animal, going hard, pulling her to him as he gripped her waist tight. She squeezed him hard to stop the juice from all coming out. Then, she got on her knees and placed it into her mouth. Eric couldn't take it. Kenya took all he had until he was empty. Steady stroking him and sucking, with her eyes looking straight into his. He backpedaled until she finally let him go. She used the stool to stand herself up.

"Are you hungry?" She asked him, then stuck her tongue out of the corner of her mouth.

"Hell yeah," he replied.

"Great. I know this place you're going to love."

Kenya walked to her bedroom. Eric looked up, as if he was looking at God, and exhaled, as if this was too much. He got his luggage and went to the guest room.

CHAPTER 34

Later that night, Eric was sitting at the table in the restaurant, a little past tipsy, waiting on Kenya to come back from the bathroom. He ordered another pitcher of red sangria. This would make their third pitcher. He had his elbow on the table, rubbing his forehead with his eyes closed.

"Are you okay?" Kenya asked as she slid back into her chair.

He moved his hand and opened his eyes. "I'm good, baby. Waiting on you, beautiful."

Kenya noticed Eric was rocking in his chair and slurring his words. "Waiter, can I get the check?"

"We can't leave now, I have another pitcher coming with your name on it."

"I'm good, but I could use a good cup of coffee. What about you?"

"I know what you're doing. You're trying to sober me up. I'm good, but I will get that coffee with you."

Kenya paid the check, and they took a Lyft to Starbucks. Eric ordered a bottle of water, cappuccino, and a piece of iced lemon loaf cake. She ordered a chestnut praline latte and a maple pecan muffin. He sat at a table, watching her put napkins, creamers, and spoons on their tray. She placed the tray on the table and sat down across from him. He opened the water, turned it up, and downed it.

"Was you a little thirsty?"

"Yes, I'm trying to snap back. I don't know if it's the sangria or the time difference. Or a combination of both."

"It's probably both, but the drinks there will put you on your backside if you don't pace yourself. Don't I know."

"You could have given me a disclaimer ahead of time. I would've paced myself! I'm not trying to ruin your night." He took a sip of his cappuccino.

"You're good, trust me, you're good. Plus, all these years I've known you, you have never once ruined my night. I'd rather take care of a drunk Eric than be with a sober anyone else. Just enjoy yourself; you're in good hands."

Eric tapped the chair next to him with his hand, suggesting that she move over towards him. Kenya took the hint and sat in the chair next to him. He put his arm around her shoulders and pulled her close to him. He looked into her eyes, opened his mouth, but didn't say anything. She side-eyed him, looking confused. Eric blew Kenya a kiss, and then he kissed her. He turned back to sit straight in his seat and started going in on his cake. He felt her looking at him, but he wouldn't look back.

They sat there, talking about some of the many nights they'd sat on her steps--talking about everything under the sun. It was well over an hour later that they were there laughing, kissing, and playing 'feely' under the table. There were a few people on their computers that they were disturbing, but they didn't care. Their chemistry hadn't changed a bit. If anything, it had intensified, but on a mature level.

Finally, they called another Lyft and went back to her crib. On the ride home, Kenya told Eric a few things she had planned for them. He watched her lips moving as they held hands, but he couldn't make out what she was saying. He kept thinking about how he'd chickened out when they faced each other in Starbucks. Eric was trying to find the right time to tell her he loved her. He hadn't told a woman he loved them since Danielle. He's told a couple of females that he had love for them and they were his people. But never once that he loved them.

"Which one you want to do tomorrow? Which one?" Kenya asked.

"I'm thinking... give me a second. Hmmm! What's the second one again?" He was trying to stall.

"What's the first one?"

"You talking about the first, first one?" He put on a goofy look on his face.

"You didn't hear nothing I said at all, did you?"

"Not a word. I was zoned out. My bad, baby."

"You good." She rolled her eyes but was still smiling.

The driver pulled up to the house. They went into the house, straight to her bedroom. Kenya went into the bathroom to freshen up.

"Put some music on," Kenya called through the bathroom door.

Eric used the remote, Googling "Smooth R&B." *Sade Essentials* popped up, so he pressed play and took his clothes off. He laid on top of the covers, waiting to see Kenya come out of the bathroom.

By the time she cut the light off and opened the door, Kenya found Eric sound asleep, laying on top of the comforter. Kenya got a small blanket and placed it on top of him. She kissed his cheek, turned down the music, and climbed in to spoon with him.

CHAPTER 35

December 23, 2017

Eric woke up to Kenya holding him from behind. He got up and padded into the bathroom. After he used it, Eric looked at his cell phone to see the time. It was 5 A.M. Even so, he felt it was later than that, since his body was still running on New York time. He got back in the bed, but couldn't go back to sleep. Eric laid there for almost an hour before he grabbed his cell phone and went to the living room to watch TV. He stopped at the guest room on his way to the living room and put on his Burberry pajama pants. He turned the TV on with the remote by pressing the Netflix button.

Eric reclined on the couch and used her profile to find something to watch. She watched a lot of documentaries on food and health. Seeing this, her eating habits suddenly made a lot more sense. He flipped through her "Continue Watching For Kenya." He stopped on *Greenleaf* because he noticed Oprah and Lynn Whitfield. He went to the first season, episode one, to see what she was watching. Before he knew it, he'd watched two episodes and started a third. Eric picked up his cell phone to see the time: 8:11. He pressed pause on the remote, then walked into the kitchen.

Eric opened the cabinets to see if she had some syrup and pancake mix. She had syrup, but no mix to be seen. He checked in her cubby--still no luck, but he found a griddle. He placed the syrup on the island and the griddle on the counter by the sink. Eric opened the refrigerator, and piled eggs, milk, green pepper, onions, cheese, and hash browns into his arms. He placed the items on the island as he thought, *If she only had some bread, I could make some french toast.* He searched for the bread, and found a bread box inside the cubby. He opened it to find a cinnamon-swirl loaf. *Bingo!* He also grabbed her spice rack and placed it on the island.

After Eric got all the bowls and utensils, he started whipping up his magic. His favorite meal of the day was breakfast. He could eat it all day, every day.

Bing! He picked up his phone to see a text from Michelle.

Michelle*: I guess you're still in the air because you never texted me to let me know you made it. Call me when you get a second.*

Eric dialed her number, placed it on speaker phone, then used his phone case's kickstand to prop the phone up while he was cooking.

Ring, ring.

"Hello?"

"My bad for not texting you--I've been running ever since I touched down. What's good? Or should I say, what's bad? You never hit me this early in the morning."

"You already know. I need to vent. I was going to call Dee, but I didn't want to offend his wife. Damn. Can you talk, Mr. Cupcake Jones?"

"Yeah, I'm good. Kenya's sleeping, and I'm making breakfast. What's up?"

"My son, damn idiot. I had to leave that day party early to bail him out of jail."

"What? For what?"

"I know, Mr. Goodie Two-shoes. Yeah, I had to bail him out on some domestic violence shit. You know I don't play any man hitting a woman, even my son. I was going to leave him in there, but my sister reminded me that, if I didn't get him, he would be there until Monday. His stupid ass going to get locked up on his day off on some *Friday the Movie* stuff."

"You silly."

"I'm *serious*. Who does that? Anyway, he said that he didn't hit her, but it's his word against hers. He's in his old room, looking crazy. He got into it with his wife over some Facebook picture that she was tagged in. She's in a picture with her ex at a party that she went to by herself."

As she told Eric the rest of the story, he missed seeing Kenya standing near the doorway, listening to the sound of Michelle's voice.

"I'm going to do what you said and get them a marriage counselor. That's enough of my silly child. How's everything going out there in California?"

"Everything is great. I can't complain. It's beautiful out here. I could get used to this warm weather."

"You know I'm not talking about Cali. I'm talking about you and ole girl."

"We good. We went out last night and had a ball. Our chemistry is amazing, almost as if we were made for each other." Eric snickered, then continued. "I don't know if it was the drinks or just living in the moment. But I almost told her I love her."

"Hold up. Not mister 'don't fall in love with me.' I can't believe this! She *must* be special. Just tell me. Was it during or after sex?"

"Neither--it was when we were at Starbucks trying to sober me up. That's a whole other conversation."

"So, what stopped you?"

"I don't know, I just punked out. I thought about it the rest of the night, but couldn't get up enough nerve to tell her. You know it's been damn near an eternity since I felt this way. Plus, it is kind of soon. We just started kicking it last month. You don't think it's too early to be saying that?"

"Yes, for most people, but not for you. It's a reason you haven't said it in a while--because you weren't there. Now that you're there, you need to move before it's too late. I don't know how your clock is ticking, but mine's moving like a Rolex. No pause, just steady moving."

"You crazy," Eric smiled as he flipped the french toast over.

"I'm for real. I don't know how many years this thing is going to get wet."

"Whoa. That's too much information."

"Calm down... but for real. You always tell me to take the shot, and now it's your turn. I don't know this woman, but I got to meet her. She got your nose wide open."

"*Too* open. I can dig in my nose with a boxing glove on."

"Damn. I like to see that."

"Me too. I'm going to get at you later. I finished cooking. I gotta wake her so we can eat."

"Do that. Bye." Michelle ended the call.

Eric turned off the griddle, wiped it off, and placed the utensils in the sink. He walked to get Kenya, and found her coming towards him in the living room.

"What's that I smell?" Kenya asked as she walked up.

"Breakfast. I know my way around a kitchen a little."

They kissed, then she walked past him and went into the kitchen. Kenya grabbed some glasses out of the cabinet and placed them on the island. Eric open the refrigerator pulled out orange and pomegranate juice. He fixed their plate and Kenya did the drinks. Eric had two plates--one with his omelette and hash brown and one with his french toast. Kenya had one plate, which had her omelette and hash browns on it. She prayed before she dug in.

“You only made french toast for you?”

“I didn’t think you liked pancakes or french toast. When we were in Atlantic City, you never would get any.”

“You right. I did that only because I bought a few dresses that were pushing my size. I love french toast over pancakes.”

“Me too.” Eric got up and got her another plate to share with her. “What about all that healthy stuff in your fridge?”

“I try to eat healthy for the most part, but I still have the things I love. I eat healthy 80% of the time, and my 20% might be really bad, but it works for me.”

“I dig that. The Crew is always asking me what I’m eating right now, ‘cause I always switch it up.”

“Exactly. Shock your body,” she said as she took a sip from her glass.

They finished eating in silence, and she put the plates in the sink. She told him to relax, that she would get the dishes in a minute. Eric sat on the couch; he pressed the pause button again to start the episode. Kenya came and laid on the couch with her head in his lap.

“Thanks, baby, for the breakfast.”

“No problem. That’s what I do--but next time I will make more french toast. You killed mines.”

“Yes, I did. They were great. Don’t start nothing you can’t finish.”

“Whatever. I should be saying the same to you. The way you gave me that facial in the kitchen yesterday? If you hadn’t stopped, you neighbors were going to have to call the cops because I was about to scream.”

“Stop,” Kenya said as she covered her face.

"Don't be acting shy now. The damage is done, and I'm going to be here for a while."

"I know. If my friends or my ex-husband knew what I was doing with you... Lord. My friends would give me a standing ovation, and he would beat me down." She caught his expression and quickly added, "Don't get me wrong--he never hit me, but he asked for things sexually that I didn't feel comfortable doing with him. I don't know if it was how he treated me or what. But with you, I feel so free, safe, wanted, and loved. And... I love you, too."

Eric was stunned. "Huh? Where that come from?"

"I told you to be honest with me when I left New York. Plus, I overheard you talking to your friend over the phone. On that note, I love you, too."

Eric took a moment, looking down at her as she looked up at him, smiling. "I love you... Kenya... Crawford," he said, with dramatic pauses.

"I know, and I always knew." Eric huffed, grabbed a pillow from behind him, and placed it on her face.

From that day forward, they told each other they loved each other multiple times a day. They stayed in the house for the rest of the day. She talked about going to a vineyard, but that never happened. They took showers and laid on her couch instead, eating ice cream and watching *Greenleaf*. They didn't even make love; they just spent some much-needed, quality bonding time.

CHAPTER 36

December 31, 2017

The last nine days had been awesome. On Christmas Eve, they spent the day shopping for gifts for the homeless. Kenya talked Eric into serving Christmas dinner at the shelter. He always wanted to do something like that, but he would usually donate money, not his time. He watched her glowing as she greeted and hugged the people coming in the cafeteria. Eric had never seen that side of her growing up. Even when they made it back to her house to eat their own Christmas dinner that she prepared for them, she still was glowing. Dinner was fabulous and very intimate. Kenya decorated the dining room with the Christmas spirit: red tablecloth, silver ribbons on the chairs, red candles, silver and red ornaments hanging everywhere. They tapped glasses while making a toast to being thankful for spending this Christmas with each other.

The other highlights of the week were visiting several wine vineyards, movies, and the Hollywood Walk of Fame. They took date night to another level, even letting their hair down, and had a burger from Mom's Burger in Compton, which was delicious. It was incredible how Queens was nearly three thousand miles away from Compton, but the grind and hidden jewels were so similar. Eric soaked up a lot of Cali culture, thanks to Kenya. There wasn't a dull moment. The only time they spent alone was when Kenya went to church on Christmas Eve. She didn't like Eric not going to church, but she didn't press him. He liked how she took him saying he didn't want to go and left it at that.

Kenya has gospel music playing on the surround sound while she was in the bathroom. Eric laid in the bed, going through his phone and looking at the pictures they took. Every image had a special memory. The ones they snapped in one particular vineyard were his favorite. It had been very romantic--plus, they looked sexy in those photos.

"What are you smiling at?" Kenya asked with a bobby pin between her teeth. She stared at him for a response as she did her hair.

"Ain't you doing your hair? How do you know what I'm doing if you're looking in the mirror?"

"I can do more than one thing at a time. What is it?"

"Nothing. Just looking at these pictures from the week."

"I've been doing the same thing. We take some good pictures together."

"Yeah. That's what Danny said."

"Oh. You're sending pictures to New York?"

"Yes, they are my pictures. You're acting like you haven't sent any."

"Well... I might have sent a few to Jackie and a few other people."

"Wow! I only sent them to Danny. Now, it's possible he showed someone. I just haven't shown anyone else. Who's everyone you sent it to?" Eric crossed his arms with a smile on his face.

"Let me think... Jackie, Charita, Rochelle, and my daughter. I think that's it."

"You think! Not you, Miss Precise, thinking and not knowing.

That don't sound right."

"I can always go through my phone so that I can be exact." She paused for a second. "I did forget Pam--we going to her New Years Eve get together. I usually bring in the New Year at church, but I want to spend it with you. Plus, I'm going to church this morning."

"I know it's more than Pam, but I'm cool. How long you've been going to church on New Years?"

"Since 2003. That's the same year I got saved. I didn't realize I got saved that long ago, wow."

"I've been noticing you praying over your food, but I didn't know you got saved. When we were kids, my parents were the ones that kept me in church religiously. Your parents didn't go, and they didn't force you to go. It's funny how life works."

"You right about that. When the last time you been to church?"

"I was slowing up when I found out my dad had a whole other family. He preached that a family that prays together, stays together. I guess he prayed harder with his other family. Then, when Danielle passed, I lost my way--or, should I say, my desire to sit in someone's church. I've had my questions for God back then and even now. I don't think the church has the answers."

"You might be right, who am I to say. But I will tell you this. Every step you take towards God, he will meet you halfway."

"You got that from church, or your own experience?" He sat up with his feet on the floor. Kenya walked in the bedroom right in front of him.

"This is my testimony. In 2003, I was going through a lot with my career and my marriage. Overwhelmed to the point that I didn't know if I was coming or going. I kept having this dream that had me walking through this dark tunnel. I could see the light, but it was way down the tunnel. Every time I made it to the light, it would blind me so much that I couldn't go any further. I told my therapist, and she asked, were I saved or religious? She explained that the light represented God and the darkness was how I was living. To make a long story short, a couple of months later, I got saved, and I had that dream one more time. When I made it to the light, I felt a sense of calmness. I was no longer blind, I could see in all directions. I saw my future and where I came from. I woke up in tears, but I knew where I was going to plant my next step." She shook, as if she had a chill. "Every time I tell that story, it does something to me. Don't get me wrong, I'm not perfect by no measure. But I can say, when darkness or unsureness finds me, the light of God shows me the way." She walked back into the bathroom to do her hair.

Eric sat there quietly, thinking about what she'd shared with him. He knew the darkness that she was talking about. He'd been there too many times. Dee shared a similar experience to him. Eric wanted to believe that this was confirmation, but he was still a bit skeptical. He had a realist mentality, that the pastor was selling hope to a troubled community. He'd always felt the pastor gets rich while the congregation waits for a blessing. He sat there, trying to process all she'd said.

The mood changed in the room when "I Surrender All" by C.C. Winan came onto the surround sound. You could drop a pin in the place and would have heard it hit the floor. The music moved him to the point he was about to ask her how long the service was, but she beat him to it.

"I really would love it if you come to church with me. It's heavy on my heart right now that you come with me. Don't say 'no' too fast. Just think how awesome it would be to finish the year on a holy or high note. If that didn't get you, do it for me." She had a look in her eyes that he couldn't say no to, but he still didn't say yes immediately.

After a while more of her getting ready, he agreed to go to church with her, and it was initially a great decision. The atmosphere was inviting and friendly. The singing was of the new Gospel's selections, very up-tempo. Everything was going great, and then the pastor gave the word. He said a lot of things, but what stood out to Eric was when he came out of the book of Jonah.

Jonah 4:10

But the Lord said, "You have been concerned about this plant, though you did not tend it or make it grow. It sprang up overnight and died overnight."

The Pastor read the text and continued to give his message. Eric held on to the scriptures he read. He stared at the bible, reading it over and over. Kenya rubbed his knee as she noticed he was stuck looking in his bible. She gave Eric a slight smile before looking back at the pastor. He sat there for the rest of the service in deep thought about what he was concerned with. *My concerns, my concerns...* He couldn't stop thinking about what was important to him, and how much he could really control.

Driving back from the church was very awkward, Eric hoped she didn't notice. He looked out the window, trying to not look at Kenya, bopping to the music and enjoying the ride.

"Did you like the service?" Kenya asked.

"Yes. Even more than I anticipated. I was surprised to see such a young following, and the pastor gave an awesome word."

"Yeah, he normally does. And it's like that every Sunday, as far as the crowd. The youth ministers do an awesome job with the youth and young adults. He preaches the future is in our youth. Therefore, he makes sure the church keeps them at the forefront. I'm glad you enjoyed yourself."

"I'm glad you invited me." Eric picked her right hand off his knee with his left hand. He interlocked their fingers, then he lifted her hand to his face. He kissed her hand and lowered it back to his knee, still holding her hand.

They went back to North Italia, where the food and drinks were great. Eric didn't overindulge in the red sangria; he paced himself that day. The last time he'd ordered the roasted salmon, and she did the chicken parmesan. They flipped the meals, but did the same sides as before. They had an even better time than before. He really couldn't place his finger on why, but he loved it.

CHAPTER 37

Eric was looking out the window as Kenya drove them to Pam's house. People still had their Christmas lights up. They grooved to The Temptations' holiday CD playing. This was Eric's first New Years party that would start as early as 7 P.M., and they were trying to be on time. He was wearing an ugly sweater. He was never one to follow the crowd; every time his job told them to wear an ugly sweater, he never did. But Kenya had sprung this sweater on him. He would have never picked out one that had two gingerbread cookies going at it. The male ginger cookie was hitting the female cookie from behind.

"You okay, baby?" Kenya asked.

"Yeah, but you know I'm not feeling this sweater."

She touched his knee and said, "That's why I put on the reindeers getting it in. We both look silly."

"I hear you, but your reindeers are small. Look how big these ginger cookies are. I might as well have a condom sweater on," Eric said sarcastically.

"Yeah, that would be something to see. I don't know why I didn't think of that."

He turned and looked at her with the slant-eye. "I'm just playing, baby. *Relax*. If you feel uncomfortable once we get there, you can put on your Giants sweater." All Eric could do was smile, because he was thinking the same thing. The G-Men had beat the Redskins earlier that day.

She pulled up to Pam's house. They had one of those drive-around driveways, and the house was huge. "Damn, what they do?" Eric asked.

"Pam retired from the Air Force like me, but her husband owns about twenty or thirty car dealerships. He took over the family business from his parents."

Kenya popped the trunk, and they got out of the car. Eric got the case of mix wine they'd gotten from the vineyards. They walked to the door, rang the bell, and stood there. Pam opened the door.

"This must be Eric "got Kenya wide open" Taylor! I'm Pam, and this is my husband Oliver," Pam said. Oliver greeted them as he walked up and took the case out of Eric's hand, and Pam hugged Eric. Kenya's face was red as an apple after Pam said that to Eric. Pam pulled Kenya by the hand as they followed Oliver.

Their house was ridiculous. They had a spiral staircase that led upstairs, and their gothic cathedral ceiling was breathtaking. *This is a mansion, not a house,* Eric thought to himself. Oliver put the case down on the counter in the kitchen. The women walked to the living room, and Oliver turned to Eric and said, "Call me O, and make yourself at home. Kenya's family--we love her, and she must think the world of you for bringing you here."

"I hope she does."

"Don't hope--she does. She's been telling us about you for the past month. I don't know what you did to her in Atlantic City, but you did it well. She even showed us your high school and college clips out the papers that she has saved. I was very impressed. I even Googled you to see your stats. I balled at Yale, but I couldn't tie your shoelaces."

"You just saying that. I'm sure you did your thing in college."

"A little bit," Oliver shrugged as he handed Eric a glass of wine.

"I don't hear the women, they must be talking about us." Oliver chuckled, and they listened hard.

Oliver walked into the living room, and Eric followed behind him. He didn't realize that Kenya had kept up on him in college. It made him smile, knowing that she wasn't in the same state but still had some newspaper clips. They made it to the living room to see the ladies looking at a variety of board games.

"I'll be right back, I forgot something," Oliver said.

As he walked away, Eric realize Oliver sweater had turd flakes instead of snowflakes. Pam's sweater was on the sexual side, like Kenya and his. She had Mrs. Claus mooning Santa while he had a boner in his pants. Eric walked over to the table to look at the games. They had Plenty, Scrabble, Monopoly, Phase 10, Taboo, and a couple of adult games. The adult games were for a date night, he assumed.

"What's this 'Phase 10?'" Eric asked as he held the box, reading the rules.

Kenya and Pam looked at him as if he were speaking another language. "You've never played Phase 10?" Pam asked with excitement in her voice.

"No. I never even heard of this game."

"We got a virgin, Honey!" Pam yelled to Oliver as he entered the room.

Oliver walked into the room with a bag of marshmallows. "A virgin to what? What did I miss?"

The first thing Eric thought was, *They must use this game to get their swinger party going. I hope not, because I'm not a sharer. Plus, they're both nice, but Pam is not my type by no means*. Eric looked at her to see how she was going to respond.

"Eric has never played Phase 10. I can't wait for Richie and Natasha to get here," Pam said.

"Cool. You're going to love it. My baby loves to break a new person in. We have a game night just to play Phase 10 with other couples, I get tired of whipping her. Ain't that right, baby?" Oliver asked Pam, then tried to kiss her.

Pam pushed his lips away from her, and he laughed. "Excuse me, don't get it twisted. Eric, I kill him every chance I get. But he's right--you are going to love it."

Oliver pressed a button on a sizeable remote. The curtain and sliding door opened in the living room to the backyard. They had a huge pool and jacuzzi, lit with neon lights. Pam put on some music, and they went into the backyard. Everyone sat on their deck bench area with the fire pit in the middle of the table. The bench didn't look comfortable with the futon-esque pillows, but, to Eric's surprise, it was. Oliver brought the bag of marshmallows and a bottle of wine, placing them on the table. Kenya sat up on Eric, damn near laying on him. Eric laughed to himself as he watched Oliver put marshmallows on a stick. He was too big to be doing that. He reminded Eric in that moment of Roc, or Charles S. Dutton. Oliver looked like he used to be muscular, but now he was borderline fat. Pam was the opposite; she had a nice physique and face. It was the dreads that had thrown Eric off. Ever since Eric found out a person couldn't wash their hair at the beginning of the dread process, just seeing them creeped him out a bit. Eric sipped his wine, smiling, listening to Teddy P.'s "Feel the Fire."

"You good, baby?" Kenya asked with her head tilted back.

"I'm good. Great wine, great company, and my baby." He squeezed her thigh. Kenya smiled and tapped his hand. Then, Eric said, "Plus, Big O whipping up those marshmallows."

"Don't knock it 'til you try it. Some people do cheese and crackers with their wine. My dad was notorious for roasting marshmallows any time there's an open flame. All he needed was his merlot and marshmallows. Ain't that right, baby?" Oliver asked Pam.

"Yeah, we can't get enough of that, baby," Pam replied, but she shook her head side to side, saying 'no.' Kenya, and Eric laughed under their breath.

Oliver kept roasting one after another, until Richie and Natasha finally joined the group. Pam introduced them as they walked on the deck. Richie had brought the biggest bottle of Patron Eric had ever seen. Pam started bringing food out near the pool.

"The food was set up in the dining room, but it's so nice out here. I hope you all don't mind eating outside," Pam said. They all responded that it was just fine.

Kenya and Natasha helped Pam bring in the food. *All* the food. Jerk chicken, curry chicken, brown stew and oxtails. Plantains, cabbage, collards, yams, rice, and beans. They sat at the table near the pool. The food was great, even when everyone ate too much. Oliver went into the house; then, he came back with a cigar case. Oliver cleared his throat to get the fellas' attention, holding the cigars and pointing to the deck area. They got up and left the women by the pool. Oliver handed Richie and Eric a cigar as they sat down.

"These are Montecristo #2 cigars. I only smoke these on special occasions," Oliver informed them as he sniffed the cigar.

"You said that the last four times you pulled them out," Richie said with a chuckle.

"And it was! To wake up above ground is always a special occasion." Oliver lit his cigar.

"You right about that," Eric said as he reached for the lighter.

The fellas smoked cigars while sipping on the wine. The women took the food back in the house. After they cleared off the table, Pam brought out the Phase 10 cards and the hookah. She got the hookah going, and the girls went in on it. The guys talked about sports, and the girls talked about the guys.

"I guess somebody done moved on. I see you glowing over here," Natasha said. Pam looked at Natasha, moving her head up and down.

“Yes, I did, and it’s long overdue,” Kenya said. Pam put her hand in the air and gave Kenya a high five.

“I’m glad, because I was tired of you wearing those granny panties,” Pam said.

“What are you talking about?” Kenya asked Pam confused.

“You were all bitter and soaking like an old hag. But not like today. I see you smiling and your breasts all perky…” Pam sniffed the air, hard. “I smell a G-string on,” Pam said in a funny voice.

Kenya choked on the smoke from the hookah. They all laughed. “All jokes aside… He has a good aura, plus he has fit in, as if we’ve always known each other. That’s a great quality,” Pam said.

“That’s Eric. He charmed you like he charmed my mother. She still asked about him, and we haven’t been together in over thirty years…”

“Hold up. So, you’ve doubled back?” Natasha asked Kenya.

“She’s not only doubling backing. She’s doing it with her first love. The guy who took her virginity,” Pam said.

“Damn! Tell all my business.” Kenya looked at Pam with the evil eye.

“Well, at least *your* first is worth doubling back. I saw my first on Facebook two years ago, and I would be ashamed to say we had sex, more or less that he was my first. He let himself go to the point he looks bad, horrible,” Natasha said with a grimace.

“Ain’t that the truth,” Pam said.

“Ironically, he’s probably finer now than when we were younger. And our chemistry now is *way* better too. I feel free sexually with Eric, more than my ex-husband.” Kenya looked up as she was thinking.

“Stop! I don’t want to hear no more. Because if I get any freer with my husband, he’ll call me a prostitute and divorce me. Okay?” Natasha said, snapping her neck. They laughed so hard the guys made it over to the table with them.

Pam turned the light dimmer up so everyone could see better. They taught Eric the rules of Phase 10. He picked up quick, and soon upped the ante. If a player didn't phase out, they had to take a shot of Patron or hot sauce. The game got real interesting. They didn't know they were messing with Mr. Competitor. They didn't lie, and the game was fun and long. They took so many breaks that the game was starting to drag even slower. Smoke, marshmallow, bathroom--they made all kinds of breaks. Natasha's alarm went off on her cell phone. It was already five minutes before midnight, Cali time. Eric had already spoken to Danny and Nana three hours ago. Pam paused the game and got some champagne glasses. Oliver poured everyone a drink as they stood by the fire pit.

They started the countdown. "10, 9, 8, 7, 6, 5, 4, 3, 2,... Happy New Year!" Everyone shouted. Eric gave Kenya a hug and a big kiss. He must have been feeling the alcohol, for him to kiss her so passionately in front of her friends he'd only just met. She looked at him, surprised, but smiled. Oliver held his glass up and made a toast.

"Here's to a new year. I hope for prosperity, great health, and spontaneous sex. Cheers!" Oliver said. They smiled at his toast while touching glasses.

"I feel the spontaneous happening already. We'll be back," Oliver said in the Terminator's voice. Oliver and Pam went upstairs. Eric looked at Richie and Natasha.

"They'll be back in ten minutes. They do this every year, no matter where we are," Natasha said.

"I give him four," Richie said. They all laughed.

Eric went to the table by the pool to get some Patron, and Kenya followed him. He made a shot, sat down, and she sat in his lap. Kenya had her legs together with her feet going over his right thigh. Her right arm lay over his shoulders as she looked in Eric's eyes.

“Happy New Year,” Kenya whispered. Eric smiled. They started kissing until his nature rose. Eric looked at Kenya with his *I want you now* eyes. Without saying a word, she got up and grabbed his hand, leading him to a bedroom upstairs.

Laying in the bed naked, breathing hard, Eric could hear Oliver yelling down the hall. “Richie, Natasha, Kenya, Eric!” He repeated their names over and over. “If you all don’t want to finish the game, I won.” Eric and Kenya laughed at Oliver, then Eric rolled on top of Kenya.

CHAPTER 38

January 4, 2018

Eric was sitting on the plane, looking out the window and daydreaming about the last two weeks with Kenya. He'd had the time of his life. He smiled, thinking about all the things they did as he twirled the bracelet in his hand. Eric meant to give it to Kenya so she would know that he was all in. Him being a sucker once again, he'd punked out. He couldn't even blame it on Danielle. Ever since Eric saw Kenya at the wedding, he hadn't been broken-hearted at all. This was the first time in almost thirty years he had felt like that.

The Captain announced that they would be arriving at JFK Airport in twenty minutes. Those words couldn't have sounded any better for Eric.

Eric stood at the baggage conveyor belt, trying to locate his bags. He was starting to get a little aggravated, especially when people from his flight were leaving with their luggage. Finally, he spotted his bags. He grabbed them, then headed outside where Danny was waiting. Eric saw Danny leaning on a black Tahoe. He was surprised, because Danny didn't own an SUV. *It must be a rental,* Eric thought. Danny took the luggage and loaded them into the trunk. Eric got in the passenger seat, then Danny got in.

"Hey, Dad. How was your trip?" Danny asked as he pulled off.

"It was great. Kenya is amazing. She showed me such a good time that I almost thought about asking her to marry me," Eric said while looking out the window. He could feel Danny looking at him. Eric turned to make eye contact. "What?"

"You're serious?"

"I'm *so* serious. I couldn't wait to tell you. I needed to hear me say that out loud, to let it resonate."

"Wow. I was joking when you left here with all that singing at y'all's wedding. But… Damn! I'm happy for you, Dad. It's just weird to hear you say that. I never thought I would ever hear you say that."

"So, you thought I would be single the rest of my life?"

"No, I thought one of your lady friends would lock you down, but I thought you would be legally married before you got married. I would have lost everything in a bet if I thought you were getting married on your own."

"I get that. I mean, I have stuck to my rules all these years. It might be my old age, or because you're no longer in the house."

"It's neither. At the reception, I saw how you were looking at Kenya. I'm sure you looked at Moms like that, but I was too young to recognize it. I told Yolanda on the honeymoon that Kenya coming to the wedding might turn out better than we thought. And she said she hopes so. You might not believe it, but a lot of people want to see you happy with someone. Kenya or whoever. You deserve it, Dad."

"Thanks, son. You're right. I wish I would have realized this years ago."

"Knowing it then or now doesn't matter. But to know it and not to act on it… Is what?"

"It's foolish, son. And you know I didn't raise any fool, and I ain't trying to be one. You're going to stop schooling me with my sayings."

"No matter who it comes from, the truth is the truth," Danny said, and Eric nodded. After a moment, Danny spoke again. "Speaking of the truth--you're about to be a grand-dad. Yolanda is three months pregnant."

Eric turned and looked at Danny. Danny nodded his head up and down with the biggest smile. "Congrats. Damn! You don't play no games, do you, son? Three months, so she was pregnant at the wedding? I'm glad she wasn't showing."

"Thanks. You're right. That wouldn't have been a good look. Just don't tell anyone. On January 14th, we're going to invite our parents over for dinner at our new place. At the dinner, we're going to announce the pregnancy."

"I got you. I will act surprised."

Eric tried to convince Danny that Eric would be a good name for a boy, and Erica for a girl. Danny tried to ignore him, changing the subject to the Giants' win from Sunday. Eric knew what Danny was doing, but he let him slide.

Danny dropped him off at the house. When Eric opened the door, he could hear the wall clock ticking from the dining room. He took his bag up to his bedroom. He got undressed and put on his Georgia Tech basketball shorts and his house shoes. Eric went downstairs to the basement to watch the Warriors vs. Rockets game on TNT in the Boom Boom Room. He turned the game on, got a Heineken, and flopped on the sofa. Eric turned it up volume with the remote to hear what Ernie and the fellas were talking about. He opened the beer, took a sip, then texted Kenya.

Eric: *Hey baby. I finally made it home.*

Kenya: *I'm glad I was starting to worry. I will call you when I get off the phone with Jackie.*

Eric: *Cool. Love you.*

Kenya: *Love you too.*

Eric placed the phone down on the coffee table. He watched TV with a slight smile, still tripping over all the love talk. The Crew would have had a roast session if they found out what the love birds were up to.

◆ ◆ ◆

"Baby? I'm home. I got your goodies," Danny yelled up the steps to Yolanda.

Danny put his car keys in a bowl on a stand in the living room. He walked into the kitchen with the bags from the store and placed them on the table. Yolanda entered into the kitchen. She went straight to the bags without saying a word to Danny.

"'Hey, baby, thanks for getting my goodies,'" Danny said, affecting a falsetto and making kissing noises.

"I'm sorry, my love, but I've been craving this since yesterday," Yolanda said, holding the box of ice cream.

She kissed Danny, and then she got a big spoon out the drawer. "I bought you three different kinds because I forgot which one you said." She looked at all three pints: butter pecan, strawberry swirl, and mint chocolate chip. She sat down with her spoon and ate out of all of them in turns. Danny got a glass of milk so he could dip his butter crunch cookies he got for himself. He pulled four Slim Jims out of his pocket and placed them on the table. She opened one Slim Jim and used it as a spoon for her ice cream. Danny squinted his eyes at her.

"You sure you're alright?" Danny asked.

"Yes. You know I have a sweet tooth, but now it's intensified. How's your dad?" Yolanda stuffed her face.

"He's great. But you won't believe what he told me."

"What?"

"He's thinking about asking Kenya to marry him."

"WOW! Not Mr. Taylor."

"That's what I thought, but he's serious. Plus, he has that look in his eyes when he's going to follow through. I hope that she right for him."

"Don't worry about that, baby. If she's not, he'll run her off like he does the rest of them. One thing I can say is when she was doing my make-up, she had this way about herself--confidence, not arrogance. It was my wedding day, but she had a glow like it was her day. Do that make sense?"

"Totally. You have that same radiance coming from you. That's why I had to make you Mrs. Taylor."

Yolanda smiled with her eyes closed. "You don't have to flatter me to get some, baby. I'm yours." She leaned over to kiss him. Danny gave her a peck, but moved back quickly. She side-eyed him.

"You know I love you, but I can't stand Slim Jims on your breath." He got up and walked away. She tore a piece of the Slim Jim off and threw it at him.

"Steph Curry hit another three. The Rockets call a timeout," said the commentator on the TV. Eric got up and put his plate in the trash. He grabbed another beer, then sat back on the couch. He opened it and took a swig. *Ring! Ring!* It was Kenya on Facetime.

"Hello."

"Hey, baby. Sorry it took me so long to call you back, but Jackie wanted every little detail," Kenya said.

"I could imagine. That's why I only let Danny know I'm back. I told The Crew I was coming back Saturday. I might hit them tomorrow, but I don't know yet."

"You haven't called your mother either?"

"No. I'm going over there in the morning. I'll surprise her; we'll do breakfast and maybe shopping. I don't know yet, but it depends on how she feels."

"That's good. You know I'm missing the heck out of you," Kenya said with a sad face.

"I miss you, too. It was only 13... 14 days, but it felt like three months. I mean that in a good way. I'm already looking at my calendar thinking about the next time we'll see each other."

"I know you meant that in a good way. If it's okay with you, I would love to come up there for Valentine's Day."

"That sounds great. Now I can play hostess."

"Good deal. Because I already booked the flight. I'll be there on the 13th and leaving out on the 17th," Kenya said with a smile.

"You kill me. What if I had plans already?"

"I would have visited my family and blew up your phone until I busted up your plans."

Eric shook his head, chuckling. "You don't have to worry about that. You are the only plans I look forward to."

"I hope so." Kenya's grin lit up his iPhone.

They talked on the phone from the third quarter of the first game to halftime of the second game. Kenya told Eric how Pam and Oliver had nothing but praise for him. He told her the feeling was mutual. They said they loved each other, and finally ended their Facetime. Eric held the phone in his hand as he thought to himself, smiling, *I usually won't talk on the phone when it's a game I wanted to see. I'm breaking all my rules with her, but I love it.*

CHAPTER 39

January 5, 2018

Eric knocked on Nana's door. *I hope she's in there,* he thought to himself. He closed his eyes, trying to listen for her. Still no response. Eric knocked again as he pulled out his keys. Before he could locate the spare key Nana'd given him, she opened the door in her night gown.

"Was you out here long?" Nana let him in and started walking to her bedroom.

"No. No longer than usual." Eric closed the door. He stopped at his trophies and wiped the dust off a couple of them. His State Championship MVP trophy was his favorite. He remembered making that game-winning shot as time ran out. Eric was only a junior that year. He'd believed that his school would play for the Championship the following year, but that hadn't been in the cards for them.

"What brings you out here, Mr. West Coast?" Nana snickered as she stood near the couch, buttoning her blouse.

"Okay, I see you got jokes. Just haven't spent time with you in a minute. Plus, I have something I need to tell you."

"Oh, Lord. Let me sit down, I don't need no more news that's going to upset me," Nana said. She took a seat in her recliner.

"What are you talking about? What other news?"

"Nothing. What do you have to tell me?"

Eric looked at her for a moment before he said anything. He knew she was keeping something from him from her body language. "You know I went to California to see Kenya, right?"

"Yes. And I know she took care of you. Now, spit out whatever you're trying to tell me."

Eric rolled his eyes. She was a mess. "I'm thinking about asking Kenya to marry me."

"Is that all? I already knew that. I thought you had some real news."

"How? Danny told you?"

"No. You told me, how you looked at her at the reception. Ever since that day, you've been walking around like you're woke. Ain't that what the young kids be saying?"

"Yes, but you shouldn't be saying that. Seriously, though, how do you feel about me asking her?

"Honestly, it doesn't matter how I or anybody else feel," Nana said as she got up and walked back to her bedroom doorway. "Earle, come out and meet my son, Eric."

Eric was confused, thinking this woman had finally lost her mind. A man came out of her bedroom and shook his hand. The man kissed Nana on the cheek and said, "I'm late for my nurse's visit." She walked him out, and then started talking like none of that had happened.

"Like I was saying. Life is too short to worry about what anyone thinks. You do what makes you happy, and that you can live with. I know I am," she said, a bit of sass to her voice.

Eric didn't say anything. He was still in shock at what had happened.

"Did you hear what I said?"

"Yes. But... how long has this Earle situation been going on?"

"That's none of your business. You need to worry about how you're going to pop the question. I've seen a couple of good ways on these reality shows. I could help you out."

"I don't know about that, but get dressed so we can get something to eat." Nana got up and went to her bedroom. All he could do was smile, a bit incredulous, about her and Earle, knowing that she was right about life being too short.

They went to eat at Richie's Place on Hillside Avenue. Eric and Nana sat there for hours, talking about anything that came to mind. She even spoke about Earle a little. He just listened and put his son antennas down. Eric couldn't remember the last time they'd had such a great conversation. When she smiled, she showed all her dentures.

CHAPTER 40

January 14, 2018

Danny walked into the dining room. As he sat in his chair, he whispered into Yolanda's ear. Eric couldn't hear what he said, because he was fake-listening to Dell, Danielle's father. It was Eric, Danny, Yolanda, Dell, May, Nana, Mr. and Mrs. B all sitting at the dining room table.

"Then after all that, the guy said--" Dell took a pause and looked at May, his wife. He smiled with his dramatic pause, as if he was going to drop the hammer. "'--The same thing happened to me.' You get it?" Dell asked in his raspy voice. May and Eric were the only ones that laughed hard. Everyone else looked a little confused--which they should've been. Eric remembered Danielle giving him some advice about laughing at Dell's corny jokes. If you don't laugh, he will tell another one.

"You know, I get it," Eric said, loud and confident. Dell gestured at him with both his pointers.

Ring, Ring.

Eric looked at his cell phone, and saw it was Kenya. "Hold on a second, baby," he said to Kenya after answering. "Son, I'll be right back." He pointed to his phone.

"Okay, Dad. Just don't take too long. You know I'm about to make the announcement," Danny whispered.

"I got you." Eric touched Nana's shoulder as he walked out of the dining room. He went to the kitchen to talk in privacy. "Hey, baby. What's going on?"

"Nothing... just had you on my mind, so I called."

"I'm glad you did, you saved me. I couldn't take one more of Dell's stories. He tells the same stories in slow motion. I try my hardest not to finish the story before he does. Hands down, he's the worst storyteller I ever heard in my life. I mess with him every time. I open my eyes real wide at certain spots of the story, so he thinks I'm enjoying it. This guy," Eric said with a chuckle.

"My bad, baby. I forgot about the dinner. Call me when you leave there?"

"Will do. Love you."

"Love you more," Kenya said, then she ended the call before he could argue it. He walked back in the dining room and sat back next to Nana.

Danny got up and placed an envelope in front of each person's dessert plate. "Before y'all open the envelopes, I want to say thanks once again for helping us on our big day. We are so thankful to have the support team that we do. We love y'all," Danny said, holding Yolanda's hand.

"Yes, we do. And I hope that y'all didn't overeat, because you're going to love this cake," Yolanda said. Danny walked off to get the cake. They all opened their envelopes and looked confused. The cards all read "**IT'S A**."

"'IT'S A,'" Ma May read out loud from the card.

Everyone looked around to the others at the table. Yolanda didn't say a word--she just smiled. Danny placed the silver cake stand, topped with a dome, in the center of the table. Danny took Nana's card from her; then, he put his hand on the cake lid.

"It's a... boy!" Danny said as he raised the lid. The cake was shaped as a baby boy, lying and looking up. He had a diaper on and the most adorable smile.

The entire room looked at Yolanda. She nodded up and down with a grin to give them confirmation. Then, the room cheered. Everyone congratulated them with hugs and kisses. Yolanda had never had that many hands on her stomach at one time.

“That reminds me when I found out May was pregnant,” Dell was saying as May stopped him.

“Can you let them have their time, honey?” Ma May asked Dell. He didn’t say another word.

“How far along are you?” Mrs. Banks asked Yolanda.

Yolanda looked at Danny before she answered. “Almost four months,” Yolanda replied.

“So that means you were… We will talk about that later, baby. You’re having my first grandbaby,” Mrs. Banks said.

“Thank the Lord. You finally gave her somebody else she can make throw-up,” Mr. Banks said as he walked out of the room. He walked to the front door as Mrs. B followed him. She cursed him out until he closed the door in her face. He went to smoke a cigarette. Mrs. B locked the door behind him.

After the outburst, Yolanda got up and started cutting the cake. She put a slice on everyone’s plate, then she sat down next to Danny. Danny fed her some of his cake before taking his own bite.

“Sweetheart, make sure you wrap up a piece of the cake and freeze it--with a label, though. I thought I was thawing out some yams, and it was some chitterlings. You know I was hot about that. I went from sugar to shit--literally,” Nana said.

Everyone laughed except for Dell. He didn’t seem to get it. Danny looked back at his plate, and Yolanda ate his cake and hers. The ladies started giving Yolanda their fondest baby stories. Dell even got a chance to tell his own story. (Eric noticed

Nana dozing at the table during that time.)

"Ma, get up. I'm going to take her home--it's past her bedtime," Eric said.

Nana and Eric hugged everyone, and then they left. On the ride home, she asked him, "How long did you know she was pregnant?"

Eric laughed, then said, "Danny told me when I got back from Cali." She didn't say anything after that. *This old lady doesn't miss anything.*

Less than two blocks from her place she had him run in the store for a Pepsi and a B.C. When Eric opened the door to get back in the car, she was on the phone, looking worried. He was about to joke, but recognized the serious look on her face. Eric sat down and waited for her to get off the phone, quietly without starting the car. She ended the call and closed her eyes, sucking in her lips.

"Are you okay, Ma?"

She opened her eyes, then blew out a long sigh. "I need you to drive me to the Kings County Hospital." Without saying a word, he started the car.

CHAPTER 41

Eric pulled up to the front of the hospital at 11:10 P.M. "After I park, I will call you and see where you are," he said to Nana.

"That's fine, but before you do, I need you to know who I'm going to see. It's your dad, baby. He's not doing too good." Nana looked worried.

"Are you serious? You're here for *what*? All that pain that he put you through, and you're here concerned about him. I can't believe this." He glared out the window, refusing to look at her; he was full of disgust.

"He did put me through a lot of pain; you know that more than anyone. But that was a long time ago, and I finally forgave him."

Eric looked back at her and said, "Well, I'm glad you did. But I'm not there right now, and probably never will be."

"I get that. Do you want to know his health status?"

"No. You can tell someone who cares, like his other family. Or, should I say, his *real* family, with his *real* wife."

Nana gave him a cold look.. "I'm going to let that slide because of your hurting. But don't you ever think that I'm the lesser of the two. Never! So, sit your ass in the car until I'm ready to go." She got out of the car, closed the door loudly, and entered the hospital.

Eric parked the car, still in his feelings. He pulled up Kenya's contact, but never pressed call. He tapped his phone on the steering wheel in disbelief. *All those years I had to hear her crying after she put my dad out. I thought her tears would never stop.*

It was 1980. Eric heard a lot of commotion coming from his parent's room. That had been going on for the last two years. His mother was getting on his father for not staying at home. His father drove a city bus and did a lot of doubles. Then, when he wasn't working, he played in a Pro-Am league. His time in the house was growing farther and farther in between. It didn't bother Eric, because he had his own life going on. He got off the bed to close his door so that he could hear Kenya on the phone. They talked for fifteen minutes longer, until the yelling escalated. Eric heard a *bam,* as if they were physically fighting--they never went that far.= He got off the phone, opened his door, and stood in the hall.

"What you want me to do? I'm trying to make everything right," Raymond said.

"Tell that hussy you can't see her and them bastards no more!" Patricia yelled back.

"Now you know I can't do that, and they're not bastards. I messed up, I understand that--give me some time to figure this out."

"No. Not another minute. When you leave tonight, make it your last time coming to this house."

"You don't mean that. And why would you try to make me choose Eric and you against them? You know how I feel about kids being raised by their father--not someone else."

"You right. That's why *I'm* your wife and that hussy ain't." Raymond looked at the floor. "Hold up. Did you marry her?"

Raymond looked at her with a shameful look on his face. "You know I wasn't going to bring a child in this world out of wedlock. That's why it's not as easy as you think."

"Yes, it is. You made that choice a long time ago. Leave! *Leave!*" She kept yelling. He turned around, only to see Eric in the hallway. He put his head down as he walked towards him. Eric slid over so that he could walk by him. Raymond stopped.

"I love you, son, and nothing will ever change that," Raymond said as he stood beside him.

"The sad thing is, you believe that. We are done! You're dead to me," Eric spat, with disgust on his face. He went back into his room and shut the door. He didn't even give his father a chance to respond. He locked the door as the tears came down his face. Eric didn't know if he was hurt or puzzled. *All these principles he's been drilling. Family! Family! Family! Damn liar.*

Two hours later, Eric came out of the room to find his mother sitting on the floor with her back on the front door. He walked over to check on her. When she looked up at him, her eyes were glassy. She didn't even look like herself. He helped her up, took her to her bed. He thought she would be better in the morning, but he was wrong. It took months before that glassy look went away.

◆ ◆ ◆

Ring. Ring.

Eric snapped out of his daze at the sound of his phone ringing. It was Kenya Facetiming him. He sent her to voicemail. He got out of the car and went into the hospital. Eric walked through the lobby, trying to find a bathroom. After using it, he headed back to the car. He stopped once he saw his mother and a lady he thought might have been his dad's other wife. He backed up next to the wall so they wouldn't see him. Eric watched the lady get back onto the elevator while his mother walked out the front door. He started following her as his phone rang. It was Nana.

"Hello."

"Come get me; I'm at the front door."

"Yes, ma'am." He walked up behind her and tapped her shoulder. She swung back and hit him in the eye. Eric grabbed his eye.

Nana said, "I *told* you about walking up on me. Now, let's go, I'm sleepy."

They walked to the car and Eric drove her home. She slept the whole ride. He walked her to her apartment to make sure she was okay. He thought she would have said something on the way home--not a word. That made him a little curious. After helping her in, he started the car and looked at the time. It was 1:15 AM. He called Kenya, since it was only 10:15 PM, Cali time. He started driving as the phone rang.

"Hey, baby. I thought you forgot about me," Kenya said as she answered the phone.

"Never that. I had to take my mother to the hospital. Then I had to--"

"Oh my God. Is she okay?" He heard the sound of bed sheets rustling, as if she'd sat up quickly.

"Yes, you didn't let me finish. I drove her up there to check on my dad."

"Your dad?"

"You heard me right, my dad."

"Is he okay? how did it go? I know you haven't spoken to him in years."

"I don't know how he's doing. It went okay, though. I stayed in the car until my mother got done seeing him. Then I drove her home."

"Hold up--let me get this right. You drove your mother to the hospital to visit your dad. Even after she told you what's wrong with him, you still decided not to visit him. Is that right?"

"Yes and no, but who cares? Let's change the subject. How was your day?"

"I will tell you about my day in a minute. Back to your dad. At some point, you need to have a conversation with him or forgive him completely. You're carrying around too much pain, and it's not healthy."

"I hear you, but honestly, I didn't ask you for your opinion."

"Oh, so you have to grant me permission to speak my mind?"

"No, and you know I didn't mean it like that."

"I took it how you said it. When you want my opinion about this matter, call me, because this conversation is not over. Bye." Kenya ended the call.

Damn! Can this day get any worse? He asked himself. Eric drove home, trying to think about how he could have worded things better with Kenya, and with his mother, as well. When he made it home, he took a shower and went to bed. Eric laid there, looking at the ceiling and trying to convince himself not to text Kenya. He was flipping her words around in his head. *She said when I call her, we need to finish that conversation. So, if I text her, I should be good.* He almost started to believe that by the time he eventually went to sleep.

CHAPTER 42

January 15, 2018

Stuck in traffic, Eric couldn't stop thinking about his conversation with Kenya. *I hope I didn't blow it with her. I should have just given in and apologized last night... No. She should have been considerate that this is a very touchy situation. She knows the run down with my dad,* Eric thought to himself as he drove into the city. He walked into the building to see Steve heading towards him.

"Mr. Taylor, I'm glad you're back. I need you to finalize some paperwork," Steve said as he started walking alongside Eric.

Eric pressed the elevator; then, he looked at Steve. "Why didn't you give it to Tina?"

"I've been giving her folders ever since you left. Mr. Murdock said this particular account needs to be done ASAP. I didn't know what to do." They walked onto the elevator.

"He said that?"

"Yes, sir, and I didn't know what to do."

Eric took the folder from Steve, open it, and then smiled. This was how Mr. Murdock gave promotions. Eric must look over the numbers--then, when he gave the folder back, it would be the terms of the promotion. "Hmmm! That doesn't look good," Eric said, ruffling Steve's feathers.

"What is it? Do I need to go over them again?" He tried to look in the file with Eric.

"No. You have done enough." Eric got off the elevator and shook his head at Steve as the doors closed with him still on it.

Eric walked towards his office, smiling. "Hey, Tina, did you keep everyone in order?"

"You know I did. How was California?" Tina asked.

"It was great. I truly enjoyed myself. Before I forget, take this folder and email Mr. Murdock. Get the promotion contract for Steve. He must have done a great job while I was gone." Eric handed her the folder.

"On it. And he did an excellent job. He reminds me of you, but he needs to put less starch in his underwear," Tina said with a chuckle.

"You're a mess." He laughed at her.

"No. *This* is a mess. Welcome back, boss." She handed him a stack of folders.

"Not 'welcome back.' This is back to reality," Eric said while shrugging his shoulders. He took the folders and went into his office.

After Eric placed the folders on his desk, he went straight to the window. Looking at everyone moving always motivated him. He hopped into the folders, head-first. Sometimes, checking over someone else's assignment was more work than doing it yourself. Eric was so locked into it he lost track of time. *Damn!* Three hours went that fast. He stopped for a moment and sent Kenya a text.

Eric: *Good morning. I hope you have a good day at work. LOVE YOU*

He waited for ten minutes, but she hadn't responded to the text. Eric checked his phone periodically as he got back to work.

◆ ◆ ◆

Pam was sitting in Kenya's office as the text came through. Her phone said there was a text message from 'Sweet Thang'. Kenya ended the voice notification without checking the text.

"Are you alright?" Pam asked Kenya.

"Yes, I have all the deadlines to meet. I will be eating lunch in the office as usual," Kenya replied.

"You're telling me as if I'm not assisting you. I'm talking about you and Eric. He is your sweet thang, right?"

"Yes. You know he is," Kenya smiled.

"Okay, then what's the problem?"

Kenya sighed, rubbing her temples as she said, "We had our first fight last night. Our first."

"Y'all first and you worried. My mother used to tell me the relationship isn't stamped until you have your first argument. It's easy to be love bird while the nest is intact. Y'all be okay."

"I don't know... he's very stubborn and prideful." Kenya read her notes. She noticed Pam didn't say anything, and looked up to see Pam staring at her with her head tilted and arms crossed.

Kenya squinted her eyes at Pam. "Girl, bye. I know that look."

"You should. You're the most stubborn person I know. And I got 5000 friends--Facebook friends," Pam said. She stuck her tongue out at Kenya as she walked out of the office.

Kenya smiled to herself, then finally opened the text and read it. *Eric thinks he's slick*, she thought to herself. She kept working and didn't respond.

◆ ◆ ◆

Later that night, sitting on the couch, Eric flipped through the TV in the Boom Boom Room. He hadn't told anyone, but he'd been sleeping in the basement ever since he got back from Cali. He didn't know if he felt guilty for feeling this way for Kenya or what. Eric wanted to spend the rest of his life with that woman. In his mind, by sleeping in the basement, he was hiding from Danielle. The funny thing was, Danielle had never stepped a foot in that house in the flesh. But her spirit filled the place, with all the pictures and mementos.

Eric sat up on the couch and got his phone off the coffee table. He checked the text messages, but she still hadn't responded. He placed the phone on his lap as he bit the inside of his mouth in deep thought. *I guess this is payback for all the females I cut short with no scissors.* Eric watched TV until he fell asleep on the couch.

CHAPTER 43

January 24, 2018

Eric was sitting at his desk, thinking about Kenya and wondering if she was still coming for Valentine's. It'd been about ten days since they talked. He didn't know if he missed her laugh more, or her intoxicating eyes on Facetime. Eric almost broke down several times and called her, but his pride wouldn't let him. He was surprised she hadn't called him yet. Eric was wondering if they were as tight as he thought they were, when--*Brrrrr!*--is phone vibrating on his desk made him snap out of it.

He picked up his phone to see a text from Dee.

Dee: *Come downstairs ASAP. I have a dilemma*

Eric shut his computer, grabbed his pea coat and scarf. He told Tina he was going to be out of the office for the rest of the day. He knew if Dee came to the city, it had to be important, because he hated the city traffic. Eric got off the elevator to see Dee pacing in the lobby as he walked up. Dee turned around, and his face said it all.

"I need to take you to the hospital to be there for your mother," Dee said.

Eric exhaled and nodded. He followed Dee. On the way to the hospital, Eric didn't say a word. He was numb to the fact that his father was gone. To him, he'd died a long time ago.

When they pulled up to the hospital, Dee placed the car in park and gave him a few words.

"Danny and his wife are in there with Nana. She's strong, but she needs you. I know you more than probably anyone in The Crew." Danny looked at Dee with a nasty look. "I can see by your face you don't want to hear this, but I don't care. You're my brother from a different mother--that's without question. You're loyal, loving, and disciplined. Did I say disciplined? But on the flip side. You're stubborn and hold grudges, or, should I say, pain. It's okay not to forget anything, but you're going to have to forgive some things. They say all sins are created equal, but they didn't say the pain that they bring is. Even a mountain climber knows what going to help him up the mountain. What will make his climb hard and what will make his climb impossible. That's why they pack their backpack accordingly. It's not up to me to tell you what you need to leave out your bag or what to take. But as your friend and brother... You gotta let some stuff go. You dig me?"

Eric nodded up and down, gave him a fist bump, then got up the car. He strolled in the hospital. After getting the room number, he walked down the hall, reading the room numbers. He passed a small lobby and saw the woman he saw talking to his mother the other day. She was surrounded by her family consoling her.

When Eric got to the room, he looked through the glass in the door. Danny was standing behind Nana with his hand on her shoulder as she sat in a chair next to the bed. They both had their backs towards him. Yolanda sat on the other side of the bed. He stood there for a second, trying to get the nerve to open the door. As Yolanda spotted him, he walked into the room. Danny turned, gave Eric a hug when he moved out of the way. Nana stood up and gave Eric the longest hug ever. While she hugged him, he looked at his father the whole time. He looked bad. Raymond had lost a lot of weight, to the point Eric could see the veins in his neck. His chest rose up and down, and Eric was surprised he was still alive. As she let him go, she slid her hands down Eric's arms. Once she got to his hands, she held them tight.

"I'm glad you came, baby. We were hoping you would come before they took him off the breathing machine. Raymond always believed when it was his time, it's his time. And, baby, it's his time." Nana released his hands, and then she waved to Yolanda and Danny to leave with her. They exited the room and Eric looked back at the door.

Eric slid the chair closer to the bed. He had his head down, his forehead laid on the bed touching Raymond's thigh. He sat there quietly, not knowing what to say. With his head still down, Eric thought about the time he wanted to quit a basketball team because he didn't get a lot of playing time. Raymond had told him, *"It's not who starts or who finishes. It's who plays the hardest and will give their all to win for the team."* At eight years old that had sounded like a parable. But as the years went by, it started to make sense. He laughed to himself. Because no matter how long Raymond hadn't been in Eric's life, he'd still sculpted him to be the man that he was today. As Eric smiled, Raymond's hand touched his head. He opened his eyes as he jumped up. Raymond's arm dangled off the side of the bed. Eric placed his arm on his chest as he stood beside him.

A nurse came in and started checking his vitals. While she was recording his vitals, Eric asked her a few questions.

"Can he hear?"

"Yes. And sometimes, he'll try to respond by certain body movement. The severity of the strokes he survived has taken their toll on his brain and body functions," the nurse replied.

"So... This might sound crazy, but... When I had my head on the bed, his hand fell on top of my head. Is it possible that he meant to do that?"

"It's possible." Eric stood there with a smirk on his face looking at him. She left the room once she got the info she needed.

"You always had to have the last word, even if it's a slam of the door or a slap on the head. But I guess today I will get the last word. I'm sorry for saying those ugly things to you the last time you were at the house. And for the time you showed up to my games and I acted like you didn't exist. You know that wasn't our relationship, but to find out you were lying to me all those years, it crushed me. You were my idol, role model, and friend. You're the one that told me if you don't have trust, you don't have anything. Therefore, to hear my mother say that about your other family and have you not deny it, I was crushed. You broke my heart to the point of no return. At that time I felt outta sight, outta mind. It might have helped in the short term, but I knew it wasn't a long-term answer." Eric paused and took a deep breath as the tears started to trickle down his cheeks. "What I'm trying to say, and I wish I were able to say it a long time ago is... I forgive you, Dad, and I missed you. I hope that you can forgive me for treating you the way I did."

Eric lifted Raymond's hand off the bed and prayed, holding it, head bowed and eyes closed. He said the prayer to himself, but said 'amen' out loud. Raymond squeezed his hand. Eric opened his eyes and squeezed it back.

Eric walked to the lobby to check on the family. It looked like he was the last one to the party. Both families were talking and enjoying themselves. Eric met his brother and sister for the first time, Carmen and Bobby. They both had two kids that were in college in Florida. They talked all night about their Dad. They got Eric up to speed on how he'd changed after he stopped seeing Nana and him. He had started having anxiety attacks, along with other health issues. Bobby said he hated to hear Dad say, "Eric." Eric this, Eric that. It was hard competing with Eric, because he was athletic like their dad. They all laughed as they told different stories. Eric felt good to see their mothers embrace each other. Raymond might have lived his life doing him, but he hand-picked two angels to do it with.

2:35 A.M. was the last time he took a breath on his own. Eric didn't have any more tears. He was happy Raymond didn't have to be there like that. Danny drove Nana and Eric home. Nana tapped his knee the whole ride to her place. After Eric walked Nana into her residence and before she closed the door, she said.

"Baby, your dad spoke to me in the bathroom. He said that he's glad you forgive him, and he said you never did anything wrong to him. He deserved it, and you taught him a lesson. That was the last time he hurt anyone he loved again with his selfish act. Then, he said you have to forgive God." Nana said through the cracked door.

Eric looked at her as she closed the door. *I don't know when he told her... she stayed in the bathroom. She gotta have the weakest bladder ever,* Eric thought to himself as he entered the elevator.

CHAPTER 44

January 28, 2018

Eric heard his phone ringing softly, and then it started getting louder. He felt under the cover until he found it. He pulled it out to see it was Nana, calling at 5:34 A.M. He sat up and answered it, puzzled why she was hitting him that early.

"Hello."

"I'm sorry to wake you, baby, but I need a ride to church. Danny texted me last night saying he wasn't going to be able to drive me. Can you do it?"

"Yes, what time do I need to pick you up?"

"Church starts at 11. So, be here by 9:30."

"Okay. I'll see you at 9:30. Love you."

"Love you too, baby."

◆◆◆

Nana was sitting on the edge of her bed with a candle burning on her nightstand. She reached down toward her left thigh and picked up a notepad that she was using to gather some information about the funeral Tuesday. (For a man to have two wives working together for his home going said a lot.) Earle rolled over and grabbed Nana's arm from behind. She looked back at him.

“You know I could have driven you,” Earle said.

“I know... but my son needs to go with me, I have this feeling about today.”

“Understood. Now, come back to bed.”

Nana blew the candle out and got under the covers facing the nightstand. Earle turned and held her from behind. She smiled, but never went back to sleep.

Eric knocked on Nana’s door. She opened the door, and he walked in. He went straight to the kitchen to see if she had some homemade lemon pound cake. *Bingo*. He got a knife, cut him a slice and put it on a napkin. He pinched off the cake as he walked to sit on the couch. She had pictures of his dad laying everywhere. Nana walked in the living room with her coat and church hat on. Eric finished the cake, and they headed out.

They stopped and sat to eat breakfast at a spot Danny often took her to. As they ate their food, he noticed she had put her wedding set back on. He didn’t say anything.

“I didn’t know you still had all those pictures of Dad.”

“Yes. I have more than that. You must understand, we were together for twenty years--which, nineteen of those years, we were married and living together. I was trying to find some of his good ones for the obituary.”

“Okay. I was making sure you weren’t having a relapse or a breakdown.”

“Relapse on what? His corpse? Hmmm!”

Eric dropped his head into his hand. He’d learned to never be surprised as to what came out of her mouth. He paid the check, and then they went to the church that wasn’t too far. Nana had seats reserved for them, so the usher led them to their seats. Eric thought that was strange--even though she'd been going to the same church for over thirty years, almost forty. When his dad left, she'd church-hopped until she found this place. He looked around as he clapped while the choir was singing to see if he recognized anyone. The praise team was getting everyone ready to worship. The spirit was in the building immediately.

They stood up as the pastor stepped to the podium to read the word. Eric knew it had been a long time since he'd been there because of the new pastor. It was a female, and she looked younger than him, very good looking. Her sermon came from Matthew 3:13-17. She preached on Jesus' baptism. As she jumped to different scriptures, Eric sat there, thinking about if he had been able to speak to his dad before he died. Not what he had in the hospital, but a real conversation. Plus, not talking to Kenya had been taking a toll on him. Eric knew he must do better than what he'd been doing. Nana tapped his knee to get his attention back on what the pastor was saying.

"If you have any doubt that if you die tonight that you have a place in heaven... You need to meet me at the altar. John said in Matthews 3:11, 'I baptize you with water for repentance. But after me comes one who is more powerful than I, whose sandals I am not worthy to carry. He will baptize you in the Holy Spirit and fire,'" The Pastor said. Then, she walked off the stage and stood in front of the podium on the floor. The whole church stood up.

The choir started singing, "Meet Me at the Altar." The pastor prayed for souls. After she prayed, she walked down the middle of the church. She was stopping at certain aisles, praying with her hand stretched out over the aisle. "It's time! Jesus has called for you," the Pastor shouted. When the people came out into the aisle, she prayed again, and the congregation clapped with joy.

The closer she got to their section, the more nervous Eric got. He'd been avoiding God for a long time and this sermon had proved it to him. Tears rolled down his cheeks. Nana grabbed his hand; she gripped it tight. The pastor did the same thing at their row. Eric closed his eyes while she prayed. His heart started beating faster, and then Nana whispered in his ear.

"Forgive God now."

Eric opened his eyes to look at Nana, but she had her eyes closed and head bowed. The Pastor said, "It's time. Jesus has called for you, Eric." When he looked at the Pastor, she stared directly at him. Nana slid back and pushed Eric toward the pastor. When he made it to the end of the aisle, the pastor grabbed his hand. She gave the usher her microphone. She placed her hands on his heart and forehead. The pastor hummed as she laid her hands on Eric, and then, she said, "Hallelujah."

The pastor took the mic back and walked further in the church. The usher escorted him to the basement of the church where there were lockers. As Eric walked, he realized the nervousness went away, and his heart slowed to a calm. They took turns changing into these sheet-like robes. Everything was happening so fast, he couldn't believe he was doing this. The ushers lined them up on stage. They moved the podium and removed some panels that led to the baptism pool. The pastor asked them, "Do you believe that Jesus died for our sins? And do you believe that he rose on the third day? Do you accept him as our Lord and Savior?" They all said yes. The pastor read Romans 10:9-10. After that, she stepped down into the pool, where she waited on them.

Everyone's family came to the front of the church. Nana, Danny, and Yolanda stood together. When Eric saw them, he felt like a child, hoping that he was making them proud. The first person stepped into the pool with the pastor. The pastor held the young man's head and back as he leaned back, holding his nose. When she raised him, the ushers passed him a towel. Then, he met his family at the stairs of the stage. The dunking took five to ten seconds. They were going one after another.

Finally, it was Eric's turn. He stepped down into the pool. She placed her hand on his back and the back of his head. He leaned back, holding his nose with his eyes wide open. Looking through the water, Eric saw the pastor in her robe, holding him.

Then, he saw her.

Danielle appeared over the pastor's head, holding a piece of paper. She ripped the paper into small pieces, tossed them down at him, and then she disappeared. When the pastor lifted him, Eric couldn't stop crying as the ushers handed him the towel. The joy he was feeling while walking to the stairs was heavenly. Eric felt God's grace running through his veins. For Danielle to be present on this day was no coincidence. He walked, drying himself with the towel. The usher held his hand as he walked down the steps. Nana and Danny were there to meet Eric.

As Eric hugged Nana, he saw Yolanda and Dee about ten feet away, standing together. They opened up, and Kenya was behind them. He let go of Nana and walked straight to Kenya. She hugged him so tightly he almost couldn't breathe, and she whispered in his ear.

"Congratulation. I love you and miss you."

"Thanks, and love you more." Eric looked at the usher as they released from the hug. The usher waved him on because he needed to go to the basement with the rest of the people that were baptized. "Don't go nowhere," Eric said to Kenya.

CHAPTER 45

Eric walked from the basement, fully dressed, and sat with his family. Nana, Danny, Yolanda, and Kenya were sitting on the same church bench. He sat between Nana and Kenya. As the pastor preached, Eric wondered who had their hand on getting Kenya here. As well as how they'd known he was getting saved that day--or any day, for that matter. They both held his hand while the pastor finished the closing benediction. After the service, they all walked out of the church. They met Dee and his wife Rachel in front of the church.

"I'm so proud that you handed your life over to God. Now we shall be roommates again, but this time it will be in Heaven," Dee said.

"Thanks," Eric responded with a raised eyebrow.

They all said their words to him as they patted Eric on the back. He vaguely heard anything they said. He just smiled as they talked. Eric was anxious to see what had brought Kenya to New York. Plus, he wanted to know if she was still upset with him. He was hoping that she wasn't going to drag this out any further.

Danny took Nana home. Kenya and Eric said their good-byes to Dee and his wife. Then, they walked to his car, got in, and drove off.

"How long are you going to be in New York?"

"I'm leaving the day after the funeral."

"I'm sorry to hear that. Who passed?"

"I can't talk about it."

"Why?"

"Well, I guess I can because you asked me. Your dad's funeral, silly."

"Danny called you? Or Dee?"

"Neither--it was your mother. She called me the same day he died. I believe you were still at the hospital at the time."

Eric looked at her, then back at the road. "No matter how you found out, I'm glad to see you. Thanks for coming."

"No problem. So... When did you decide to get saved?"

"During service. I've been thinking about it after we went to your church in Cali. But I couldn't get up my nerve to make a decision."

"So, how did your mother know it was happening today?"

"*Hmm*. You got me. That lady knows me better than anyone."

"And it worked out. Once again, I'm so proud of you."

"Thanks."

"I need you to drive me to Jackie's house."

"Why? You're not staying with me?"

Eric looked at Kenya to see how she answered him. She closed her eyes with a smirk on her face. "I will come by later. I don't know if I will be staying over, but we can finish our conversation. You do know what conversation I'm talking about, right?"

"Yes, do I ever. I know, I owe you an apology. I should have--"

"Stop. We are not going to do this now. I need to do something with Jackie. Let's wait until I come over later. Okay?"

"That's cool. I will be looking forward to the conversation."

He glanced at her with a creepy smile after she said that. Then, he looked back at the road. They listened to 101.1 FM. Eric tried to pray for one of their songs to come on, but they didn't. No one said a word until Jackie's house. He pulled up at Jackie's home and double-parked for a second to let Kenya out of the car.

"I will text you later before I come your way. It should be around 7 or 8."

"Okay, see you then."

Kenya opened the door, got out the car. Then she went into the house. Eric drove to the house, thinking about how he was going to apologize.

"What you doing here?" Jackie asked Kenya.

"Nothing. Going to take a nap before I go out later."

"You couldn't stay at Eric's place?"

"Yes, I could have, nosey. Damn. You act like you don't want me here."

"You know it ain't that. But, wasn't that you crying on the phone missing Eric? Telling me that you might have been a little too hard on him? Wasn't that you?"

"Yes, you know that was me. For your information, I didn't go over there because I was feeling weak, and there wasn't going to be any talking going on. I need to focus on getting an understanding and not getting under him."

"I hear you, but I don't agree. You could get under him, standing. I'm sure that will work it out, or work you out. Whatever comes first," Jackie said, gyrating up and down.

"You so nasty. 'Whatever comes first.'" They both laughed.

Eric went straight to his bedroom once he got into the house. He gathered everything that reminded him of Danielle, not wanting Kenya to feel some type of way. He placed the pictures and mementos on the bed. Eric scanned the room one more time to make sure that he got everything, and then he sat on the bed. He looked through the pile of items. While smiling, he remembered seeing her through the water at the baptism. He didn't understand what that image was about.

Why was she ripping up a piece of paper? Why would she throw it on me? Eric asked himself. He all but jumped up as it dawned on him about their Promise. He went straight to the safe to recover the contract. Eric pulled out the envelope and tried to pull out the letter, but only pulled out a piece of the letter. Eric looked in the envelope to see that it was ripped to pieces. He turned the envelope upside down on the bed. Shreds flipped through the air, as if in slow motion, to the bed. The ripped pieces fell on Danielle's pictures.

Eric dropped to his knees with a cold feeling spreading through his body. He looked to the ceiling as if he was looking to heaven. *You released me from our Promise. At the church, you Annulled Our Promise.* Tears started falling from his eyes, down his cheeks, while he looked at the ceiling. "Was Thank you! Thank you! Thank you!" Eric cried out uncontrollably. He balled his fist holding the envelope as he kept repeating, "Thank you!"

CHAPTER 46

Eric paced back and forth in the living room, waiting for Kenya to show up. He looked at his cell phone to view the time Kenya had texted him. It was over thirty minutes ago when he'd sent her his address. He'd been trying to get his words together for the last fifteen minutes. He felt like he was going to court, rather than having a conversation with his lady.

The doorbell rang. Eric looked at the door, then exhaled as he walked to it. He opened the door, and Kenya let herself in.

"Hey. I was starting to worry that you got lost, Miss. Cali girl. You know these New York streets is rough." Eric shut the door and locked it. "Do you want to talk in the living room or kitchen?"

"Let's do it in the kitchen. Can I have something to drink? My throat is dry."

"Cool. You want water or juice?" Eric asked as they walked to the kitchen.

"Juice is fine."

Kenya took her coat, scarf, and hat off. She draped them over the chair next to her as she sat down. Eric opens the fridge and grabbed a container of passion fruit juice. He closed the refrigerator door, then snatched a glass out the dish strainer. He rinsed out the glass. Eric sat across the table from Kenya, pouring her a glass of juice, and then he slid it to her.

"Thanks." She picked the glass up and took a sip.

"No problem." Eric bit the side of his cheek for a second; then, he went right into it. "Let me start by saying, I'm sorry for snapping at you. I was upset before I spoke to you, and I took it out on you, which I shouldn't have. Usually, I'm pretty good with not letting my problems or attitude affect others around me. I was dead wrong, and I hope you can forgive me. Also, I need to apologize for letting it get this far. The last thing I want to do is lose you."

"Hold on before you go any further. Let me apologize."

"For what?"

"For not being more understanding. I didn't take into consideration that you were processing a lot with your dad popping up. At times, I get in my way of trying to push the right thing on people, instead of being in their corner for support. I have to do better. My daughter got on me because I did the same thing to her."

"I get it. We both gotta do better. I want us to do it by each other's side--not separated." Eric stood up and walked around the table. He grabbed Kenya by the hand to lift her. They stood there, facing each other, holding hands. "I love you, and I'm glad that you came for my father's funeral. More importantly, I'm happy that you're back in my life."

"Yes, I am, and I'm here to stay."

They shared a passionate kiss that Kenya eventually broke up. "I'm not going to ruin the day that you gave your life to God so fast with this lust."

"Baby, this is *love*. And what's better than makeup sex?"

Kenya smiled as she rolled her eyes. "Anyway. Since this is my first time at your house, I need the grand tour. Starting with the infamous Boom Boom Room."

"Follow me, and I will show you exactly why they called it the

Boom Boom Room," Eric said, licking his lips.

He showed her the house, starting with the Boom Boom Room. She laughed at his wall bed, but he didn't mind. Eric was happy to have Kenya in his presence; she could have teased him all night. He ordered some pizza, which they ate in the basement. She spent the night, and they slept in his bed upstairs. Eric had never had a woman in his bedroom.

Before they went to sleep, he prayed, and felt like it was answered as he held his blessing in his arms.

CHAPTER 47

The day of the funeral. Eric dressed in all black, sitting in the front row, thinking about his dad as the pastor gave the eulogy. He'd read the obituary and was in awe of all the things his father accomplished, or was a part of. A tear rolled down his jaw, but he had a smile on his face. Kenya handed him some tissue from out of her purse. Eric wiped his face without taking his shades off.

He saw so many coaches and teammates from Raymond's playing days. He was surprised to see so many of them still alive and kicking. The pastor had the ushers open the casket for the people to view the body. After they viewed the body, they paid their respect to the family as they walked by. The homecoming was beautiful, due to circumstance. Two wives, three kids, five grandchildren, and one great-grandchild on the way. Eric knew his dad would be smiling, knowing he left a legacy behind.

At the repass, Eric was standing with Dee, Maleek, and Bruce in the church cafeteria. He looked across the room to see Kenya wearing an apron and helping the servers. She caught him looking at her. She crossed her eyes at him and stuck her tongue out. All he could do was smile.

"Snap out of it, Lover Boy, she ain't going nowhere. You are acting like Kevin Costner over here. You still on duty, fake bodyguard?" Bruce asked as he laughed.

"Whatever."

Maleek and Dee laughed at Bruce. Eric looked at Bruce with the side eye; he couldn't help it. "I got something to knock the edge off," Maleek said. He showed them the top of his flask in his inside suit pocket.

"That better be some holy water. You know we're in the church, right?" Dee asked.

Maleek said, "Relax, Saint Donald. Damn! This is holy Patron, so be quiet and receive your blessing."

They all had a look on their faces, as if they were down with hitting the flask--except for Dee. "Let's take it outside of the church," Eric said, trying to convince Dee.

"I will come with y'all, but I'm not drinking," Dee insisted.

They went outside and passed the flask around two times without Dee taking a swig. It reminded them of when they were kids, sitting in I.S. 8 Park sharing a 40oz of Ole English. Dee finally jumped in and joined the rotation. They stayed out there until the whole flask was finished. Maleek went to the car to fill it back up. Dee went back into the church.

"All jokes aside. How does it feel to have more family than Mrs. Pat?" Bruce asked.

"It's still a little weird, but it's more a blessing for Danny than me. He gets to experience an uncle and aunt, plus cousins. By Danielle being an only child and me not dealing with my Dad's other family, Danny missed out."

"What about The Crew?"

"You right. And I'm thankful for y'all, but blood has a different type of bond. Plus, none of y'all are a woman. My sister already wants to help Yolanda with the baby shower."

"I dig that. Ain't nothing like family. Blood or extended."

"That's a fact."

"That why... I've been focusing more on mines than ever. Between you and me, I haven't stepped out on Angel once this year." Eric raised his eyebrows as Bruce talked. "I know, this year is only a month in, but I'm trying. It's been hard, and I'm taking it one day at a time. I'm too old to be chasing waterfalls--plus, Angel deserves to have me all to herself."

"Wow!"

Bruce stared at Eric, then said, "That's all you got to say after I shared that with you."

"Bro. Some things don't need an ad live. You said it all."

Eric gave Bruce dap as Maleek walked up. "What did this guy say?" Maleek asked.

"Nothing, pass the Patron," Bruce said.

They stood out there for another ten minutes until Eric saw the car pull up that he was waiting on. "Let's go back inside so I can thank everyone for coming out showing love to the family." The Crew walked back into the church.

When Eric entered the cafeteria, he spotted Kenya sitting with his mother at the table. He walked over to Nana and kissed her on the neck from behind. She looked up and smiled as she patted his hand that was on her shoulder. Kenya smiled so hard as she watched them. He walked around the table to Kenya and reached out for her hand. She took his hand with a baffled look on her face. They stood up, still holding hands, and walked to the front of the cafeteria.

"Let me get everyone's attention," Eric shouted over the room. He waited for a second until the room got quiet. "I want to thank everyone for coming out sending my dad off with the love that he deserved. It meant a lot to my family to see this type of turn out. To my family. That's my mother and stepmother. My brother, sister, son, nieces, and nephews. Thanks for coming together and making this day a reunion in dad's honor, not a cry fest. Taylors truly know how to come together when they're needed. Thanks, once again. Thanks to the pastor and the church for a beautiful service. Also, thanks to The Crew for being my shoulder--plus, pushing me to be strong for my mother. Thanks." The Crew beat their chests with their fists, two times to show they'd felt his words.

Eric turned to Kenya, took a deep breath with a long pause. She looked at him as if she was trying to say *don't embarrass me.* She could be very shy at moments. "Kenya Crawford. If y'all don't know her name, y'all know it now." The crowd laughed. "But seriously. I want to thank you for everything. For your support, love, and encouragement. You challenge me in the way that it brings the best out of me, and I'm grateful. Thanks for everything. When I was a kid, still in high school, I was in love with this lady. At the time, I tried to find a way to tell her how much she meant to me. I made her this friendship bracelet in shop class using both of our favorite colors. With our color, I felt like that together, intertwined, nothing could break us apart. When I presented it to her, I was giving her my heart." Awws echoed across the cafeteria. "You're my first love, and no one else can have that title, ever."

Eric reached into his pocket, holding the bracelet in his hand. "They say if you love something, let it go, and if it's yours, it will come back. I know it's been over thirty years since I first gave you this, and they say lightning doesn't strike in the same place. But the Devil is a liar. When I saw you at Danny's wedding, I was struck all over again. What I'm trying to say is that I love you, and I don't have another thirty years to see if lightning will three strike times. I'm offering you this bracelet as I offer my heart. By you taking this bracelet, you're accepting my love."

Eric grabbed her hand and turned it palm facing up. "Do you accept my love?"

Kenya smiled, her eyes misty. "Yes, I do. Do you accept mine?"

"Absolutely." He placed the bracelet in her hand, then took a step back.

There was a weight to the end of the bracelet, and when she looked, she saw there was an engagement ring tied to the end.

She started breathing hard, as if she was hyperventilating. Eric took a knee and looked at her. Jackie and Kelsea walked up behind her to check on her. She didn't even know they were there. Kenya looked at them, then looked back at Eric as she tried to regulate her breathing.

"Will you marry me?"

Without missing a beat, she said, "Yes, yes. I will marry you!"

Eric stood up and kissed her. Everyone clapped. He hugged her as she cried in his chest.

Bobby looked at Carmen and said. "If that ain't Dad." Carmen smiled back at Bobby.

Everyone came to the front to congratulate the two of them. Eric knew he was going to get it later by the look on Kenya's face. He shrugged his shoulders with a smug smile.

CHAPTER 48

Two weeks later. Kenya and Eric were sitting on the deck, getting some sun while sipping mojitos. The Maldives were beautiful, and the Honeymoon Water Villa was perfect. They loved how the suite was over the water. He glanced at her lovely skin to see the guest service agent walking toward them.

"I hate to bother you, but Mrs. Taylor has a message," the agent told Eric, because Kenya had her eyes closed with her headphones on. He tapped her to get her attention. She sat up, and he pointed to the agent.

"I have a message for you, Mrs. Taylor."

"Can you be a doll and read it to me?" Kenya said.

"Mrs. Taylor, Mrs. Taylor, Mrs. Taylor. It is time for your two o'clock nose lick." The agent looked at them, puzzled at what he read.

"Thank you, I almost forgot."

The agent placed the message on the table as he walked away. "I thought you said your headphones weren't working?" Eric asked.

"They don't. I need to hear 'Mrs. Taylor' as many times as the law allows. Chop chop, you heard the man, it's that time." Kenya got up and walked into the villa to the bed. Eric got up, placing his shades and hat on his seat.

"Coming, Mrs. Taylor!"

THE END.

Epilogue

"Lord knows everyone thinks Nana's old and senile. But what they didn't know is that I called Kenya two weeks before I allowed Danny to see that picture. See, when Yolanda told me about Danny and her plans to hook up Eric, I knew their planning wasn't going to work. I know my son, and he's as stubborn as they come. He's truly what they call an old dog. It must be his way, and how he likes it. They say you can't teach an old dog new tricks. But they didn't say you couldn't trick an old dog," Nana said, sitting on the edge of her bed.

"What you say? The cold fog?" Earle asked, laying behind her in the bed.

"Just hush, Earle." Nana rolled her eyes as she wiped her feet to get in bed.

www.ingramcontent.com/pod-product-compliance
Lightning Source LLC
LaVergne TN
LVHW091119080826
845145LV00008B/1980

* 9 7 8 1 7 3 3 8 6 4 1 2 1 *